BLOODLINE

DICK FRANCIS'S
BLOODLINE

FELIX FRANCIS

G. P. Putnam's Sons
New York

PUTNAM

G. P. PUTNAM'S SONS
Publishers Since 1838
Published by the Penguin Group
Penguin Group (USA) Inc., 375 Hudson Street, New York, New York
10014, USA • Penguin Group (Canada), 90 Eglinton Avenue East, Suite 700, Toronto,
Ontario M4P 2Y3, Canada (a division of Pearson Penguin Canada Inc.) • Penguin Books
Ltd, 80 Strand, London WC2R 0RL, England • Penguin Ireland, 25 St Stephen's Green,
Dublin 2, Ireland (a division of Penguin Books Ltd) • Penguin Group (Australia),
250 Camberwell Road, Camberwell, Victoria 3124, Australia (a division of Pearson
Australia Group Pty Ltd) • Penguin Books India Pvt Ltd, 11 Community Centre,
Panchsheel Park, New Delhi–110 017, India • Penguin Group (NZ), 67 Apollo Drive,
Rosedale, North Shore 0632, New Zealand (a division of Pearson New Zealand
Ltd) • Penguin Books (South Africa) (Pty) Ltd, 24 Sturdee Avenue,
Rosebank, Johannesburg 2196, South Africa

Penguin Books Ltd, Registered Offices: 80 Strand, London WC2R 0RL, England

Library of Congress Cataloging-in-Publication Data

Francis, Felix.
Dick Francis's bloodline / Felix Francis.
p.   cm.
ISBN 978-0-399-16080-6
1. Sportscasters—Fiction.   2. Brother and sister—Fiction.   3. Women jockeys—Crimes
against—Fiction.   4. Horse racing—England—Fiction.   I. Title.   II. Title: Bloodline.
PR6056.R273D525   2012   2012025458
823'.914—dc23

Printed in the United States of America
1   3   5   7   9   10   8   6   4   2

Book design by Nicole LaRoche

This is a work of fiction. Names, characters, places, and incidents either are the product of
the author's imagination or are used fictitiously, and any resemblance to actual persons, living
or dead, businesses, companies, events, or locales is entirely coincidental.

With my special thanks to
Mike Cattermole,
race caller and TV presenter,
to all my friends at
Channel 4 Racing
and
BBC Radio 5 Live
for their help and encouragement,
and, as always, to Debbie

BLOODLINE

1

They're off!"

I looked down at the image of the horses on my TV monitor and shielded my eyes from the bright September sunshine. An unremarkable straight, mile-long sprint for maiden two-year-olds at Lingfield Park with twelve runners—just another horse race, one of more than fifteen hundred such races I would watch live this year.

But this particular race was to change my life forever.

THE HORSES broke from the starting gate in a fairly even line, and I glanced down at my handwritten sheet that showed the runners in their draw positions as they faced me almost a mile away.

The mile start at Lingfield was slightly obscured from the grandstand by some overhanging trees, so I leaned closer to the monitor to get a better view.

"They're running in the Herald Sunshine Limited Maiden Stakes, and Spitfire Boy is the early leader," I said, "with Steeplejack also showing early pace. Sudoku is next on the rail, tracked by Radioactive, with Troubleatmill running wide. Postal Vote is next, then High Definition and Low Calorie, with Bangkok Flyer on the far outside in the green jacket, followed by Tailplane with the white cap and Routemaster in the orange hoops. The backmarker at this stage is Pink Pashmina, who is struggling and getting a reminder as they pass the three-quarter-mile marker."

I lifted my eyes from the monitor and looked down toward the horses using my high-powered binoculars. At three-quarters of a mile I could now see them all clearly as they raced directly toward me, the foreshortening effect of the binoculars making the horses' heads seem to bob up and down unnaturally.

Races like this, with the horses running headlong down the straight track, nearly always made life difficult for race callers, and this one was no exception. The twelve runners had split into two groups, with eight horses running close to the nearside rail and the four others making their way right down the middle.

The punters in the grandstands understandably wanted to know which horse was leading, but the angle from which I was looking did not make it an easy task to decide.

"The red jacket of Spitfire Boy leads the larger group on the nearside, with Radioactive making a challenge. Troubleatmill and Bangkok Flyer are running neck and neck in the middle of the course with half a mile to go."

I looked intensely at the field as they galloped toward me. It may have stated in the race program that Bangkok Flyer's colors were dark green, but, silhouetted in the sunshine, they looked very black to me, and I didn't want to confuse them with the navy jacket of Postal Vote.

No, I was sure. It was Bangkok Flyer, with his sheepskin noseband, and he was living up to his name.

"Bangkok Flyer, with the sheepskin noseband, now stretching away on the far side. He has opened up a two-length margin over Troubleatmill, who seems not to be staying the distance. And on the nearside, Spitfire Boy has been caught by Radioactive. But here comes Sudoku between horses under Paul James in the white jacket, who has yet to move a muscle."

I lowered my binoculars and watched the horses unaided.

"Sudoku now sweeps to the front on the nearside as they pass the eighth-of-a-mile pole, but he still has the short-priced favorite, Bangkok Flyer, to beat. Sudoku and Bangkok Flyer come together as they move into the closing stages. Sudoku in white and Bangkok Flyer in dark green, it's a two-horse race." The tone of my voice rose higher and higher as the equine nostrils stretched for the finishing line beneath me. "Bangkok Flyer and Sudoku stride for stride. Sudoku and Bangkok Flyer." My pitch reached its crescendo. "Sudoku wins from Bangkok Flyer, Low Calorie runs on gamely to be third, Radioactive is fourth, followed by the longtime leader Spitfire Boy, then Routemaster, High Definition, Troubleatmill, Steeplejack, then Tailplane and Postal Vote together, and finally the filly, Pink Pashmina, who has finished a long way last."

I pushed the button that switched off my microphone.

"First, number ten, Sudoku," said the judge over the PA. "Second, number one. Third, number four. The fourth horse was number eight. The distances were a neck, and two and a half lengths."

The PA fell silent.

The race was over. The excitement had come and gone, and the crowd would already be looking forward to the next contest in thirty minutes.

I looked out across the track and felt uneasy.

Something there hadn't been quite right.

It wasn't my commentary. I hadn't confused the horses or called the wrong horse home as the winner—something that every race caller had done at some time in his life. It was the race itself that hadn't been quite right.

"Thanks, Mark. Great job," said a voice in my headphones. *"And well done mentioning every horse, and thanks for the finish order."*

"No problem, Derek," I said.

Derek was a producer for RacingTV, the satellite broadcaster that was showing the racing live. He would be sitting in the scanner, a large blacked-out truck somewhere behind the racetrack stables, with a bank of television images in front of him, one for each of the half a dozen or so cameras, and it was he who decided what pictures the people at home or in the betting shops would see. The TV company didn't have their own race caller, so they took the course commentary—namely, me. But they liked it if all the horses were mentioned at least once, and they were pretty insistent on the full finishing order being given. That was fine with twelve runners, but not so easy when there were thirty or more, especially in a sprint like this when the whole thing was over in less than a minute and a half.

"Derek?" I said, pushing a button on the control box.

"Go ahead," he replied into my ears.

"Could you make me a DVD of that race? To take home. Every angle."

"But she didn't win."

"I still want it," I said.

"OK," he said. *"It'll be ready."*

"Thanks," I said. "I'll collect it after the last."

"We'll still be here."

There was a click and my headphones went silent once more.

"But she didn't win," Derek had said.

"She" was my sister—my twin sister, to be precise, Clare Shillingford—a top jockey with more than six hundred winners to her name.

But that race had not been one of them. She'd just come second by a neck on Bangkok Flyer, and I thought it was her riding that hadn't been right.

I LOOKED AT MY WATCH. There were twenty minutes before I needed to be back here in the commentary booth for the next race, so I skipped down the five flights of stairs to ground level and made my way around behind the grandstand to the weighing room.

I put my head through the open doorway of the racetrack broadcast center, a small room just off the main weighing room that was half filled with a bank of electronic equipment all down one wall.

"Afternoon, Jack," I said to the back of a man standing there.

"Hi, Mark," said the man, turning around and rubbing his hands on a green sweater that appeared to have more holes in it than wool. "Everything all right?"

"Fine," I replied.

Jack Laver was the technician for the on-course broadcasting service that relayed the closed-circuit pictures to the many television sets throughout the racetrack, including the monitor in the commentary booth. His dress sense might have been suspect, but he was an absolute wizard with electronics.

"Fancy a cuppa?" he asked.

"Love one," I said, and he disappeared into an alcove, re-emerging with two white plastic mugs of steaming brown liquid.

"Sugar?"

"No thanks," I said, taking one of the beakers.

Weighing-room tea would never have won any prizes for its taste, but it was hot and wet, and both were good for my voice. A race caller with a sore throat, or—worse—laryngitis, was no good for anything. Peter Bromley, the legendary BBC race caller, always carried with him a bottle of his special balm—a secret homemade concoction containing honey and whisky. He would take a small swig before every race to lubricate the throat.

I was never as organized as that, but I did like to have a bottle of water always close at hand. And tea was a bonus.

"Jack, can you show me a replay of that last race? Just the last quarter mile will do."

"Sure," he said, moving toward the electronics. "Did you get something wrong?" he asked, glancing over his shoulder at me with a huge grin.

"Get stuffed," I said. "And, no, I didn't."

"You'd never admit it anyway. You bloody commentators, you're all the same."

"Perfect, you mean."

"Ha! Don't make me laugh."

He fiddled with some of the controls and the previous race appeared on one of the tiny screens on the front of his equipment.

"Just the last quarter mile, you say?"

"Yes, please."

He used a large ball-type mouse to fast-forward the race, the horses moving comically along the track at breakneck speed.

"There you are," said Jack, slowing the runners to a normal pace.

I leaned forward to get a closer look.

I hoped I was wrong. In fact, I wanted desperately to be wrong.

"Can you show me that again?" I asked Jack.

He used the ball to rewind the recording to the quarter-mile pole.

I watched it once more, and there was no mistake.

I had absolutely no doubt that Clare Shillingford, my twin sister, had just been in contravention of rules (B)58, (B)59, and (D)45 of the Rules of Racing, rules that state, amongst other things, that *a rider must ride a horse throughout the race in such a way that he or she can be seen to have made a genuine attempt to obtain from the horse timely, real, and substantial efforts to achieve the best possible placing.*

Put more simply, Clare had not won the race when she could have done. And, furthermore, I believed she had not won it on purpose.

THE NEXT HOUR passed in somewhat of a blur. Good commentating requires solid concentration to the extent that all other thoughts need to be excluded. No one actually complained about my race calling in the next two races, but I knew that I hadn't been at my best, and Derek made no further appreciative comments into my ears.

I made another trip down to the weighing room between the third and fourth races. Clare had a ride in the fourth, and I wanted to have a quick word with her, but it was nothing to do with my unease over her riding Bangkok Flyer. We had a long-standing arrangement to have dinner together that night, and I wanted to confirm the plans.

"Hi, Clare," I called out to her as she exited the weighing room in a set of bright yellow silks with blue stars across her front and back. "Are you still on for tonight? I've booked a table at Haxted Mill for eight o'clock."

"Great," she said, smiling up at me as I walked alongside her. "But I'm going to see Mom and Dad first, so I'll meet you there."

"Fine," I said.

I slowed to a halt and watched her walk away from me and through the small crowd into the parade ring.

I wondered whether I really knew her anymore.

We had arrived into this world by cesarean section just thirty seconds apart, she being born first, as she never failed to remind me.

Our childhoods had been totally intertwined, with us sharing first cots, then bedrooms, schools, and finally a rented apartment on the outskirts of Edenbridge in Kent when, aged nineteen, we had together summoned the courage to tell our overbearing father that we no longer wanted to live under his roof.

That had been twelve years ago, but our sharing of an apartment had lasted barely six months before she had moved out and gone north to Newmarket.

We had both wanted to be jockeys for as long as we could

remember and had ridden imaginary races and stirring finishes, first on rocking horses and then on ponies in the paddocks behind our parents' home in Surrey.

Twins we might be, but we didn't have all the same genes.

While Clare remained short and slight, I became tall and broad.

She ate heartily and stayed annoyingly thin, while I had starved myself half to death but still grew heavier by the day. While we both became jockeys, we never rode against each other as we had done so often on our ponies. Hers became the life of a featherweight flat jock at racing's "Headquarters" in Newmarket, while I rode precisely five times as an amateur over the jumps before my battle with my ever-increasing body mass put paid to that career path.

So, instead, I had rather pretentiously announced my desire to be a racehorse trainer and had moved briefly to Lambourn as an assistant to the assistant at one of the top steeplechase training stables. By this time I was twenty years old but, somehow, my body had still been growing at an age when everyone else's had stopped. When it decided that enough was enough, I stood at six feet two inches in my socks, with shoulders to match, and, in spite of severe undernourishment, I was too heavy even to ride out with the string.

Riding had been my passion, and I had soon discovered that driving a Land Rover up onto the Berkshire Downs each day to watch the horses at work was not what I'd had in mind as my future. I missed the adrenaline rush of riding a Thoroughbred racehorse at high speed, with the wind and rain stinging my face, and watching others do what I craved somehow made the agony all the worse.

Strange, then, that I had ended up as a race caller doing just that, but the adrenaline rush was back, in particular on big race days when my audience could be millions.

"Hello, Mark," a voice said behind me. "Are you rooted to that spot?"

I recognized the voice and turned around, smiling. "Hi, Harry," I said. "I was just thinking."

"Dangerous stuff, thinking."

As far as I could tell, Harry Jacobs was a man of leisure. Only twice over the years had I asked him what he did for a living and both times he'd replied in the same way: "Nothing, if I can manage it." He was too young to be of retirement age. I estimated him to be in his late fifties, but he would've hardly had time for any paid employment as he seemed to spend every day of his life satisfying his passion for racing.

I'd first met him when I'd been an eighteen-year-old budding amateur jockey and he had agreed to me riding one of his horses in my first-ever race. I hadn't expected it to be the beginning of a firm friendship, especially as I'd missed the start, never recovered my position, and finished tailed-off last. But Harry hadn't appeared to mind, and he had slapped me reassuringly on the back. We'd been firm "racetrack" friends ever since, although I'd no idea where he lived and, I suspect, he had no idea where I did either.

"Fancy a drink?" he asked.

"Harry, I would have loved to, but I'm commentating, and they're almost on their way out of the paddock. Some other time."

"You workers." He laughed. "No sense of priority."

I wondered again where his money came from. He had a sizable string of racehorses, both jumpers and flat, and there was no shortage of readies available for entertaining in private boxes around the country's racetracks.

I made it back into the commentary booth just in time to describe the horses for the fourth race as they emerged onto the course and made their way to the one-mile start.

"First going down is Jetstar, in the red jacket with the white crossbelts. Next is Superjumbo, in white with a red circle and black cap." I looked down at my notes and also at my folded copy of the *Racing Post* with its diagrams of the jockeys' silks. "Rogerly comes next, in the blue and white quarters and hooped cap, followed by Scusami, the favorite, in the yellow jacket with the light blue stars and cap." I watched Clare cantering Scusami down the course and wondered again what was going on in that head of hers underneath the light blue cap. "Lounge Lizard is next, in the green and white stripes, with Tournado—in the pink with dark green epaulettes and cap—completing the lineup for the John Holmes Construction Limited Stakes over a mile, the big race of the day here at Lingfield."

I clicked off my microphone.

Six runners over a mile on the round track. Easy-peasy.

I pushed a button on my control box and the latest betting odds for the race came up on my monitor.

"Scusami is still the favorite, and his price has shortened to five-to-four. Superjumbo is at threes, as is Rogerly. It's five-to-one for Tournado, sixes Lounge Lizard, with Jetstar the rank outsider at twenty-five-to-one."

I turned off my mike and switched the monitor to show the horses as they circled at the start.

For a race with a very large field, like the Grand National, I would have spent some time the previous evening studying the colors, but mostly I learned them in the last few minutes before the off. If I tried absorbing six or seven races' worth all together, I would simply get them confused in my head.

So I learned them race by race and probably couldn't describe them ten minutes after it had finished. I started each race with a clear mind, and describing the silks as the horses cantered to the start was as much part of my learning routine as it was for the benefit of the racegoers in the grandstands. Now I watched the horses circle on the monitor and put my finger on the image of each animal in turn while saying its name out loud. With more runners I might have gone to see them in the parade ring to give me more time, but with six . . . piece of cake.

"Going behind the gate," I told the crowd. "Scusami is still the favorite at five-to-four, Rogerly now clear second at three-to-one, with Superjumbo at seven-to-two; five-to-one, bar those."

I flicked the monitor back to the horses and went on, putting my finger on their images and saying aloud each horse's name.

"Now loading," I said.

Derek spoke into my ear. *"Mark, coming to you in five seconds. Four. Three. Two . . ."* He counted down to zero while I described the horses as they were being loaded into the starting gate. As he reached zero, I paused fractionally so that I wasn't actually speaking as the satellite viewers came online.

"Just two to go now," I said. I briefly flicked back to the odds on my monitor. "Scusami is still favorite but has drifted slightly to six-to-four, with Rogerly still at threes. Just Superjumbo now still to be loaded."

I took a small sip of water from my bottle.

"Right, they're all in. Ready. They're off!"

Easy-peasy indeed. Even my grandmother could have called this race.

Scusami jumped out of the gate first and, as an established front-runner, he never relinquished the position. He was only briefly challenged in the home stretch by Superjumbo, but when Clare asked him for a response it was instant and dramatic. She raised her whip only once, riding the horse out mostly with hands and heels, to a comfortable three-length victory, with the others trailing past the winning post in line astern.

"I'll make you a copy of that one too," said Derek into my ears. *"What a great horse. Must be a good bet for the Guineas."*

"The opposition may have made him look better than he really is," I replied. But I did agree with Derek. Perhaps I'd make a small investment in the ante-post market. The 2,000 Guineas was not until May, and a lot could happen in the next eight months.

Indeed, much would happen in the next eight hours.

LINGFIELD WAS my local course, and I was home by half past six, even though the last race didn't start until five twenty-five. And I had remembered to collect the DVD from Derek with the two recordings on it.

I sat on my sofa and played them back over and over.

The difference between a moderate jockey and a great one is all about weight management and timing. All jockeys stand in their stirrup irons and lean forward, placing their weight over the horse's shoulders, and all jockeys move their weight back and forth slightly with the horse's action, but the greats are those who use this movement to bring the most out of their mounts. They dictate to, rather than just follow, the horse beneath them.

Riding a finish with "hands and heels" has far more to do with the positioning of weight than anything actually done to the horse with the hands or the heels. Most jockeys, especially those on the flat, ride far too short to be able to give the animal a decent kick with their heels anyway, and the hands on the reins move back and forth with the horse's head.

I watched again the recording of Clare riding Scusami to win that afternoon's fourth race. As Superjumbo came to challenge, Clare gave her mount a single smack with her whip down its flank, then she rode out a classic finish, lowering her back and pushing her hands back and forth along the horse's neck and moving her weight rhythmically to encourage it to lengthen its stride, which it duly did to win easily.

I compared that with her riding of Bangkok Flyer in the first when she was beaten by a neck by Sudoku.

In the final eighth of a mile she appeared to give the horse three heavy backhanded smacks with the whip, but the head-on camera showed that these strikes were, in fact, "air shots," or superficial hits at best, with her hand slowing dramatically before the whip made any contact with the flesh. As on Scusami, she had lowered her back, and there had also been plenty of elbow motion, but little of this had actually transmitted to her hands, the elbows going up and down rather than back and forth.

But the most telling thing was what had caused me to question her riding in the first place. Clare's body movement had been all wrong. Instead of encouraging the horse to lengthen its stride as she had done on Scusami, her actions had had the opposite effect. It was like in a car engine: if the combustion in the cylinder occurred when the piston was moving up and not down, the effect would be to slow the engine rather than to speed it up.

So it had been with Clare's riding, and hence Bangkok Flyer had been easily caught and passed by Sudoku.

But she had been very clever. It was a real art to make it appear that she was riding out a finish for all she was worth while actually doing the opposite.

Indeed, the only reason I had been suspicious was because of a game we had loved to play when riding our ponies as kids.

The "Race Fixing Game," we had called it—pulling up our ponies to a halt while looking like we were riding a tight finish. We had practiced for days and days so that even our aged great-uncle couldn't tell what we were doing, and he'd been a regular steward for decades at racetracks all over the country.

There had been no inquiry, so the Lingfield stewards obviously hadn't spotted it. And the racing press clearly hadn't noticed anything either, as there had been no difficult questions asked of me in the press room when I'd visited there after the fifth race.

But I could see only too clearly that Clare had definitely been playing the Race Fixing Game on Bangkok Flyer.

2

I was at Haxted Mill on time, at eight, and I chose a quiet corner table inside the restaurant, although they were still serving dinner on the terrace alongside the River Eden. The day may have been unseasonably warm for September, but the temperature was dropping fast with the setting sun.

Clare arrived at ten past in faded blue jeans and a pink polo shirt.

"Sorry I'm late, Marky," she said, sitting down opposite me.

"No problem. What would you like to drink?"

"Fizzy water."

"You can have a bed for the night if you want to drink."

"No, thanks," she replied. "I have to get back. I'm riding work in the morning, then racing."

"Newmarket?" I asked.

She nodded. "I've got three rides including one in the Cesarewitch Trial."

"I'll be at Newbury so I'll watch you on the television."

A waitress arrived with the menus, and I ordered a large bottle of sparkling mineral water.

"Don't let me stop you from having something stronger," Clare said.

"You won't. I'll have some wine with my dinner."

We perused the menus in silence for a while.

"How are Mom and Dad?" I asked.

"Oh, god-awful as always. They're getting so old."

The waitress returned with the water and poured two glasses.

"Are you ready to order?" she asked.

"Just the haddock for me," Clare said. "And without the mashed potato."

"No appetizer?" I asked.

"No, thanks. I'm riding at one hundred and ten pounds to-morrow."

"My," I said. "That is light."

"Too bloody light."

"I'll have the steak," I said to the patient waitress. "Medium rare, but no fries." I could hardly eat fries with Clare watching enviously. "And a glass of the red Bordeaux, please."

The waitress took our menus and left us.

"I found it really depressing going home," Clare said.

"Why?"

"Dad's lost all his sparkle, and Mom's not much better. I swear Dad gets more grumpy every day."

"But, as you said, they're getting old. Dad will be seventy-eight next month, and Mom's only a couple of years behind him."

Both our parents had been in their mid-forties when we had unexpectedly come along. We had three much older siblings.

"Getting old's a real bugger," Clare said. "I've decided I'm never getting old."

"It's better than the alternative."

"Is it?" Clare replied. "I can't imagine a time when I couldn't ride anymore. I wouldn't want to go on living."

"Willie Shoemaker was nearly sixty when he stopped riding."

"Yeah, I know," she said. "And he was fifty-four when he won the Kentucky Derby for the fourth time. I looked it up."

My, I thought, she's really worried about retirement and she's only thirty-one. In my experience, when jockeys started thinking about it, they usually retired pretty quickly. Lots of them would say they would in five years and then stop in about five months, some in five weeks or even less.

The waitress brought me my glass of wine and offered us bread, which we both declined.

"And the house is looking old too," Clare said.

"Well, it would, wouldn't it?" I said. According to the date-stone on one of the gables, it had been built in 1607.

"You know what I mean," she said. "It needs some TLC."

"A lick of paint on the windows," I agreed, nodding. "But Dad's a bit too old to do that himself. He may be quite fit, but I don't think ladders are a good idea anymore, not at his age."

"I think they should move," she said decisively. "Into somewhere smaller, or into an old folk's home. I told them so."

"I bet that didn't go down too well."

"No," she agreed. "Dad was angry—as usual. But they have to be practical. That house is too big. I think they should go into a home now while they still can."

"Don't be daft," I said. "They don't need to yet. And where would they put all their stuff?"

"What worries me is what the one will do when the other dies. That place is far too big for both of them, let alone just one. The one left will have to move, then."

"I hope that'll be years away. Anyway, we'll cross that bridge when we come to it."

"That's typical of you," Clare said, pointing her slender left forefinger at my chest. "Always burying your head in the sand and doing nothing."

"That's not fair," I said.

"Yes, it is," she said defiantly. "You always put things off. That's why you still live in that dreadful rented apartment in Edenbridge."

"You liked it, once," I whined.

"I did when I was nineteen, but life moves on. You should have bought yourself a house years ago. You must be earning enough by now."

She was right. She usually was.

Our meals arrived, and we ate for a while in silence.

"How's your love life?" Clare asked finally.

"None of your business," I replied, laughing. "How's yours?"

"Absolutely wonderful. I have a new man. Three months now. What a lover!" She grinned and then laughed. He clearly made her happy.

"Who is it?" I asked, leaning forward.

"Now, that's none of *your* business," she said.

"Come on, Clare. Who is it?"

"I'm not saying," she said seriously, drawing a finger across her mouth as if zipping it shut. She opened it, however, to pop in a bite of her haddock. "Are you still seeing Sarah?"

"Yes," I said.

She looked down at her plate and shook her head.

"And what's that meant to mean?" I asked.

"Mark, it's high time you had a proper girlfriend."

"I do."

"Sarah is not a proper girlfriend. She's someone else's wife."

"She's working on it," I said defensively.

"She's been working on it for five years. When are you going to realize she won't ever leave Mitchell? She can't afford to."

"Give her time."

"God, Mark, you're so weak. For once, do something about it. Tell her it's now or never and you're fed up waiting. You're wasting your life."

"You should talk," I said. "Your love life has hardly been a Hallmark Romance." Clare had dated a string of what my father had rather generously called "unsuitable young men," and not all of them had been that young either. "Which misfit is it you're seeing now anyway?"

"I told you, that's none of your bloody business," she replied curtly, and without the humor that had been there earlier. "But at least I'm not living a lie."

"Aren't you?" I said.

"And what is that meant to mean?" she asked belligerently.

"Oh, nothing."

We ate again in silence.

Why did we always seem to fight these days? When we were kids, we had been so close that we didn't even need to speak to know what the other was thinking. But recently our twin-intuition had waned and faded away, at least for me. I wondered if she could still read my mind. If so, she probably wouldn't like it.

The waitress reappeared to collect our plates.

"Dessert?" she asked.

"Just coffee," Clare said. "Black."

"Same for me, please."

The waitress went away, and we sat there awkwardly once more.

"Good win on Scusami," I said.

"Yes," Clare replied, keeping her eyes on the table.

"Do you think he'll win the Guineas?"

"I doubt it. That Peter Williams colt, Reading Glass, he'll take a lot of beating. But Scusi's good, and it would be nice to be the first lady jockey to win a Classic." She looked upward wistfully. "One year anyway."

"But you'll ride him?"

"Maybe," she said thoughtfully. "That'll be up to Geoff." Scusami was trained by Geoffrey Grubb in Newmarket.

The coffee arrived.

"Shame about Bangkok Flyer," I said.

Clare sat in silence and looked down at her cup.

"Don't you think?" I prompted.

"I'd forgotten you were commentating."

"You don't deny it, then?" I asked.

More silence.

"Why, Clare?"

"It's complicated."

"How can it be complicated?" I asked incredulously. "You fixed the bloody race."

"Don't be silly," she said, looking up quickly. "I didn't fix it. I just didn't win it."

"Don't split hairs with me," I said sharply.

"Ooh! Look at you, getting on your high horse."

"Be serious."

"Why should I?"

"Because it's a serious matter," I said. "You could lose your license, and your livelihood."

"Only if I get caught."

"I caught you."

"Yeah, but what are you going to do about it?"

I sat and watched her. I could tell that she already knew the answer.

"Nothing. But someone else will be bound to notice if you do it again."

"No one has done so far."

I looked at her in disbelief.

"Are you saying this wasn't the first time you've done this?"

She smiled at me. "Of course not."

"Clare!"

The couple at a table nearby looked over at us. I lowered my voice but not my anger.

"Are you telling me that you regularly don't win races you should?"

"I wouldn't say regularly," she said, "but I have."

"How often?"

She pursed her lips.

"Three or four times, maybe five."

"But why?"

"I told you, it's complicated."

I didn't know what to say. She was so matter-of-fact about it all. If the British Horseracing Authority knew she had "stopped" horses three, four, or five times, they probably would have taken away her license for good and banned her from all racetracks for life.

And she didn't seem bothered.

"Well, don't ever do it again," I said in my most domineering tone.

"And what will you do about it if I do?" She was mocking me.

"Clare, please. Don't do this. Don't you understand? I love you, and I don't want to see you destroy all that you've built up."

I glanced around to make sure no one was listening.

"Don't be so patronizing," Clare said.

I sat there, stunned.

"I've had to claw my way up in this business," she said with feeling, leaning across the table. "No one gives you an inch. Lady jockey—ha! Don't make me laugh. Half of those in racing think we're no bloody good and should leave it all to the men, while the other half are a bunch of dirty old men who fantasize about us wearing tight breeches with whips in our hands. I've had to bow and scrape to them all, and sweat blood, to get where I am today, and now at last it's me who's in control of them."

"Is that it, then?" I asked. "Is this all about control?"

"You bet. Control over the bloody trainers, and the owners."

Control, I thought, could be a powerful force. What was that old adage? *Power corrupts; absolute power corrupts absolutely.* Absolute power and unbridled control over others had led to the Nazis, and a world war was needed to wrest control from their fingers. Control over others was a dangerous concept.

"I thought I knew you," I said slowly, "but I don't."

"I've changed," she said, "and I've hardened. I've had to climb the slippery pole while others kicked me in the teeth. Success didn't just fall into *my* lap by chance."

We both knew what she meant.

I had been in the right place at the right time.

It was now eight years since that day at the Fontwell Park races when the paddock presenter for RacingTV had been taken seriously ill with a heart attack just before he was due to go on the air. The backup presenter, the much respected wife of an up-and-coming young trainer, turned out to be the main presenter's mistress, and she had insisted on going with him to the hospital in the ambulance.

I was only there as a guest to watch because I'd carelessly put my hand up at a charity auction to spend a day with the RacingTV team. But I found myself putting up my hand again and volunteering to stand in.

"Do you know the horses?" the agitated producer had demanded while pulling out clumps of his already thinning hair.

"Yes," I'd replied.

And I had. As my sister had so correctly pointed out, I tended to drift rather a lot, and I hadn't actually acquired a proper job since returning from my brief sojourn in Lambourn two years before. Rather, I'd decided to earn my living as a professional gambler and had consequently spent most of my time studying the form. I knew the horses very well.

"Only for the first race, then," the producer had said. "I've sent for a replacement, but he won't be here until two o'clock."

I had talked easily to the camera about each horse in the first race and had even tipped the winner. When the replacement had arrived, he'd just sat and watched me all afternoon as I'd tipped the winner in three other races as well.

"What are you doing tomorrow?" the producer had asked as they were packing up.

"Nothing," I'd replied honestly.

"We're at Wincanton. Fancy a job?"

Since that day, I had never looked back, spreading into commentating again by accident when the race caller at Windsor had been held up by a big car crash on the local highway and I had been asked to stand in.

Nowadays I split my time three ways—commentating at the racetracks, paddock presenting for RacingTV, and also hosting the TV coverage on Channel 4, the terrestrial broadcaster of horseracing in Britain.

But Clare firmly believed that I still didn't have a "proper" job and that I would soon drift off into something else.

Maybe she was right.

"I much preferred the old you," I said to her.

"Oh God!" she said. "Don't start all that again. I live in a competitive world. I have a competitive job. I have to compete. Otherwise I'd be trampled on."

"Do you have to compete on everything?"

"What do you mean?" she asked.

"I just feel that whenever we have a conversation these days, it's a points-scoring exercise."

"Don't be ridiculous."

I wasn't going to argue with her. There was no sense in it. For whatever I might say, she would have a riposte. Losing was not an option for her, except, of course, when she clearly lost on purpose.

I paid the bill, and we went out together to the parking lot.

"Is there anything I can say that would stop you from doing it again?"

She turned to me. "Probably not."

"I might report you to the authorities."

"I don't think so."

"Don't bank on it," I said.

"Mark, don't be such a prat. You know perfectly well that you won't tell anyone. For a start, it would reflect badly on you. So just keep your eyes and mouth shut."

"I can hardly do that in my job."

"Then you'll have to turn a blind eye instead."

"Clare, seriously, if you do that once more when I'm commentating, I'll never speak to you again."

She opened the door of her silver Audi TT.

"Your loss, not mine."

She climbed into the sports car and slammed the door shut.

Again, I was stunned. Maybe it had been a careless thing to say, but I hadn't expected such a brusque answer.

What had happened to my lovely twin sister?

She gunned the engine, and spun the rear wheels on the gravel, as she shot off without a wave, without even a glance.

AS I ARRIVED back at my apartment, the phone in the hallway was ringing, and the caller ID on the handset showed me that it was Clare calling from her cell.

I wondered what else she had to say to hurt me some more. Maybe she had thought up another barbed comment to thrust into my heart.

I let the phone go on ringing.

Eventually the answering machine picked it up, and I stood there in the dark listening for any message. There wasn't one. Clare had hung up.

My own cell phone started vibrating in my pocket, but I also let that go to voice mail.

I didn't want to talk to her. I was hurting enough already. Even if she was ringing to apologize, which I doubted, she could wait. It wouldn't do her any harm to feel guilty for a while.

I flicked on the light and looked at my watch. It was still only nine-twenty. Far from enjoying a leisurely dinner with my loving twin sister to mull over our news and catch up on family gossip, I was back home less than an hour and a half after leaving.

I felt wretched, and cheated.

I walked into my sitting room–cum–kitchen–cum–dining room–cum–office.

Perhaps Clare was right about my apartment. Maybe it was time to move on.

We had initially found the place through a student accommodations company, and, looking at it now, I had to admit that it certainly still had a "student" feel about it.

Once I had talked the landlord into redecorating, but that had been about eight years ago, and the cheap paint he had used had faded and cracked. I knew I should ask him to do it again, but I didn't relish all the upheaval that would be produced moving my stuff. Better to live with a few marks on the walls and a slowly yellowing ceiling.

I sat down at my table and opened my laptop computer. I logged on to the *Racing Post* website and looked through the cards for the following day's racing at Newbury, where I would be presenting for Channel 4.

As hard as I tried to concentrate on the horses, looking up their form and making notes, my mind kept drifting back to Clare and our conversation over dinner.

How could she be so stupid? And for what? Did I really believe she was stopping horses from winning just to play some weird game of control over trainers and owners? There had to be more to it than that. Surely there had to be some financial implications.

"It's complicated," she had said.

It sure was.

My phone rang again, and I went on ignoring it. I was sure it was Clare, but I was angry and upset and I wouldn't speak to her. It stopped ringing, and, as before, there was no message.

I forced myself back to the horses running at Newbury the following day and spent the next hour going through all eight races in detail. Only three of the eight were due to be shown live on Channel 4, but, as I still tried to supplement my income with some winnings, I was looking for horses that I believed showed especially good value in the prices currently offered on the Internet betting sites.

One particular horse, Raised Heartbeat, running in the third race, was quoted at decimal odds of 7.5; in other words, if I placed a bet of one hundred pounds, I would get seven hundred fifty pounds back altogether, including my hundred-pound stake. That was equivalent to fractional odds of thirteen-to-two. I felt sure that the horse would actually start at maybe six-to-one or even five-to-one. If I placed a bet now at the longer price and then "layed" the horse at shorter odds tomorrow, I would effectively have a bet to nothing. If it won, I would win a little, but if it lost I wouldn't lose anything.

It was a technique I had employed for some time with considerable success. But the system wasn't foolproof. The horse could drift in the market, making my bet seem rather undervalued. I could then still lay the horse to limit my exposure, but that would guarantee a financial loss whether the horse won the race or not.

However, due to my job, I watched the same horses run day after day, week after week, even year after year, and I knew them as well as anyone. Experience had proven that I was more often right than not about the way the odds would change.

I logged on to my account and placed my bet on Raised Heartbeat—a hundred-pound stake to make six-hundred-and-fifty profit.

If I was right and the price shortened to, say, five-to-one, I would then lay it. That is, I'd take a hundred-pound bet from someone else for them to win five hundred. Now, if the horse won, I would win six hundred fifty on my bet and pay out the five hundred on the bet from someone else, giving me a profit of a hundred fifty pounds. If the horse lost, then I would lose my hundred-pound stake, but I'd also keep the hundred from someone else, leaving me even. Whereas it wasn't quite win/win, at least it was win/not lose.

The phone rang once more. I looked at my watch. It was ten past eleven. I was tempted to answer it, but I was still smarting from earlier and I didn't want another row. I would speak to her in the morning when we had both cooled off a little.

I closed the lid of my computer and went along the corridor to bed.

The only significant change I had made when Clare had moved out to go to Newmarket was to transfer from the smaller bedroom into the larger one. Now I lay awake on the double bed in the darkness and thought back to those months we had spent here together.

Undoubtedly it had been the happiest time of my life. We had escaped the nightmare of living in a house where our father had become so prescriptive about what we could and couldn't do that he had refused permission for us to go out to a friend's New Year's Eve party in spite of the fact that we both were over eighteen. When we had defied him and gone anyway, we had found the house locked and bolted on our return. We had rung the bell and battered on the door, but he wouldn't let us in, so we had spent the night shivering in Clare's Mini and planned our getaway.

This apartment had seemed like a palace—somewhere we could leave the lights on without being shouted at, and where we didn't have to account for our every waking minute.

How I longed for a return to those halcyon days.

Perhaps I should call Clare after all.

I turned on the bedside lamp and looked at the clock. It was a quarter to midnight. Was it too late to call? It was a good half hour since she had last tried me. Would she be asleep?

I tried her anyway, figuring that she could always turn her cell phone off if she didn't want to be disturbed.

It went straight to voice mail.

"Clare, it's Mark," I said. "I'm sorry this evening was such a disaster. Call me in the morning. Love you. Bye."

I hung up and then turned my phone off. I needed to sleep and didn't want her calling me again tonight.

I WOKE to the sound of someone hammering on my front door.

My bedside clock showed me that it was just past three o'clock in the morning.

The hammering went on.

I turned on the bedside light and collected my dressing gown from its hook on the back of my bedroom door.

"OK, OK, I'm coming," I shouted as I walked down the corridor.

Bloody Clare, I thought. Go home.

I opened the front door, but it wasn't Clare. Someone shone a flashlight right into my face so I couldn't see anything.

"Mr. Shillingford?" said a voice in an official tone. "Mr. Mark Shillingford?"

"Yes," I said, holding my hand up and trying to see past the light. "What is it?"

"Kent Police, sir," said the voice. "Constable Davis." He held out his warrant card.

My skin went cold. Personal calls from the police at this time of night were never good news.

"I'm sorry, sir, but I have some very bad news for you," the constable went on. "It's your sister, Miss Clare Shillingford." He paused. "She's dead."

3

"Dead?" I said, my voice box seemingly detached from my body.

"Yes, sir," said PC Davis. "I'm afraid so."

"Where?" I asked in a croak.

I felt weak and swayed somewhat.

"Shall we come in, sir?" he said, stepping forward and supporting me by the elbow.

There were two of them, the other a female officer, and they guided me into my sitting room and down onto the sofa.

"Liz, get some sweet tea," the policeman said to his colleague.

I watched as she went over to the kitchenette and opened cupboards, looking for mugs.

"Top right," I said automatically.

Time seemed to stand still as the kettle boiled and a cup of hot tea was pressed into my hand.

"Drink it, sir," said the constable. "It will do you good."

I took a sip and winced. "I don't take sugar."

"You do tonight, sir. Drink it."

I drank some of the sweet liquid, but it didn't make me feel noticeably better.

"Where is she?" I asked.

"Sorry, sir," he said, "what do you mean?"

"Where is she?" I asked again. "I must go to her."

"All in good time, sir. We need to ask you some questions first."

I just looked at him.

"Are you, in fact, Miss Shillingford's next of kin?" the female officer asked.

"I don't know," I said. "Her parents—our parents—they're still alive. Does that make them the next of kin?"

"No husband?" she asked. "Or children?"

"No."

I drank some more of the tea.

"How did you find me?" I asked.

The two police officers looked at each other.

"We had your address, sir," said the man.

"How?" I asked again.

"It was amongst Miss Shillingford's possessions," he said.

"Where was she killed?" I asked.

"In central London. Park Lane."

I looked up at him. "How odd."

"Why odd, sir?"

"She wouldn't normally drive up Park Lane going from here to Newmarket."

"Was she here this evening?"

"Yes," I said. "Well, she was at Haxted Mill, down the road. We had dinner there together."

The policeman made a note in his notebook.

"But she didn't drink and drive, if that's what you're thinking. She only had fizzy water."

"What time did she leave?" he asked.

"About ten past nine," I said. I thought back to her spinning the wheels of her sports car as she left the parking lot. "I always said that bloody car would be the death of her."

"Oh no, sir," said the female officer. "It wasn't a car crash that killed her."

I stared at her.

"What, then?" I asked.

The police officers looked at each other once more.

"It appears that Miss Shillingford may have fallen from the balcony of a hotel."

I sat there with my mouth open.

"Where?" I said finally. "Which hotel?"

"The Hilton Hotel on Park Lane."

"But when?"

"At half past eleven."

Oh God! She had tried to call me twenty minutes before that.

"How are you sure it was her?" I asked in desperation. "It must be someone else."

"I am told, sir, that it is definitely Miss Clare Shillingford."

"But how can they know for sure?"

"I don't know that, sir. But I am told it's one hundred percent certain. Maybe there were witnesses."

"But it was an accident, right?" I asked forlornly.

"The incident is still under investigation. It will be up to the coroner to determine the cause of death."

There was something in the way he said it that gave me no comfort.

"Are you implying it wasn't an accident?"

"As I said, sir, that will be a matter for the coroner."

"But what was she doing at a hotel anyway?" I asked. "She said she had to go straight home to Newmarket."

"I can't say, sir," the policeman replied. "The investigating officer will no doubt look into that."

I sat on my sofa not knowing what to think or what to do. How could Clare be dead? It didn't seem real. She had been so alive just a few hours ago. I found I couldn't even cry. There were too many unanswered questions in my head.

"Now, sir, do you have the address for Miss Shillingford's parents? As next of kin, they need to be informed. There will also be a need for an official identification."

Oh God, I thought. That would kill my mother.

"How exactly did you have my address?" I asked.

"Apparently it was written on an envelope found in Miss Shillingford's hotel room."

"What was in the envelope?" I asked, perhaps not wanting to know the answer.

"I can't say, sir."

"Can't or won't?" I asked.

"Can't," he said. "I was not at the scene and was simply informed about the presence of your address on the envelope. My colleague and I are not from the Metropolitan Police, we're from Kent headquarters at Maidstone. Now, where do your parents live?"

"Oxted," I said.

"Surrey," the policeman said to his colleague with obvious displeasure. "We'll have to contact Guildford."

"It's only five miles away."

"Still outside our patch," said Constable Davis. "What address in Oxted?"

"I'll go and tell them," I said.

"Fine, sir. But I will still need their address as they will have to be officially informed. There are procedures to follow."

"Yes, of course." I gave him the address, and he wrote it in his notebook as well as relaying it over his personal radio. "Tell them to give me time to be there first."

He spoke again into the radio, but I couldn't hear the reply.

"The Surrey Police will be in no hurry, sir," he said. "They will probably visit your parents later in the morning."

"Thank you," I said. I bet the Surrey Police would be delighted not to have to perform what must be a dreadful duty. I certainly didn't relish the task. "I'll go and see them right away. I'd also better call my two brothers and my other sister."

"I would recommend that, sir. The incident is already being reported on the BBC radio news, and it will only be a matter of time before Miss Shillingford's name is mentioned, her being something of a celebrity and all."

"You've heard of her, then?" I was pleased.

"Oh yes, sir. I follow the horses a bit. Like to have a flutter now and again. And I've watched you on the telly lots of times. I saw you last Saturday on Channel 4."

Last Saturday suddenly seemed like a long time ago.

"Will you be all right now, sir? We can stay a while longer if you'd like."

"No, thank you. I'll be fine. I'll get dressed and drive over to Oxted."

IT WAS the worst journey of my life. Afterward I could hardly remember a single yard of the five miles from my apartment to my parents' house.

Lots of questions struggled to get a hearing in my consciousness.

What was she doing in a Park Lane hotel in the first place when she'd told me she was going straight home to Newmarket? Had our row at Haxted Mill somehow caused her to change her plans? Had she gone to the hotel to meet someone? How could she have fallen from a balcony? Why? Why? Why?

I couldn't get out of my head the image of her driving off from dinner without even a glance at me. I didn't know whether to be angry or sad.

And then there were the phone calls I had ignored.

Had she been calling me for help?

I should have answered them, I thought. What had I been doing? She was my sister, for goodness' sake, my darling twin sister. And she had needed me.

The tears started, and I had to pull over as I couldn't see the road. I sat in the driver's seat of my trusty old Ford and sobbed.

How could she be dead? She had been more full of life than anyone I had ever met. It must be a mistake.

I HAD SAT there for a full fifteen minutes before I had been able to continue, but it was still just before four when I pulled my Ford through the gates and down the sweeping driveway in front of the familiar Jacobean pile on the southern edge of Oxted.

My parents had moved here when Clare and I had been babies, my mother inheriting the place from her parents, but they had never had the money to decorate and furnish the house in the manner that its architectural grandeur demanded.

Dad had been a banker before his retirement. At least that

is what he regularly told everyone. In fact, he had spent his working life in the accounts department of a City of London investment bank, doing the paperwork for all the deals that other people had made.

I sat now in my car and looked up at the imposing façade lit only by the glow from the streetlights on the road at the far end of the drive. I suppose I must have had some happy times here when I'd been a young boy, but all I could remember were the fights of my teenage years.

By then, Dad had been in his late fifties, but he had somehow seemed much older. In spite of him having been only twenty-five at the start of the Swinging Sixties, pop music had passed him by, and he had regularly shouted at Clare and me for playing it at anything above a whisper, even in our bedrooms with the doors closed.

The thought of having any of our school friends around for a bit of a party was completely out of the question. For a start, he'd say, they then would know what we had in the house and would send burglars around when we were away. The fact that we had nothing much in the place that anyone would want to steal anyway seemed to have been beside the point.

By the time Clare and I had moved out to the apartment in Edenbridge, which we had done in secret one day when Dad had been in London for a reunion lunch at his bank, I had come to hate this house so much that I'd not returned to it for the next five years.

But I suppose as time moves on and we grow older, family ties become more important. Or maybe it's that our unhappy memories fade. Either way, I was now a regular visitor here, helping in the battle against dry rot and damp inside and organizing a man to assist with the garden outside.

Not that Dad and I had become close. He still liked to boss me around. The difference now was that I took no notice of him and went home when I could stand it no longer. Nowadays instead of rows, we simply had long periods of noncommunication. Clare had been right when she had said I'd rather put my head in the sand than do something more constructive. I had found it to be the recipe for a quieter life.

Well, now I *had* to do something, although I would have happily found some sand-hole in which to hide my head.

I turned on *BBC Radio 5 Live* and listened to the four o'clock news bulletin. Clare was the lead story, but they didn't mention her by name. "Police are investigating how a thirty-one-year-old woman fell to her death from the balcony of a central London hotel late last evening."

I clicked off the radio and got out of the car.

I decided that standing on the step and battering on the great oak front door, as I had done with Clare all those years ago, was not the right approach. Knowing my father, he would probably think I was a burglar, trying to get in, and call the police.

Instead, I used my cell to call their number.

I could hear the phone ringing in the hallway and, presently, my father answered it in the bedroom.

"Yes," he said, sounding very sleepy.

"Dad," I said, "it's Mark. I'm outside. Could you come down and let me in?"

"What do you want?" he asked, clearly irritated.

I could hear my mother in the background, asking who it was.

"Dad, just come down and open the front door."

"It's Mark." I heard him telling my mother. "He's outside and he wants to get in."

I didn't hear her reply, but he came back on the line. "OK," he said. "I'm coming down." He had that tone which implied he was doing me a huge favor.

If only he knew.

How, I thought, am I going to tell him that Clare was dead?

I USED THE POLICEMAN'S TRICK and made them both hot sweet tea.

My mother sat in an armchair and wept, rocking back and forth with a tissue pressed to her nose, while my father expressed any grief he might have with anger, most of it directed toward me as if abusing the messenger could somehow change the message.

"How did this happen?" he demanded, standing full square in the middle of their drawing room.

"I don't know," I said.

"Well, you bloody well should know," he bellowed. "Why didn't you ask the police?"

"I did," I said. "But they couldn't say."

"Nonsense!" he shouted at me. "You just didn't ask them in the right way."

"Would it make any difference?" I shouted back. "Knowing exactly what happened won't bring her back."

My mother uttered a whimper, and I went over to comfort her as her stupid fool of a husband marched around the room, bunching, then relaxing, his fists. I suppose grief affects people in different ways. He clearly wanted to lash out at something—to have someone to blame, someone to hit.

In truth, part of me felt the same way.

"We had better call James, Stephen, and Angela," I said. "Before they hear it on the radio."

"You do it," my father instructed.

Oh thanks, I thought.

"I'll ask them all if they'd like to come here. Is that OK?"

"Yes," my mother said between sobs.

I thought my father was about to say something, but he obviously had second thoughts and kept quiet, just nodding.

I went into his study and used the phone on his big oak desk in the bay window to pass on the bad news to our siblings, waking each one in turn.

"Oh God, Mark," said James, my elder brother, "I'm so sorry."

He made it sound like it was more of a loss for me than for him, which, I suppose, was true. Losing one's twin, I was discovering, was like losing half of oneself.

They all agreed to come to Oxted, although in Stephen's case it would take all day to get there as he and his wife, Tracy, were on holiday near Saint-Tropez in the south of France.

"Just come as soon as you can. We all need to be together."

I wondered why I had said that to him. Did we all need to be together? We had hardly been together in the past. Other than Clare, Stephen was the youngest of my siblings, but he was still some sixteen years older than me. I had no memory of him living at home because he had also flown the nest as soon as he'd been able, just as we all had.

Once or twice over the years we had gathered together for Christmas, but they had never been great social successes, mostly descending into bitterness and recrimination rather than uplifting us all into happiness and goodwill.

The last time all five of the Shillingford children had been under the same roof had been at a London hotel where we had gathered two years ago to commemorate my parents' golden wedding anniversary.

Now we would never all be together again.

I sat at my father's desk and was again close to tears. But I made one final telephone call, to Lisa, the producer of *The Morning Line*, the Saturday racing program on Channel 4. I knew she wouldn't still be in bed. She would already be at Newmarket racetrack getting ready for the live broadcast that started just before eight o'clock.

She answered on the second ring. "Lisa here," she said.

"It's Mark," I said.

"My, you're up early," she said. "And you're not even on the show. Aren't you at Newbury today?"

"That's partly why I'm calling," I said. "Can you tell Neville I won't be able to make it to Newbury today?"

"You tell him," she said with some humor in her voice.

"Lisa," I said. "My sister's been killed."

"Not Clare?" she asked.

"Yes," I said. "Have you heard the radio news this morning?"

"Yes," she said slowly.

"Clare was the woman who fell from the hotel balcony."

"Oh my God!" She paused. "Can we use it?"

Always the journalist.

"Yes," I said. Why else had I rung her?

"Any details?"

"No, nothing other than you'd know from the news. And be kind."

"Of course," she said. "Mark, I'm so sorry. And leave Neville to me."

"Thank you, I will. And Lisa, no one else knows."

"Right," she said. "Thanks."

A **POLICEMAN** arrived at the house at eight o'clock, but he wasn't from the Surrey constabulary, he was from the Met.

"Mr. Shillingford?" he asked when I opened the door.

"Yes," I said.

"Detective Sergeant Sharp," he said, holding out his ID card.

"Detective?" I said.

"Every unexplained death is investigated by a detective. Can I come in?"

I took him through into the drawing room where my mother was still sitting in the same armchair, wearing her dressing gown. My father had been upstairs to dress, and we had also been joined by Angela, my elder sister, and her husband, Nicholas, who had arrived from their home in Hertfordshire. I made the introductions, and the sergeant sat down facing us.

"I am very sorry for your loss," he said to the five expectant faces. "Can any of you suggest why Miss Shillingford would take her own life?"

4

"uicide?" my father said loudly. "But that can't be so."

"I'm afraid it appears to be," said the detective sergeant. He opened his briefcase and removed a clear plastic folder containing a single sheet of paper. "This was found in Miss Shillingford's room at the hotel."

He held out the folder and, as I was nearest, I took it, which was appropriate because the sheet of paper inside was a brief, handwritten letter addressed to me on Hilton Hotel–headed notepaper.

Dear Marky,

Thank you for dinner tonight. I am sorry it was such a disaster. You are right—you're always right. I don't know what has been happening to me these last few months. Please don't think badly of me.

I am so sorry

There was no signature, but I recognized the handwriting, and only Clare had called me Marky. I couldn't stop the tears running in streams down my cheeks. I passed it to Angela, who also sobbed.

"What was it you were right about?" the detective sergeant asked.

"Just something about her riding at Lingfield yesterday," I replied, wiping my face with my fingers.

Suddenly it didn't seem to be that important.

"Was there anything she said at dinner that might have indicated she was troubled?"

"No," I said. "Quite the reverse. She was looking forward to riding today at Newmarket. And she was hopeful of being the first lady jockey to win a Classic next May. I can't believe she would kill herself."

"She wouldn't," my father said decisively from over by the window. "Clare was here only yesterday, and she was talking about coming back to see us in two weeks. Why would she do that if she was contemplating suicide? It's all nonsense."

"And," I said, "she hardly ate anything at dinner last night because she was due to be riding very light today. Why would she bother?"

The phone vibrated in my pocket. In my business, ringing phones on the air were severely frowned upon, and I had been caught out too often in the past. Nowadays I permanently left mine on "vibrate only."

It was Sarah, the lady Clare had called my non-proper girl-friend.

"Excuse me a moment," I said, walking out into the hallway.

I answered the phone. "Hello."

"Mark, my darling, I've been watching *The Morning Line*. I can't believe it. Oh my love, I'm so sorry." She was crying.

"Thank you for calling," I said inadequately. "I'm at my parents' house, and it's a bit bloody here at the moment."

"I don't suppose you'll be at Newbury, then?"

"No," I said. "Sorry."

"OK. I'll call you later," Sarah said.

"Right. Bye, now."

She disconnected, and I stood for a moment in the hallway, thinking. What was it that Clare had said? *When are you going to realize she won't ever leave Mitchell? She can't afford to.*

Mitchell was her husband—Mitchell Stacey—her much older husband. He was one of the country's leading steeplechase trainers, with over eighty top horses in his yard in the village of East Ilsley, north of Newbury.

It had been five years now since that Friday night at Doncaster when Sarah and I had carelessly ended up in bed, professing undying love for each other.

We had both been there for the two-day Christmas National Hunt Meeting. I had been commentating at the course, and Mitchell had had runners on both days. He and Sarah had stayed over in the same hotel as me, where we had all dined together in a large party of racing folk. Mitchell and the others had gone straight to bed after dinner, as was the norm, in my experience, with racehorse trainers, while Sarah and I had shared, first, another bottle of red wine, then a nightcap liqueur or two, followed by a passionate sexual encounter in my bedroom.

Since then we had survived on snatched hours here and there, sometimes even a night or two together whenever Mitchell was away at the sales, and I had run up huge telephone bills calling her cell.

We had been due to see each other at the Newbury races this afternoon and then for a while afterward at a carefully selected, discreet motel near Hungerford, one more fleeting assignation in our ongoing dangerous liaison.

Another of Clare's pearls of wisdom came floating into my mind—*Tell her it's now or never and you're fed up waiting. You're wasting your life.*

Was I?

I was thirty-one, and Sarah was four years my senior. Mitchell, however, was now in his sixties, having been married twice before. How he had wooed and won the then-twenty-one-year-old Sarah remained a mystery to me, but perhaps it was something to do with his immense wealth, most of which he had inherited as a baby from his grandfather, an eccentric oil magnate.

They didn't have any children of their own—Sarah told me that Mitchell had had a vasectomy before they met—but there were three boys from his previous marriages, and Sarah was being the dutiful stepmother. The youngest was about to finish school, and Sarah told me that then she would leave Mitchell and come and live with me. But, in truth, it was the latest in a long list of prospective departure dates, and maybe Clare had been right: Sarah never would leave Mitchell. She couldn't afford to.

But did I care? Was I, in fact, not content with how things were? The old joke—*I used to be indecisive, but now I'm not so sure*—seemed to have been written for me. As things stood, sex was fairly frequent and exciting, but I also quite enjoyed the freedom of living on my own.

However, there was also the worry of being found out. Mitchell Stacey was a hugely influential character in racing, and

I wasn't at all sure my job would be safe if he discovered that I'd been seducing his wife behind his back. But would it be any better if we came clean and Sarah left him for me? Probably not. The best thing, I decided, was simply to carry on as before and not get caught.

Nicholas, my brother-in-law, came out of the drawing room, looking for me. "This policeman needs to ask you some more questions."

"Sorry. I'm coming."

DETECTIVE SERGEANT SHARP remained for another two hours, asking mundane questions and annoying us all. My brother James, the eldest of the Shillingford offspring, arrived in the middle with his scatterbrained wife, Helen, so much of the ground had to be covered again.

Finally, the policeman seemed content with the answers he had, not that any of us were able to give him any reason why Clare should have thrown herself to her death from the balcony of a hotel room on the fifteenth floor.

"Are you sure that's a suicide note?" I'd asked him as he'd shown it to James. "It doesn't say anything about dying."

He'd said nothing, but his expression had shown that he thought I was grasping at straws. Maybe I was.

"I'm afraid there will need to be a formal identification of the body," he said in the hallway.

To his credit, Nicholas volunteered immediately.

"It would be better to be a blood relative," said the detective, "rather than an in-law."

"Can't you do it by DNA?" I asked.

"We can, sir, yes. But that takes time."

And money, I thought.

"The coroner will likely want to open an inquest first thing on Monday, and he will want evidence of identification at that point."

"The policeman who came last night told me that you were one hundred percent certain it was Clare. He said there were witnesses. Who were they?"

The detective somehow seemed reluctant to tell me.

"Who were they?" I pressed.

"There had been a charity gala dinner in the ballroom of the Hilton Hotel. Most of the guests had left before Miss Shillingford fell." He paused. "But there were a few that had stayed on after the dinner for a drink in the bar. She narrowly missed landing on this group as they were waiting for a taxi."

Oh God, I thought.

"The gala dinner," he went on, "had been in aid of the Injured Jockeys Fund."

Of course. I remembered getting an invitation to buy tickets for the event, but, as usual, I had left it so late before deciding that all the spaces had already gone.

"And the group had included a Mr. Reg Nicholl, an ex–police superintendent who, I understand, is now the head of the racing security services. It was he who confirmed the identity of Miss Shillingford."

"I still can't understand what she was doing there in the first place," I said, "let alone having booked a room. I feel this is just a huge mistake and that Clare is at home, safe, in Newmarket."

"I'm afraid it's not a mistake, sir. It would appear that your sister turned up at the hotel without having made a reservation.

There had been a cancellation, and Miss Shillingford checked in using her credit card at . . ."—he consulted his notebook—". . . ten-twenty p.m."

An hour and ten minutes after leaving me. She must have gone almost straight from Haxted Mill to the hotel. But why?

In the end it was decided that James would go with Detective Sergeant Sharp to perform the gruesome task of making a formal identification, and Nicholas would go with him for support.

I couldn't decide whether I should go as well. Part of me really wanted to in order to see Clare for one last time, but I was frightened. Fifteen floors was a long way down, and I didn't like to think about what the impact might have done to her. But, equally, I was distressed by my memory of the last time I had seen her alive, staring straight ahead in anger as she drove away from the restaurant.

THE AFTERNOON dragged by, with my mother taking herself off to bed, while my father wore a groove in the carpet, endlessly pacing up and down the drawing room. Helen and Angela, meanwhile, adjourned to the kitchen to find us all something to eat, and I settled down in the small sitting room on my own to watch the racing on Channel 4 from Newmarket and Newbury.

The program started with a short tribute to Clare, showing video clips of her winning many races on a variety of horses. The flags at Newmarket racetrack were flying at half-mast, and there was even a minute's silence before the first race, with some racegoers clearly in tears.

I watched the races, but less than half my mind was on the action. I kept coming back to the same two questions. Why had

Clare gone to a hotel in central London? And why had she killed herself?

So distracted was I that I only remembered my hundred-pound bet on Raised Heartbeat when the horse was being loaded into the starting gate at Newbury. As I had predicted last evening, his price had shortened from thirteen-to-two to five-to-one, but with my computer still at my apartment it was too late now to lay the horse on the Internet exchanges. My money would just have to take its chances on the nose.

The horses broke from the gate in an even line, and I found myself commentating on the race inside my head. However, as was always the case, my eye was drawn unintentionally toward the horse I had backed. It was why I almost never had a bet in those races on which I was commentating, it was simply too distracting.

Raised Heartbeat lived up to his name, lifting my own pulse a notch or two, as he fought out a tight finish with the favorite, going down to defeat only in the final stride.

My hundred pounds was lost, but it was a minor inconvenience compared to the greater loss of my twin sister.

I sat there alone for quite a while and wept.

I cried in grief, but also I cried in frustration. Death was so final, so permanent. There was no "undo button" like there was on my computer.

Why oh why hadn't I answered the phone when Clare had called me? Perhaps I could have prevented this disaster.

STEPHEN AND TRACY arrived from Saint-Tropez at four o'clock, just as James and Nicholas returned from the morgue, looking drawn and shell-shocked.

I didn't need to ask how it had been, and I was suddenly thankful that I'd decided not to go with them.

James just nodded at me before disappearing into the cloakroom. I wondered if he was going to be sick.

"Bloody awful," said Nicholas. "Literally, bloody awful. But it was her. No mistake."

I hadn't really expected there to be a mistake, but the confirmation of what we already knew was, nevertheless, another cause of distress, especially for my mother, who had come down to greet the new arrivals.

We sat once more in the drawing room, this time for some tea, except that my father refused to sit down, again pacing back and forth near the French windows.

None of us could imagine why Clare would have taken her own life. We speculated about what might have been troubling her but came up short providing any answers.

"I absolutely refuse to believe she committed suicide," said my father resolutely. "It had to have been an accident."

"Or murder," said Stephen.

Everyone looked at him. Even my father ceased his pacing.

"Don't be ridiculous," he said. "Why on earth would anyone want to kill our Clare? Everyone loved her."

But who would think that anyone would have wanted to kill John Lennon? People had loved him too.

"What about the note?" said scatterbrained Helen. "It certainly looked like a suicide note to me."

I watched as my father, over her head, gave Helen a contemptuous stare. He had never been slow in expressing his disapproval of James's choice of wife, and she clearly was not endearing herself to him right now.

"But why would she kill herself?" Angela wailed, putting into words once more what we were all asking ourselves.

"Maybe because living in this family is not always easy," Helen said somewhat tactlessly.

I thought my father was going to explode behind her.

"Shut up, you silly woman," he bellowed from somewhere close to her ear.

Helen instantly burst into tears and was comforted by James, who tried to defend his wife.

"It's true," he said. "Helen is right. We are all so competitive."

Yes, I suppose we were.

It was how we had been brought up. *Top of the class, top of the class, you must strive to be top of the class.* It had been drummed into us as children. *School, university, first-class degree, job in the City.* It had been like a mantra for our father.

He had been appalled and outraged when both Clare and I had announced that we had no wish to follow our older siblings to Oxford or Cambridge, or to any other university, but were determined to go straight into racing. Not that racing had been a departure for the Shillingford family.

Prior to his retirement to a villa in southern Spain, our uncle, my father's younger brother, had been a multi-Classic-winning Newmarket trainer, and he had himself taken over the stable from our grandfather. Two of my cousins were also in the racing business, one as a trainer in the family yard and the other as the owner of a racehorse transport firm. Indeed, the Shillingfords were a much respected racing family and had been owners, trainers, and occasionally jockeys, in and around Newmarket since the days of Charles II and the founding of the Jockey Club.

It had been my father who had been the one to take a different route, becoming the first Shillingford of record to get a university degree, let alone a first-class from Merton College, Oxford.

But there was no doubt that the family as a whole, whether in the City of London or on the racetrack, had a huge competitive streak in its makeup. Clare certainly had, and she'd said so at our dinner at Haxted Mill.

Only I amongst the Shillingford clan, it seemed, hadn't been born with fire in his belly to be *The Very Best of the Best*. But even I could be pretty competitive if pushed, and I didn't like it much when people said that I wasn't the best commentator in racing, although I knew what they were saying was true.

"Perhaps we drove her to it," James said gloomily.

"What utter nonsense," my father stated, resuming his pacing. This time, however, he didn't pace aimlessly back and forth but made a beeline for the liquor cabinet in the corner. "I need a drink," he said, sloshing a hefty slug of whisky into a tumbler and knocking it back in one gulp.

I looked at my watch. It was only a quarter to five, but it felt much later. I'd already been up for almost fourteen hours, and I'd had far less than a full night's sleep before that.

I, too, could have done with a drink, but I didn't say so.

And I did tend to agree with my father on one point: I also couldn't envisage how the family could have driven Clare to kill herself. Sure, we were all competitive, but, if anything, Clare was more competitive than the rest of us put together. And she had thrived on it.

People who took their own lives, I'd always believed, were driven to it by failure and rejection, not by success and widespread affection. But I knew that wasn't universally true. I could recall several high-profile suicides whose deaths had staggered the public, where an outward persona of joy, happiness, and huge achievement had masked some inner depression and hopelessness.

The real truth was that one never knew what was going on in someone else's head.

And the big question that wouldn't leave mine was whether Clare's death was related to me confronting her about her riding of Bangkok Flyer and her subsequent admission of race fixing.

Her note might seem to imply this, but her unconcerned, almost blasé reaction at dinner hardly seemed to fit with her being so tormented by it that she had thrown herself from a balcony only two and a half hours later. However, I decided that now was neither the time nor the place to introduce this new factor into the discussion.

Nothing prepares a family for death, particularly the death of one of its youngest members. But my family had responded in true Shillingford fashion, shouting one another down and refusing to countenance any opinion but their own. Only Nicholas demonstrated any real decorum, and I realized he was the only one amongst them I actually liked.

I finally escaped from this hotbed of accusation and blame, using the excuse that there were insufficient bedrooms for us all to stay and, as I lived closest, it was easiest for me to come and go.

So I went, and just as soon as I could.

5

On Monday I went to the races and back to work. It seemed like the logical thing to do.

I had sat at home alone all day Sunday, feeling miserable, answering the hundreds of e-mails that kindly people had sent, and dealing with the fifty or so voice messages on my phones. How I wished Clare had left a message on Friday evening.

Why hadn't I answered her call?

By Monday morning I'd been desperately in need of some human contact, but the thought of going back to my family in Oxted had filled me with horror. So much so that I'd invented a sudden nasty cold in order to escape from them.

"Are you sure you can't come?" my mother had asked when I'd called early Sunday morning.

"Quite sure," I'd replied while holding my nose. "I don't want to give this cold to Dad."

I'd been on safe ground. She knew as well as I did that my father was obsessive about avoiding people with colds. Indeed, he was obsessive about lots of things. How she had put up with him for fifty-two years I couldn't imagine.

"I DIDN'T THINK you'd be here today," Derek said from behind me as I climbed the half dozen steps up to RacingTV's scanner, the blacked-out production truck parked in a compound near the Windsor racetrack stables. "I've arranged for Iain Ferguson to present."

"That's fine by me," I said, turning around. "I'll just help where I can. To be honest, I don't feel up to much anyway."

"No," said Derek. He paused. "Look, mate, I'm really sorry about Clare. I can't actually believe it."

"Thanks, Derek," I replied. "I can't believe it either. Half the time I feel that life has to go on as normal and then, the next minute, I wonder why I bother to do anything at all. I think it's the frustration that's the worst, frustration that I can't turn back time, can't bring her back."

I was close to tears once more and I knew it was evident in my voice. Open displays of emotion could be unsettling, and I could tell that Derek didn't quite know what to do.

"It's OK," I said, breathing deeply. "You must be busy. You get on."

"Right," he said, clearly relieved. "I had better. Are you coming to the production meeting?"

"I thought I'd sit in at the back."

Whether I was working for Channel 4 or for RacingTV, the first task of my day was always to attend the production meeting, where the running order for the show was discussed and agreed upon. The meeting took place in the scanner at least three hours before the broadcast was due to begin.

The producer, Derek in this case, began by handing out the printout of the draft running order. That afternoon, RacingTV was covering all seven races at Windsor, and also seven from Leicester racetrack a hundred or so miles to the north, the paddock presenter there joining us via live video link.

The program was on the air from two o'clock to six, four hours of high-octane adrenaline. If things went wrong and off script, as they usually did at some point during the afternoon, then we just had to carry on regardless. The thing about live television was that mistakes were history as soon as you made them, there was nothing you could do to unmake them. There was no saying, "Let's do that again," as you might in a recorded program where you could do it over and over until it was perfect.

In all, there were three race meetings taking place that afternoon, with Hamilton being broadcast on the other satellite network. Even though a race was scheduled only every half hour at each track, the times were staggered so that, across the three venues, a race was due to start every ten minutes, from ten past two until five-thirty, which was fine as long as all of them went off roughly on time.

If a horse got loose or lost a shoe on the way to the start, or if a stirrup leather or bridle broke, the delay could throw out the whole schedule, resulting in races at different courses running simultaneously. And that gave the producer a big headache.

Added to the actual broadcasting of the races were interviews with winning trainers and jockeys, trophy presentations, video footage of prior races of the main participants, as well as comments from the paddock presenters. And somewhere there also had to be found the time to fit in a set number of breaks for advertisements and also promos for future races.

Manic, it was not, but it was full-on nevertheless, and everyone would breathe a collective sigh of relief come three minutes to six o'clock when the production assistant would say *"Shut up"* in everyone's ears, meaning the show was over and we were off the air.

Derek called the production meeting to order. "There's to be a minute's silence here at Windsor in memory of Clare Shillingford." Everyone in the scanner instinctively turned around to glance at me. "It will be before the first race at two twenty-five, after the horses have gone out onto the course. There will be a loud beep over the public address to start and also to finish the minute. Iain, do the introduction, please, but don't talk during the minute, your mike will stay live. During it we will show the flag on the grandstand, which is flying at half-mast, and then slowly fade to a picture of Clare after forty seconds. If we are on schedule, it should come comfortably after the first from Leicester. If there's a delay at Leicester and the silence occurs during their race, we will record the silence here at Windsor and play it back immediately after as if live. Iain, your cue to speak will be the second beep, and we'll go pretty much straight to a commercial break after a few words. Understand?" Iain nodded. "And full silence, please, everyone, for the whole minute, not even any talk-back."

Talk-back was what played continually into everyone's ear through an earpiece on a coiled wire like those worn by Secret Service agents. The producer, his assistant, and the director would all speak, giving cues to presenters, or instructions to cameramen and the vision mixer, or counting down time while the clips were shown or commercials transmitted.

One became used to listening to all the chatter but picking up only the material that was relevant to you. The art of great presenting was to absorb and react to the talk-back while speaking live on air at the same time. Only the very best could carry on an interview, listening and responding to an interviewee's answers while at the same time taking in appropriate talk-back information.

Derek went through the rest of the planned running order, assigning jobs to be done and detailing all the many expected "Astons," the captions that are overlaid pictures to give the viewers information, be it betting prices, horses' and jockeys' names, details of non-runners, and so on and so on. It was the full-time job of two staff members sitting at the back of the scanner to type Astons and have them ready whenever the producer called for them.

And then there were the video clips of prior races to be annotated and spoken about, all of which would be recorded before the program went on the air so that the clips, or VTs, were stored and ready to broadcast. *VT* stood for "video tape," and the term was still used even though the recordings were stored not on tapes these days but on a computer hard drive.

The magic of television allowed two complete afternoons of racing, one from Leicester and the other from Windsor, to be fitted into the time of just one of them.

By careful use of VTs, the runners could be shown in the parade ring while they were really on their way to the start. Interviews with trainers at Windsor might be recorded while races from Leicester were being run, then played back at a time when the trainers would have been unavailable, busy saddling their horses.

Often the only things that were "live" in the whole broadcast were the races themselves, and that was a "must do" rule. The rest didn't matter. Interviews recorded after the first race might be shown later in the afternoon, if time permitted, or dropped altogether if no slot could be found. Everything was timed and cut to fit together like a jigsaw puzzle around the immovable races, filling up four hours of television that then seemed to whiz past in a flash.

I spent the first part of the afternoon in the scanner, sitting behind Derek and getting an unfamiliar view of the production as he marshaled his troops at the two racetracks, slotting everything together like a dry-stone waller taking irregular-sized segments and fashioning them to form a coherent, solid structure. It was an art, and Derek was one of the best.

Immediately after the third race at Windsor, I ventured out of the dark cavern of the scanner into the bright Berkshire sunlight.

As I walked across to the parade ring through the fairly meager Monday-afternoon crowd, it became apparent to me that the bereavement of others can be a disorienting and distressing experience for some. No end of people, including some I knew quite well, averted their eyes and hurried away as if they didn't want to burst some imaginary grief bubble that surrounded me. Even those who did talk to me seemed uncomfortable doing so.

I think it was the concept of suicide, rather than the death itself, that made for the embarrassment. Somehow, it seems that taking one's own life carries an even greater stigma than taking someone else's.

I was beginning to wish I hadn't left the comfort and security of the scanner, but I was a man on a mission—I was looking for Geoff Grubb, the trainer of Scusami, who had a runner in the fourth.

"Good God, Mark. What are you doing here?" said a man, grabbing me by the arm as I was walking by. "I thought you'd be at Oxted."

It was Brendan Shillingford, my cousin who trained in my grandfather's old yard in Newmarket.

"I'm working with RacingTV. At least I'm meant to be, but I don't really know myself what I'm doing here. I just had to get away from the rest of the family."

Brendan nodded. He knew all about his relations.

"I spoke to both James and Stephen yesterday at Uncle Joe's. They said things were pretty awful. What a bloody business."

"Yeah," I said. "A real bugger."

"Any news yet on a funeral?"

"Not as yet," I said. "The police have to agree."

"Police?" Brendan asked. "Why are they involved?"

"Something about all sudden deaths having to be investigated. They released a statement yesterday that there were no suspicious circumstances, so I don't suppose we'll have to wait too long. The coroner may have already said we can go ahead. I just haven't heard yet."

"Do you have any idea why she did it?" Brendan asked.

"None at all," I said. "Clare and I had grown slightly apart these last few months. But I know she'd been seeing someone she didn't want anyone to find out about. Perhaps that had something to do with it."

"Who was it?" he asked.

"I've no idea. I'm looking for Geoff Grubb in the hope that he might be able to tell me."

"That'll be a waste of time," Brendan said. He forced a smile. "Geoff wouldn't know about anything unless it's got four legs and a tail."

"I think I'll ask him anyway. Give my love to Gillian." I started to move away.

"Let me know about the funeral," Brendan called after me. "I need time to organize flights for Mom and Dad from Marbella. And try to avoid Thursday, Friday, or Saturday next week. It's the Cambridgeshire meeting."

Good point, I thought. I had better make sure that my father or brothers weren't in the process of fixing a funeral date without first referring to the racing calendar.

I found Geoff Grubb hurrying out of the weighing room with a tiny racing saddle over his arm.

"Geoff," I said. "Do you have time for a word?"

He slowed. "Only a quick one. I've got to go and saddle Planters Inn."

"I'll walk with you," I said, falling in beside him.

"I'm really sorry about Clare. Bloody nuisance, too, I can tell you. I've had to find different jockeys for all my runners."

I considered that to be a minor inconvenience, in the circumstances, but I let it pass.

"Geoff, I know that Clare had been seeing someone recently."

"Seeing someone?" he asked.

Perhaps Brendan had been right about it being a waste of time.

"Yes," I said. "Seeing someone—you know, a boyfriend."

"Oh, right," Geoff said, nodding.

"Do you have any idea who it might have been?"

"It wasn't me," he said seriously.

"No," I agreed. Not even for a nanosecond did I imagine that my sister had been having an affair of the heart with Geoff Grubb. He might have been outstanding with his horses, but his people skills were almost nonexistent. "But do you know who it was?"

He shook his head. "Sorry."

"Did you ever see anyone coming and going from Clare's place?" Clare had lived in a cottage attached to Geoff's training stables.

He shook his head again. "Not that I recall."

"Was there ever a car parked outside?"

"That sports car of hers was there," he said unhelpfully.

"Any others?"

"A few, now and again, but not a regular one," he said. "Not that I can remember anyway."

It wasn't that his memory was bad. He could have told me in detail about every race run by every horse in his expansive yard, not just this year but throughout their whole lives. He simply didn't notice anything else going on around him, not unless it impacted on the training of his horses.

"Do you mind if I come and have a look round her cottage?"

"Help yourself," he said. "The rent's paid for the rest of the month. Will you be clearing her things?"

"Probably. Me or someone else in the family."

"There's a spare key in the yard office."

"Thanks," I said. "I'll try to be up there sometime this week."

He hurried off toward the saddling stalls, and I watched him go.

Clare had ridden as his number one stable jockey for the past four years and they had made a good team. I wondered if he had been the one that Clare had liked to control. But she hadn't ridden exclusively for Geoff Grubb. As was the case with all jockeys, she had also been engaged by other trainers when Geoff didn't have any runners.

And I knew that Bangkok Flyer wasn't one of Geoff's.

BACK IN THE SCANNER, the afternoon was progressing on schedule. There had been no significant delays in the races, and Derek was calm, which meant that everyone else was also calm, all of them working smoothly together.

I, in contrast, wasn't doing anything useful, merely being a spectator. I thought about leaving and going home. But that wouldn't make me feel any better. At least here I had something to watch, something to take my mind off Clare.

Guilt was a soul-destroying emotion and I had lain awake half the previous night, staring into the void, into the emptiness of despair and self-condemnation. Why hadn't I answered the bloody telephone? How could I have ignored her when she had needed me the most?

"There's a dog on the course at Leicester," Derek said through the talk-back while looking at the pictures coming down the line. *"Can we get a close-up?"*

Dogs on racetracks, although rare, were always good for "atmosphere" shots, provided they didn't actually delay the races and screw up the schedule. Most racing folk loved their dogs as much as they did their horses, and there was nothing like a loose puppy to provide a bit of "Aahh" appeal to a broadcast. It made a welcome change from the crying babies with runny noses that the cameramen usually found amongst the crowd.

The afternoon continued without any significant problems. I watched on the transmission screen as Iain Ferguson interviewed guests in the paddock and talked about the horses, performing the role that I should have had. He was good. Too damn good, I thought. I'd better be careful or he'd have my job permanently, and I certainly didn't want that.

I loved my work, and I specifically enjoyed the variation that came from splitting my time between presenting for Channel 4 and RacingTV, and also doing the racetrack commentaries. And I had no intention of allowing someone else to take over any of my seats. I'd better sort my head out fast and get back to my jobs while I still had them.

The production assistant counted down to a commercial break. *"Two minutes and forty seconds,"* she called, and everyone relaxed as the preset sequence was played direct from the RacingTV headquarters building near Oxford. The commercials were the only downtime during the whole four-hour broadcast, and the crew in the scanner used the break to get coffee, visit the bathroom, or just to stretch cramped legs.

"You all right?" Derek asked, standing up and turning around to face me.

"Fine," I said. "Makes a change for me to see you at work rather than just to hear it on the talk-back. It's very interesting."

"Well, don't get any ideas of taking my job." He smiled at me, but he wasn't exactly making a joke. In times of recession and cuts, everyone, it seemed, was watching their backs, and none more so than in the TV business.

"Coming out of break in twenty seconds," called the production assistant. Everyone sat down again at their places. *"Five, four, three, two, one."* She fell silent, and the whole juggernaut rolled back smoothly into motion bang on cue.

"FOUR MINUTES TO SHUT-UP," said the production assistant through the talk-back.

It was now precisely seven minutes to six, and all the races were over for the afternoon. Iain was doing the roundup, the last few moments of each race being shown in turn with his voice-over, mostly discussing possible future plans for each of the winners.

"Two minutes to shut-up," said the assistant.

Iain went on talking without a pause as the production assistant's voice spoke in his ear, not only with the countdown to the shut-up but also those to the end of each piece of VT.

"Iain, coming to you in picture in five seconds," said Derek, adding to the chatter.

"Thirty seconds to shut-up," said his assistant at the same time. *"Four, three, two, one, cue Iain."*

"Well, that's it for this afternoon," said Iain, his smiling face now being broadcast to the viewers. "Join us later here on RacingTV for American racing live from Belmont Park in New York."

"Twenty seconds."

"And tomorrow we'll be back for live flat racing from Folkestone, and also six contests over the sticks from Newton Abbot."

"Ten seconds. Nine, eight . . ."

"So this is Iain Ferguson here at Windsor wishing you a very good evening."

". . . two, one, shut up," said the assistant as Iain fell silent and the program titles and theme music were brought up by the vision mixer.

"Well done, everybody," said Derek. *"Production meeting tomorrow morning at Folkestone at eleven. And Iain, can you come to the scanner before you go home?"* Derek flicked off his microphone and leaned back in his chair, stretching his arms high above his head. He yawned loudly. "God, I'm tired."

So am I, I thought, yawning in sympathy, but, unlike him, I hadn't done a stroke of work all day. In my case it was probably something to do with not having had any proper sleep for the past three nights.

Derek twisted around in his chair to face me. "What do you think about tomorrow?"

I was scheduled to present from Folkestone. "I'll be fine if you want me."

"I actually think we should stick with Iain for the rest of this week," he said. "It might be construed as somewhat insensitive on your part to return too soon. But how would you feel about doing a full tribute piece about Clare for broadcast on Saturday from Newmarket?"

"Channel 4 have already asked me," I said. "I'm filming it on Thursday, and it'll be shown on *The Morning Line* on Saturday, and also during the afternoon. I think I'd better check with them before I do another."

"It's all right," said Derek. "I'll ask Iain to do ours."

Iain, it seemed to me, was being asked to do far too much.

"You could always ask Channel 4 if you can use the same piece." Cooperation between the broadcasters was rare but not completely unknown.

"Maybe. But using Iain will give us a slightly different slant." He paused. "Sorry, I didn't mean that to sound how it did."

"It's OK," I said. "That's sensible."

And it was. I'd have done the same thing in his position.

"Do you think it'll it be OK for me to use the RacingTV database in Oxford for my tribute piece?" I asked.

"I'm sure it will," said Derek. "You know we've had that new indexing system installed."

"That's exactly why I want to use it."

"It's really fabulous. Just put in Clare's name under 'Jockey' and then click on 'Winner' and it will list all the races that she's won, together with the other runners, the prize money, the distances, the prices, everything. Then you just have to click on any entry in the list to play the VT straight back. It's absolutely brilliant."

"Great," I said.

"But you don't have to go all the way to Oxford, you know. You can access everything just as easily from the scanner. Not now, of course, because the link will be down, but tomorrow from Folkestone. The link will be up by about ten and there'll be about three hours clear before racing."

"Thanks," I said. "But I still think I'll go to Oxford. Then I've got all day."

"Suit yourself," Derek said rather dismissively. He obviously thought that I surely could find the videos I needed of Clare winning races in three hours and he was well aware that my home in Edenbridge was a lot closer to Folkestone than it was to Oxford.

That was all true, but I didn't really want Derek looking over my shoulder all the time I was accessing the video database because I was actually far more interested in searching for races that Clare had purposely lost.

6

It was a bit like the searching for the proverbial needle in the haystack.

During the past four months, the height of the flat-racing season, Clare had ridden almost every day, often four or five times in an afternoon, and sometimes at an evening meeting as well.

According to the database, since the beginning of June there had been four hundred and twenty-nine races run in which Clare had been one of the jockeys and she'd been on the winner in thirty-seven of them, including her last-ever ride at Lingfield the previous Friday on Scusami.

What was it that Clare had said when I asked her how often she had stopped a horse from winning? *Three or four times, maybe five.* And what had she written in her note? *I don't know what has been happening to me these last few months.*

I assumed, therefore, that the three or four races, or maybe five, would have been in the last few months. I had better start at the beginning of the four hundred and twenty-nine and just go through them all, ignoring only the ones she had actually won. That left three hundred and ninety-two races to watch. I settled myself into the studio chair for a lengthy session.

But first I watched again her ride on Bangkok Flyer the previous Friday to remind me of exactly what I was looking for. The more I saw it, the more obvious it seemed. I was sure that I'd have no trouble spotting it again in a different race. All I really needed was to watch the final eighth of a mile.

I also looked to see who trained Bangkok Flyer. I knew most things about the horses that I watched regularly, including their owners and trainers, but Bangkok Flyer was a two-year-old maiden, and Friday had been the first time I'd seen him run.

According to the database, he was trained in a Newmarket stable by Austin Reynolds, for a long time the "nearly man" of British flat racing. Austin was now in his mid- to late fifties, and he had never quite fulfilled his potential in the sport.

Perhaps too much had been expected of him because he'd enjoyed such phenomenal success very early, winning the Derby, the Oaks, and the St. Leger in only his second year as a young trainer. Since those heady days of more than twenty years ago, he had never again saddled a Classic winner, and he'd precious few other big-race victories to his name either.

Nowadays he mostly sent his horses north to race on the Yorkshire circuits, marketing himself to businessmen from the area—prospective owners who might appreciate his fashionable Newmarket address.

Bangkok Flyer had raced three times prior to his run at Lingfield, once each at Redcar, Catterick, and York, finishing second on all three occasions. But Clare hadn't ridden him in any of those previous outings.

Nevertheless, I watched the VTs of all three. There was nothing untoward in any of them, at least there was nothing that I could spot. In fact, the colt had run exceptionally well last time out at York, beaten only half a length by a good horse that had itself recently gone on to win one of the major two-year-old races of the season. No wonder Bangkok Flyer had started as a red-hot favorite under Clare. According to form, he should have won the race at Lingfield with ease, as he surely would have without Clare's untimely intervention.

EVEN WITH ME watching only the final eighth of a mile of each race, the first two hundred took me more than three hours to review. In them I found three "definites," as well as a further two "possibles." Perhaps Clare had been understating reality when she had said she'd "stopped" a maximum of only five.

By this stage, I had watched so many race finishes that the horses were beginning to dance before my eyes. I took a break for a coffee.

I felt absolutely wretched.

In a way, I suppose, I should be pleased to have found something, but I was seriously dismayed to have had it confirmed that her irregular riding of Bangkok Flyer had not been an isolated incident.

The phone vibrated in my pocket. It was Sarah.

"Hello, my darling," I said, answering it.

"Where are you?" she asked in a slightly pained voice.

"Oh God, I'm sorry. I've been so busy I forgot."

I looked at my watch. It was twenty past twelve, and we'd agreed to meet at noon in a pub overlooking the River Thames just west of Oxford.

"I'm on my way. Order me a glass of rosé. I'll be there in ten minutes."

I told the database technician I'd be back later and skipped out to my car. I was still excited every time I was on my way to see Sarah. If I wasn't, I suppose, I'd have moved on by now.

The lunchtime traffic was bad, and it was a good fifteen minutes before I turned into the pub parking lot and pulled my battered old Ford into the space alongside Sarah's brand-new BMW.

I hurried inside.

"What was making you so busy in Oxford that you forgot to come and meet me?" She wasn't really cross, just curious.

"I've been at the RacingTV studio."

"Doing what, exactly?"

"Oh, bits and pieces. Sorting out my work schedule for the coming months."

I wondered why I hadn't told her the truth.

"And I'm also looking at some past races that Clare rode in for a tribute that I'm making on Thursday for Channel 4."

"Well, in that case you're forgiven." She patted my hand. "How have things been?"

"Pretty awful," I said. "I seem to be wandering round in a daze. Nothing seems real."

"Have you fixed a date yet for the funeral?"

"Monday, at three," I said. "But that's another thing I'm not very happy about."

"Why?" she asked.

"I spoke to my brothers last night. The coroner has given us the go-ahead, but my father wants it to be immediate family only, and near Oxted where *he* lives."

"Why is that a problem?"

"Because Clare didn't really get on with her immediate biological family. Racing was Clare's world. They were her real family, and I think she would have preferred it if her funeral was held at Newmarket, where *she* lived, and all her racing friends could be there."

"Darling," Sarah said, turning to me, "you can always have a memorial service in Newmarket later. And, in all honesty, it isn't really what Clare would have wanted that's important now."

"I know." I sighed. "And my father can be very obstinate. But for some goddamn reason my brothers and sister seem to agree with him. I've tried my best but I've been voted down on this one. Personally, I think they only want a small quiet funeral because they're embarrassed by the manner of her death."

She took my hand in hers and squeezed it. There was nothing to say, so we sat there in silence for a while. As always, I couldn't get the image out of my head of Clare falling fifteen floors. I was again close to tears.

"Where's Mitchell?" I asked, purposely changing my pattern of thought.

"At Newton Abbot races, thank goodness." She shivered. "God, he was so horrible to me this morning before he went. He can be such a bully."

"Why don't you just leave him?"

She didn't answer, and I tried to read her mind. Perhaps she was afraid of him. Or had Clare been right and Sarah simply couldn't afford to leave?

"When will he be back?" I asked in the silence.

"Not for hours. He's got a runner in the last, so he won't be home until well after eight at the earliest." She paused. "I don't suppose you fancy coming back with me for a while?"

In spite of everything, I was tempted.

"How about Oscar?" I asked. Oscar was the youngest of her stepchildren, the only one that still lived at home.

"School play rehearsal. He won't be home until ten. Please do come." She was almost pleading. "I need you. It's been really dreadful knowing you've been in such pain and not being able to comfort you."

I sighed. "I've got to go back to the RacingTV offices to finish what I'm doing. It'll take another two or three hours at least."

"I'm only twenty minutes down the road. Come if you can."

"The offices close at six, and the technician told me he wants to be gone by half past five, so I've got to be finished by then. I could come after that for a little while, as long as you're sure it's safe."

"Safe as houses. I'll watch Newton Abbot on the television just to make sure Mitch is still there for the last race."

So would I.

Having been slightly irritated with me for arriving late, she now tried her best to hurry me away, so much so that I was back at the database studio, reviewing more of Clare's races, well before two o'clock.

IN ALL THE RACES that Clare had ridden in and not won since the beginning of June, I found what I was pretty sure were seven examples of her purposely trying to lose, even though in one of them she didn't really have much of a chance to win anyway. And there were a further four races where I thought she'd not been doing her best to win when she might have, although I couldn't be sure that she was actively "stopping" the horse.

I used the database system to copy the eleven races in question on a DVD, together with the information about all the horses that had run in each one.

There didn't seem to be any factors in common.

Of the seven definites, there was one pair that had the same trainer, but the five others were all different. Nine of the eleven had been trained in Newmarket, with one in Lambourn and the other at a stable near Stratford-upon-Avon. And all had different owners.

In addition to Bangkok Flyer, there was one other horse from the Austin Reynolds string, Tortola Beach, an exciting two-year-old prospect that Clare had ridden into third place at Doncaster in August when he had looked certain to win with just an eighth of a mile to go.

One of the others was from the Newmarket stable of Carla Topazio, a large, domineering lady trainer of Italian descent who loved to sing operatic arias at every opportunity, mostly in the winner's enclosure whenever her horses had won.

In another of the eleven, Clare had ridden a three-year-old filly called Jasmine Pearls, trained by our own cousin Brendan, which had finished a close fourth in the City Plate at Chester after having led comfortably into the final eighth of a mile.

The only common thread I could see was that in none of the eleven suspect races had Clare been riding a horse trained by Geoff Grubb, her principal employer. Perhaps she had thought it would have been too great a risk. She had so much to lose if Geoff, for whatever reason, became unhappy with her riding— not just her stable-jockey job but her home as well. Even though she had mocked me, at that final dinner, for not buying a house of my own, she hadn't either, choosing to live in Geoff's rented Stable Cottage.

I stared at my list of definites and possibles, hoping that some other common denominator would leap out at me.

It didn't.

Six of the eleven had started as the favorite, three at a price less than two-to-one, but two of the other five had been relative outsiders, with odds greater than eight-to-one.

I looked up the trainers of the race winners, but they were mostly different as well. As were the jockeys and the owners. Surely the eleven horses were not simply a random selection? Was there some shared characteristic that I wasn't spotting? Maybe it was because I didn't yet have all the necessary information to look at, and I needed to look at races earlier than June.

Perhaps Clare had been playing the "Race Fixing Game" for much longer than just these last few months.

I glanced at my watch. It was ten past five, and the technician was hovering and clearly itching for me to go. Any further searches would have to wait.

I quickly made another DVD, with four of Clare's big race victories on it, as well as her final race on Scusami. Sadly, I couldn't find a VT of her first-ever ride or even her first winner, but I still had more than enough to make the tribute piece for Channel 4.

I collected my two DVDs, thanked the technician, and left the studio.

The one thing that was certain about every TV company I had ever known was that in the reception area you would find a large-screen television showing the current output, and RacingTV was no exception.

I stood next to the office security desk and watched the sixth, and last, race from Newton Abbot. Mitchell Stacey's horse won it easily at a canter, and the happy trainer was shown beaming from ear to ear as his victorious animal was led into the winner's enclosure.

Newton Abbot racetrack to East Ilsley was about a hundred and sixty miles. Even taking into account that most of the journey was on freeways, and also allowing for the excessive speed at which Mitchell Stacey regularly drove, there was absolutely no way he could be at home within the next two hours.

I climbed excitedly into my old Ford, sped the twenty minutes down the road, and jumped straight into bed with Sarah.

"**MY POOR DARLING,**" Sarah said as we lay together after lovemaking, "this is such a horrid business." She lightly stroked her fingertips across my bare chest, causing shivers to go right down my legs. "It's so unbelievable."

Indeed, it was unbelievable, and I still hoped that I'd soon wake up from this nightmare and everything would be all right. Somehow it felt wrong that I could go on eating, sleeping, breathing, and even lying here with Sarah. Should I feel guilty for that too?

"What I can't understand," I said, "is what she was doing in London anyway. She told me she was going straight home."

"But people do change their minds," Sarah said.

I shook my head, not because I didn't believe Sarah but in distress at what Clare had done. "She also told me she would be riding at Newmarket on Saturday morning. How was she going to do that if she was staying in London?"

"Which hotel was it?" Sarah asked.

"The Hilton. You know, that tall one at the bottom of Park Lane."

Too tall, I thought.

Sarah suddenly sat bolt upright in bed. "But Mitch and I were at the Hilton on Friday night for that big Injured Jockeys dinner. We had a table of our owners."

"Didn't you see anything?" I asked. "An ambulance or something?"

"No. Nothing at all."

"What time did you leave?" I asked.

"Not very late. You know what racing people are like about going to bed early. The dinner started at seven, and it was over by half past ten."

"Clare fell round eleven-thirty."

"We'd gone long before then. We were back here by midnight."

"But did you see her in the hotel lobby? According to the police, she checked in at twenty past ten."

Sarah shook her head. "I would have remembered if I'd seen her because she always reminded me of you. You have the same cheekbones."

She smiled and lay back down next to me again, putting her arm around my waist.

"How many people were at the dinner?" I asked.

"Hundreds," she said. "The place was packed. They had that comedian with the funny spiky hair—you know, the one that does all those amazing impressions." She laughed at the memory. "I was actually quite surprised you weren't there. I remember spending most of the evening looking out for you."

"The tickets had all gone by the time I got round to applying."

"You should have told me. We had a spare place at our table. Someone dropped out at the last minute."

"I couldn't have come anyway. By then, I'd arranged to have dinner with Clare."

"Oh yes," Sarah said quietly, "so you had."

How different things might have been if only I'd been a bit more organized.

ON THURSDAY MORNING I drove to Newmarket and went to Clare's cottage.

I collected the spare key from the yard office, as Geoff Grubb had suggested, and let myself in through the front door.

There was a stack of unopened mail on the doormat, most of it addressed not to Clare, but to me. I knew what it would be. I'd spent most of the previous day answering condolence letters, but the people who'd sent these obviously didn't know the address of my apartment.

I collected the letters all together. There were only a couple of other items—a bill from a cell phone company and a notice from Suffolk County Council about a change to refuse collection in the area. I opened the telephone bill and scanned through the list of the numbers that Clare had called. I recognized my own, and also that of my parents, but what I was really looking for was a number that she had called regularly— say, every day—a number that might have belonged to her mystery boyfriend.

No single number stood out, but there were quite a few she had called more than ten times or so during the monthly billing period. Sadly, the bill did not include the numbers she had called last Friday night after leaving me. Perhaps I would ask the phone company for those. I put the bill down on the desk in the sitting room to look at later and went upstairs.

It was strange going through Clare's things. It felt like I was invading her privacy.

Of course I'd been to this cottage many times during the preceding four years, regularly staying overnight whenever I was working at Newmarket or anywhere farther north. But I'd been a guest, always sleeping in the guest room. Here I was searching Clare's own bedroom, pulling open drawers overflowing with what Americans would call "intimate apparel." And intimate it was too. She'd clearly had a fondness for sexy black lace underwear, and I was rather embarrassed to find it.

There was precious little else to find.

Even as a child, Clare had been frugal in the clothes department, and her wardrobe, with the exception of the lace undies, was fairly sparse, consisting mostly of jeans, polo shirts, and sleeveless puffer jackets—her usual attire.

There were only a couple of dresses hanging in the closet, one of which she had worn to our parents' golden anniversary party. It was the only time in years I could recall her not wearing pants, blue jeans mostly. She had always tried to avoid occasions where she was expected to dress up.

I knew that coming to her cottage would be difficult, but I hadn't realized just how much I would miss her. Every single thing I touched reminded me of the blissful times I had enjoyed in this place.

My heart ached and ached and ached for her.

I sat down wearily on the side of her bed and longed for her to come back, to be here once more, to laugh, to bounce up the stairs with her endless energy, to be alive again—oh, to be alive again, alive, alive.

This bout of grief lasted ten to fifteen minutes, my body plagued by both pain and guilt. There was little I could do but let it take its course, a continuous stream of tears pouring down my cheeks.

In a strange way, the session made me feel a little better. Perhaps it was the body's natural healing mechanism at work.

I would have to come back later though, I thought. Her loss was still too recent, too raw, too painful. I simply couldn't do much sorting of her things at the moment.

I collected the condolence letters, went out to my car, and drove away.

I WAS DUE to record my tribute to Clare at Newmarket racetrack.

Channel 4 was broadcasting both the Friday and Saturday of the Cambridgeshire meeting, and Thursday was the day that the equipment would be set up in preparation.

The tribute was to be a short piece of me talking straight to the camera in front of the Newmarket weighing room, then my voice-over of the four VTs of her major race successes, including her two Group One victories, her win in the Northumberland Plate, and also the Windsor Castle Stakes at Royal Ascot in June when her horse had won by a nose with a perfectly timed late run. Then there was to be another short piece to shoot in front of the camera, then another voice-over for her last race, on Scusami at Lingfield, then another very short piece to camera to finish. Three minutes and forty-five seconds in total.

I just hoped I would be able to get through it without breaking down.

I parked my car as always in the area reserved for the press and walked to the Channel 4 scanner, the huge blue truck that was already parked in the fenced-off compound behind the northern grandstand.

The technical team was busy laying thick black cables between the scanner and the signal-relay vehicle that was parked alongside, with its arrays of receiving domes and transmitting dishes on the roof. The images from each of the seven cameras around the racetrack, together with the pickups from the numerous microphones, would all be transmitted back here by microwave link, ready for mixing in the scanner.

It was also from where the final fusion of sound and pictures was sent via faraway satellite to the Channel 4 main studios in London for broadcast through the ether to people's televisions at home. And all in the blink of an eye, or maybe two blinks.

"Are you ready?" asked Neville, the *Channel 4 Racing* producer.

"As I'll ever be," I said, taking in a deep breath.

"You'll be fine," Neville said. "And we can always do it again."

Yes, I thought. Thank goodness it wasn't going out live.

But I needn't have worried. As soon as the camera's Cyclops-like lens pointed my way outside the weighing room, my professional instincts took over and I managed to do all the straight-to-camera pieces in just one take.

Afterward, I sat in the scanner for over an hour putting together the whole thing, editing the VTs and doing the voice-overs, shuffling things around until both Neville and I were happy with the final tribute. I played it right through from start to finish, and, once more, it brought me close to tears. I hoped that it might have the same effect on those who watched it on Saturday.

By the time I emerged from the scanner into a light September drizzle, the Thursday-afternoon races were well under way. But I'd had enough for one day and decided to take myself home to Edenbridge. If I was lucky, I'd get around London before the rush hour.

Mitchell Stacey was waiting for me in the parking lot.

Oh shit, I thought. What the hell's he doing here?

Mitchell trained nothing but steeplechasers or hurdlers, and there were only flat races at Newmarket. So why was he leaning on my car? I slowed to a halt about twenty yards away, but he came over quickly toward me, sticking his right forefinger up under my chin.

"Now, listen to me, you bastard!" he shouted at me from about ten inches distance. "Stop fucking my wife!"

There wasn't much to say, so I kept quiet.

Sorry somehow seemed inappropriate.

"If it wasn't for this business with your sister," Mitchell went on, "I'd have had your legs broken. Do you understand me?"

I remembered what Sarah had said about him being a bully. I could see what she meant.

"Do you understand me?" he said again, pushing his ruddy face up close to mine.

"Yes," I said.

"Good." He thrust a folded piece of paper into my hands.

I unfolded it. On it was printed a large colored photograph. It was rather grainy and slightly out of focus, but it was clear enough. The photograph showed Sarah and me in bed together the previous evening, and there was little doubt as to what we were doing.

"I won't divorce her, you know," he said. "And she won't

divorce me either because she knows she'd end up with nothing. Not a bean. We have a prenuptial contract."

I wasn't sure that prenups were legal documents under
English law, but I decided against mentioning it to him at that
particular moment.

"If you ever come near my wife again, I'll kill you." Mitchell said it with real menace.

He suddenly turned and walked away from me without
looking back.

My skin felt cold and clammy, and I found I was shaking.

I stuffed the photograph into my pocket and made it over to
my car, sitting down heavily in the driver's seat.

Bloody hell! How did he get that picture?

I called Sarah's cell phone.

"He knows," I said when she answered. "Mitchell knows
about us. He's just been here at Newmarket and he confronted me."

"I know," she said.

"Then for God's sake why didn't you warn me?"

"He threatened me, that's why." She was crying. "Told me
he'd break my legs if I contacted you."

I could believe it.

"Mark, I'm so frightened."

So was I.

"He showed me a picture taken yesterday of us in bed."

"A picture?" She sobbed. "He's got the whole bloody video.
He made me watch it this morning after Oscar went to school.
He'd set up one of those spy cameras in our bedroom. It was
awful. I thought he was going to hit me."

"Pack a bag and leave right now," I said. "Come and live

with me at my place. Mitchell won't be back for a good couple of hours even if he goes straight home."

"He took my car keys."

"So what? Call a taxi and get the train from Newbury. I'll collect you at Paddington."

I could hear her sigh. "I can't."

"Why not?"

There was no reply.

"Why not?" I asked her again.

"I just can't," she said again with a resigned tone. There was a long silence on the line. "I should have paid the little shit."

"Paid who?" I asked.

"Oh nothing," she said dismissively. There was another silence. "It might be better if we didn't talk again."

Neither of us said anything. There may have been no actual words, but the silence between us spoke volumes.

"Bye, bye, my darling," she said finally. "And thanks for everything."

She hung up, leaving me sitting there holding the dead phone to my ear.

My whole world seemed to be falling apart around me. My gorgeous twin sister had killed herself, I was arguing with the rest of my family, my lover of five years had just dumped me, and Iain Ferguson appeared to be taking over my job.

7

I sat at home all day Friday and Saturday, moping around my apartment, feeling sorry for myself, and occasionally watching the racing on the television.

I should have been at Newmarket presenting the programs for Channel 4 and RacingTV, not sitting at home watching them.

Two or three times I shouted at my TV set in frustration. I also laughed out loud when Iain Ferguson made a classic mistake, calling the trainer he was interviewing by the wrong name, not once but twice. Idiot, I thought. It was a basic rule of presenting to get an interviewee's name right because the audience at home would have it written across their screen on an Aston. They would all realize your error and think you were foolish, which indeed you were.

Perhaps Iain Ferguson wasn't such a threat to my job after all.

On Saturday, after my tribute to Clare, and shown interspersed with the flat races from Newmarket, were four others from the jumping meeting at Market Rasen.

According to my early-morning-delivered copy of the *Racing Post*, Mitchell Stacey had three horses running at Market Rasen, one in each of the first three races. I hoped they'd all lose.

I had tried to call Sarah's cell four times on Thursday evening to ensure she was all right. On the first occasion, the phone had rung a couple of times, then gone to voice mail, as if someone at the other end had declined the call. Thereafter it went straight to voice mail, as if it was switched off.

I sent her a text message. There was no reply.

In desperation, I'd called the Staceys' home number, but Mitchell himself had answered, so I'd immediately hung up. I didn't dare call again.

Now I studied the TV coverage from Market Rasen with particular attention to see if I could see Sarah, perhaps accompanying her husband into the parade ring before the first race. As always, the cameraman dwelt on the horses and not the people, and the horses were moving while the people were not. I caught a glimpse of Mitchell Stacey, his weather-beaten reddish face reminding me all too well of our close encounter at Newmarket on Thursday.

I couldn't spot Sarah, but if Mitchell was definitely at Market Rasen, I could at least try to call her safely on their landline if she was at home.

"Please, Mark," she said, answering after three rings, "I said we were not to speak again. Not ever."

"I just wanted to make sure you were all right."

"I'm fine," she said.

"Are you sure?" I said. "You sound a bit funny."

There was no reply.

"What happened?" I asked. "Did he hit you?"

"It's nothing," she said.

It was as if she was speaking through cotton wool.

"Did he split your lip?"

"I told you, I'm fine."

"What did you mean yesterday about paying the little shit?"

"Nothing," she said.

"It must have been something. And why would you pay Mitchell anyway?"

"Leave it, Mark. Move on. Forget me. I've already forgotten you. Good-bye."

She hung up.

Dammit, I thought. Why did she let him get away with hitting her?

And, to top it all, Mitchell's bloody horse went on to win the first race at Market Rasen, his horrible red face appearing joyful once again as the horse was led in to unsaddle. Oh, how I would have loved to punch his lights out, to split his lip, and see how he liked it.

AS SATURDAY AFTERNOON faded into Saturday evening, I lay on my battered old sofa, drinking a can of beer, wondering where my life was going and what I should do about it.

I looked up at the peeling and cracked ceiling of my sitting room.

If the truth be told, it really was well past the "slightly yellowing" stage and was beginning to resemble the nicotine-stained walls of an East End pub before the smoking ban. Not that I smoked. I didn't. But the "whiteness" of the paint had been fairly suspect when it had been thinly applied by my landlord in the first place, and the eight years since had not been kind.

I sat up and looked at the whole room with fresh eyes.

I had to admit that it was pretty awful.

It was not just the paintwork that was overdue for a change, it was the dilapidated and soiled furniture as well. Not to mention the carpets and the drapes, both of which were unchanged since I'd first moved in twelve years ago, and they hadn't been new even then.

To think I'd asked Sarah to give up her luxurious East Ilsley mansion to come live in this squalor. Was it any wonder she'd turned me down?

"Right," I said out loud, "it is high time I made a change."

Past time, in fact.

I quite surprised myself with my decisiveness and, after about three hours of surfing the Internet, I had a pretty good idea of how much houses cost in most of the Home Counties.

By the time I went to bed at one o'clock in the morning I had a list of eight places where I might be interested in living and the telephone numbers of six realtors to call first thing Monday morning.

I found it all quite exciting, and, if nothing else, it took my mind off Sarah, Clare's funeral, and the precariousness of my employment.

ON SUNDAY MORNING I drove into central London, to the Hilton Hotel on Park Lane.

I always knew that I'd have to go there eventually, but I hadn't before felt mentally ready for the ordeal. But now seemed to be the right time, before the funeral, not that I was especially relishing the trip.

I parked my old Ford in South Audley Street, behind the hotel, and walked through to the grand frontage of the Hilton, with its overhanging stainless-steel canopy.

Not surprisingly, there was nothing to indicate where Clare had fallen to her death nine days previously. No roped-off area, no bouquets of flowers, not even a mark on the sidewalk to show the spot where half my being had disappeared forever.

I looked above me at the vertical line of balconies that stretched upward and tried to count fifteen floors. Tears filled my eyes and stopped me. Did it matter? Fifteen wasn't important. Ten would probably have been enough, or even five. According to a telephone call from DS Sharp to my father, the autopsy had established the cause of death as multiple injuries consistent with Clare having fallen a considerable distance onto a hard surface.

I approached one of the uniformed and top-hatted doormen.

"Excuse me," I said, trying to control my voice. "Where did the girl fall?"

"Never you mind," he said somewhat brusquely. "Now, move on, please, sir." He spread his arms and walked straight toward me, forcing me back.

"She was my sister," I said to him quickly, "and I need to know where she died."

"Oh, I'm so sorry," he said, stopping and holding up his hands in apology. "I thought you were another of those ghoulish creeps we've been getting here all week." He must have spotted that I was not doing too well, as he took me by the arm. I think it was his intervention that may have stopped me collapsing altogether.

He guided me inside the hotel.

"Would you like to sit down, sir?" he asked. "You don't look well."

I nodded weakly, and one of his colleagues pulled up a chair.

"I'm sorry," I croaked.

Someone arrived with a glass of water, and I slowly recovered my composure.

"Sorry," I said again to my savior. "I didn't realize how much it would affect me."

"It's no problem, sir," he said. "When you're ready, I'll take you back outside."

"Thank you."

And, in due course, he did just that, showing me exactly where Clare had met her end.

I stood staring at the unremarkable spot on the concrete paving and offered up a silent prayer for Clare's soul. Then, once more, my eyes were drawn upward toward the balconies high above me.

She had fallen quite a distance away from the building, and I wondered if she had purposely jumped outward. She must have only just missed the overhanging steel canopy. In a funny sort of way, I was glad. Its edges appeared very sharp, although that surely would have made no difference to Clare or to the outcome.

But why had she done it? Why? Why? Why?

"Will you be all right now, sir?" asked my friendly doorman.

"Yes. Thank you," I said. "I'll be fine."

He nodded at me, then moved away to help some people into a black London taxi. I, meanwhile, remained rooted to the spot for a few moments longer, even bending down to stroke the rough, cold surface, as if in doing so I was somehow offering a final caring touch to my dead sister.

Finally, I stood up and moved away. It had been a necessary journey to see where she had died, but I would always remember Clare as brimming with life. I once again thanked my lucky stars that I hadn't accompanied James and Nicholas to see her battered and broken body. That was one mental image I could readily live without.

I waved to my doorman and went back into the hotel.

I suspect that the lobbies of all the larger London hotels are busy places at eleven o'clock on Sunday mornings, and the Hilton was certainly no exception. There were several lines of guests waiting at the reception desk to check out after a big Saturday-evening event in the hotel ballroom, while a large group of brightly dressed American tourists hung around aimlessly, desperate to check in and sleep after their overnight red-eye flight across the Atlantic. And there was baggage everywhere, lined up in long snakes like dominoes waiting to be toppled.

I went over to a young woman sitting at a desk marked "Guest Relations" and asked if I could please speak with the hotel's general manager. To my eyes, she hardly looked old enough to be out of school, and she instantly became defensive, asking me what I wanted him for. Perhaps she believed that anyone who wanted to talk to the manager was going to complain about something. I told her that it was a personal matter, but she still refused to pass on my request.

"Are you sure I can't help you?" she asked with an irritating smile.

"It's rather delicate," I said. "Would you please just call the general manager."

"I'm sorry, sir, I can't do that without knowing why you need him." She continued to smile at me in her annoying way.

OK, I thought, I had tried, but with no result. Now I was getting slightly irked by her attitude. "Young lady," I said loudly and somewhat condescendingly, "my name is Mark Shillingford. And I'm trying to discover why my beautiful twin sister fell to a violent death from one of your hotel balconies. Now, can I please talk to the general manager?"

She looked rather shocked, and, in truth, I had also somewhat surprised myself by my own determination and resolve.

"He's not here on Sundays," she said, the smile now having vanished altogether.

I sighed slightly. "Then I will speak to whoever is in charge of the hotel at this very moment."

She used the telephone on the desk. "Someone is coming," she said to me, putting down the handset.

I stood and waited, looking around me. A man wearing a suit soon appeared and came over toward us.

"Mr. Shillingford," he said, holding out his hand, "I'm Colin Dilly, duty manager. How can I help?"

He was about the same age as me but shorter and with a slighter build.

"I notice you have lots of CCTV cameras in this hotel." I pointed up at the one positioned above the Guest Relations desk. "I would like to see the images for the Friday before last."

"I'm afraid that won't be possible," said Mr. Dilly. "The images are recorded on a rolling seven-day cycle. Those for that Friday will have been overwritten by this past Friday's."

Dammit, I thought. I should have come sooner.

"Didn't the police make copies?" I asked in desperation.

"I believe they did, sir, but you will have to ask them if

you want to see them." He said it rather dismissively. "Now, is there anything else I can help you with?"

"I'd like to speak with whoever checked in my sister on Friday evening nine days ago."

He pursed his lips. "I'm not sure that will be possible either. It's not hotel policy to provide that sort of information."

"Then I will spend all day, and all night if necessary, asking every member of your staff that I can find until someone tells me who did check her in. They must know. It's the sort of thing one might remember, don't you think? Being the last person to see a suicide alive."

Mr. Dilly looked at me for a few moments. Perhaps he was deciding whether to have me thrown out.

"And if you chuck me out," I said, "I promise you I'll cause a fuss. I'll call the newspapers and the TV companies. I'm quite well known in media circles, and I don't think it would be good publicity on your part."

"Perhaps you had better come into the office," said Mr. Dilly. "I am sure we can find the information for you."

"Very wise," I said.

I followed him through a door that was disguised as a wooden panel and into some offices behind.

"Please sit down," he said, pointing to a chair in front of a desk. "I'll look up the work sheets for last week."

He sat opposite me at a computer, and I could hear him tapping the keys. "Now, let me see," he said. "Friday the sixteenth. Evening, wasn't it?" He tapped some more keys. "Right. I've found it."

I stood up and went and looked over his shoulder. If he didn't like it, he didn't say so.

There were six reception staff listed for the period from three o'clock in the afternoon until eleven at night on the sixteenth, with four others for the night shift, which ran from eleven on Friday until seven on Saturday morning.

So the staff on duty when Clare had checked in had been different from those when she'd fallen.

Nothing was ever simple.

Colin Dilly wrote down the names of staff from both shifts, but he didn't give me the list. Rather, he compared it to the record of the staff currently on duty that he also brought up on the screen.

"There is one person who was on duty that night who is also working right now. If you wait here, I'll go and fetch her."

Mr. Dilly went off to find the woman while I went on studying his computer screen, but there wasn't much of interest on it.

Presently, he returned with a small, neat woman who I took to be in her mid-thirties.

"Mr. Shillingford," Colin Dilly said, "this is Mrs. Rieta Dalal. She was working on reception during the evening of Friday the sixteenth, and she says she remembers your sister arriving even though it wasn't she who actually checked her in."

"Then how do you know it was my sister?" I asked.

"Because my colleague and I talked about her," said Mrs. Dalal quietly. "Because she had no luggage. No bags at all. Not even a handbag or a makeup bag." She smiled. "It's very rare indeed for a guest to check in with no luggage, especially a woman with no makeup. I remember her specifically because of that. It was only much later I heard that she had been the poor lady who fell from the balcony."

"Was she with anyone when she checked in?" I asked.

"No, sir, she was not," said Mrs. Dalal. "But she was talking on the telephone the whole time. That is why my colleague mentioned her to me in the first place. My colleague thought it rather rude, and she was quite cross about it."

"Which colleague was it?" Mr. Dilly asked.

"Irena."

"Irena Zelinska," he said, consulting his handwritten list. "She's not working today."

"She has gone home to Poland," said Mrs. Dalal.

It was definitely not going to be simple.

"Did my sister specifically ask for a room with a balcony?"

"I don't know, sir. Have you checked her reservation?"

"I don't think she had a reservation."

She seemed surprised. "We were very full that night, we always are when there's a big event in the ballroom. If she didn't have a reservation, we must have had a cancellation. She must have just been lucky to get a room with a balcony."

"Lucky" was not the term I would have used.

"But even then," Mrs. Dalal went on, "she would have had to ask to have the balcony door unlocked. All the balconies are normally kept locked to prevent suicides."

There was a silence as we all digested what Mrs. Dalal had just said.

"Are you saying that someone had to have gone to her room to open the balcony door?" I asked.

"Yes," said Mrs. Dalal. "We have to call security if guests request that the balcony door be unlocked. It is a common thing. It happens almost every day."

"Why do you keep them locked if you then unlock them on request?"

"The hotel policy," said Mr. Dilly, "is that there has to be a minimum of two registered guests in a room for the balcony door to be unlocked."

"The policy seems to have failed in this case," I said rather pointedly.

Neither of them said anything.

But it had also been the hotel policy not to give me the name of the person who had checked Clare into the hotel, and I'd found a way around that. Clare was infinitely more pushy than I was, and I didn't doubt that the "double occupancy" rule would have been as easy for her to circumvent.

Or had there, in fact, been two people in the room?

"Do you know who my sister was talking to on the telephone while she was checking in?" I asked Mrs. Dalal.

My question made her blush, her olive-brown skin distinctly flushing around her neck. And she looked down as if embarrassed.

"Sorry, I do not know," she replied while still studying the floor.

"Then why are you unsettled by the question?" I asked.

"It is nothing," she said, but she still wouldn't look up at me.

"It must be something," I said. "Tell me."

She looked up at Colin Dilly. "Tell him," he said.

"I am so sorry," she said to me, "we thought your sister was a prostitute. Irena was absolutely sure of it. Irena told me that she must be talking to her next client on her telephone. That is why she had no luggage. Irena said she would only have condoms, and they'd be in her pockets."

"But she paid for the room with her credit card," I said with some degree of anger. "A prostitute wouldn't do that."

She looked up again at Colin Dilly. "Sometimes they do,"

she said. "At least we are pretty sure they do. And Carlos then checks."

"Carlos?" I asked.

"He is one of the bellmen," she said. "If Irena gives him the nod, then he likes to check."

"How does he check?" I asked.

"When Irena gives Carlos the nod, he goes up ahead of the girl onto the same floor as her room and then waits and watches to see if a man comes."

"And did she give him the nod on that Friday night?" It was Colin Dilly who asked the question that I was itching to ask.

"Of course," said Rieta Dalal. "Especially after she'd been so rude at reception."

"And what did Carlos discover?" I asked.

"I do not know that," Rieta said. "I went home soon after your sister arrived." She again glanced at Colin Dilly. "I always worked right through my breaks so that I could leave early. I don't like to travel home by myself on the tube after ten o'clock at night. But that was my last late shift and now I've been switched to the early one." She smiled, clearly much happier with the new arrangement. "I have not seen Carlos since that night."

"Did you tell any of this to the police?" I asked.

"Police?" she said. "No one from the police has asked me anything."

"Do you know if the police spoke to Carlos? Or to Irena?"

"I'm sorry," she said, shaking her head, "I know nothing more than I've told you. Can I go now, please, Mr. Dilly?"

"Yes," Colin Dilly said while looking at me with raised eyebrows for confirmation, which I gave by nodding. "Thank you, Rieta. You can get back to work now."

She went out of the office, and Colin Dilly closed the door behind her.

"Surely the police must have interviewed the people who saw or spoke to my sister that night."

"I don't know," he said. "I was off last weekend."

Why was I not surprised?

"I'd now like to talk to Carlos," I said. "And also to the security man who unlocked her balcony door."

"What difference will it make?" Colin Dilly asked, his tone clearly indicating that he thought I was wasting my time, only making things harder for myself.

I looked at him. "At nine o'clock that Friday evening my sister told me she was driving straight home to Newmarket from Edenbridge in Kent. Instead, an hour and twenty minutes later she checked into this hotel without any luggage and without having a reservation. And just over an hour after that she was dead."

I paused and looked at him.

"I cannot believe she would have suddenly decided, after leaving me, to drive all the way into central London on the off chance that this hotel might have a free room and that that room would just happen to have a convenient balcony on a sufficiently high floor so that she could jump off it to her death."

I paused again to let what I was saying sink in.

"I think she had to be coming here to meet someone, someone she must have spoken to after she left me. I also think that committing suicide, if indeed it was suicide, must have been a last-moment decision. If she had been planning to kill herself, she would, at the very least, have made a reservation for a high balcony room."

I paused once more.

"So I'd like to talk to Carlos to find out if she did meet someone in her room here that night. And if Carlos didn't see anything, the security man might have."

Colin Dilly sat down once more at his computer and tapped away again on the keyboard.

"Carlos Luis Sanchez," he said, "the bellman. He's working today from three o'clock until eleven." I looked at my watch. It was ten minutes to midday. He tapped some more. "I can't find the details of the security men who were working that night."

"I'll come back at three o'clock to see Carlos. Can you find me the details by then?"

"I doubt it," he said, "but I'll try. I don't have access to the security company's work sheets, and their office will be shut today. I'm actually off duty at three, but I'll wait round to hear what Carlos has to say. Ask for me at reception."

"OK," I said. "I will. And thank you."

We shook hands, then I emerged through the wooden secret-panel door and back into the bustle of the hotel lobby.

"**TWO MEN,**" Carlos Luis Sanchez said. "One follow the other." He made no attempt to disguise his disgust.

"The lady was not a prostitute," Colin Dilly assured him.

"Huh," Carlos replied. "Then why she have two men in her room?"

It was a good question.

"How were the men dressed?" I asked him.

"Dressed or undressed, it makes no difference."

"No," I said, realizing that he hadn't understood the question. "What were they wearing when you saw them in the corridor?"

"Suits," he said. "You know, black suits with ties." He moved his hands back and forth at his neck. Bow ties.

"Both of them?" I asked.

"The first one. Yes. I see. The second . . ." He shrugged his shoulders.

"Did you see the second man?" I spoke slowly.

"Mario see him."

"Who is Mario?" I asked.

"My friend," Carlos said. "One more porter. He work nights. He say he see second man coming out later, during all fuss over falling girl."

"What?" I said, suddenly taking in what he was saying. "Are you telling us that the second man was in her room when the girl fell?"

"I not know," he said. "You ask Mario. But Mario say so to me, yes."

8

Clare's funeral was brief—far too brief, I would have said—but it wasn't up to me, as I had left all the arrangements to my father, my brothers, and my sister. I'd thought that was the best policy for avoiding further arguments and shouting. But as I sat in the Surrey and Sussex Crematorium chapel at three o'clock on Monday afternoon, I deeply regretted that decision.

Not that the day had started well either. I had tried to call Detective Sergeant Sharp to ask him about the CCTV from the London Hilton only to be informed that he was away on leave for the week and that no one else seemed to have any knowledge of any recordings or indeed of anything else to do with Clare's death. Call back next week, I was told most unhelpfully, and speak to DS Sharp.

Next I'd called the Injured Jockeys Fund to ask them about the guest list for their gala dinner. Mrs. Green, the organizer of the event, was in Portugal, I was told, enjoying a well-earned break after all her hard work. She also would be back next week.

Then my father's insistence on "immediate family only" at the funeral further added to my frustration.

The arrival at the crematorium, ten minutes before the service, of my father's younger brother, my uncle George, and his wife, Catherine, from Spain had not been a welcome addition to the immediate family as my father obviously defined it. When Cousin Brendan had then turned up, along with his wife, Gillian, and their two teenage children, closely followed by his brother Joshua plus second wife, I thought my father was about to postpone the whole thing, but the minister had then made a timely appearance, ushering us all into the chapel.

So there were a total of seventeen of us who sat in the first three rows of chairs as four pallbearers from the undertaker's carried the simple oak casket past us and placed it on the high dais at the front. Five other mourners stood at the back near the door, having been banished there by my father, who had loudly accused them of invading his grief.

Not that I was particularly pleased to see one of them, Toby Woodley, the diminutive racing correspondent from the *Daily Gazette*, a tabloid best known for celebrity exposés and rumor-mongering.

As well as trying to comfort my mother, I spent time looking out for the mystery boyfriend, but none of the five non-family attendees appeared to fit the bill. Apart from Woodley, there was an elderly couple I vaguely recognized, and two young women who told my father that they had known Clare from school, not that he had made them any more welcome for it.

Just as the minister was starting the service, the back doors of the chapel creaked open and one further individual joined the congregation. Geoff Grubb came forward and sat down in an empty row behind Uncle George and Aunt Catherine. My father stared angrily at him from across the aisle, but if Geoff noticed, he didn't react.

If it hadn't been so sad, it might have been funny.

My father couldn't see past his anger with Clare for bringing this on us all. He couldn't grasp that the death of a much-loved daughter and sister transcended the method of her passing and that her memory should be cherished for what her life had been, not vilified for how it had ended.

The service was embarrassingly short, with just a single hymn, "The Lord's My Shepherd," sung badly by us over a recorded sound track, a few prayers, and a concise Bible reading that was delivered not by a member of the family but by the minister himself.

The whole thing lasted less than ten minutes. There had been no eulogy, no family recollection of childhood, no . . . love.

I sat there fuming. How could my siblings have allowed this to happen?

I started to get up. Surely someone had to speak.

"Don't," my brother-in-law Nicholas said while grasping the tail of my jacket to stop me. "Trust me. Don't."

I turned and looked at him, and also at my cousin Brendan sitting next to him.

"Leave it," Nicholas whispered. "This is not the time or place."

"And not with him here," Brendan added, nodding toward Toby Woodley at the back of the chapel.

"But this is precisely the time and place and it's so wrong," I whispered back to them.

"I know it's wrong," Nicholas said. "We have all said so, but your father won't be moved."

Well, I was moved.

As the minister was starting the committal to conclude the proceedings, rather to his surprise, and mine, I stood up and went forward to stand close to the coffin.

I turned to face the Shillingford family and looked straight at my father. As was so often the case, his face was puce with rage, but I didn't care. This service was for Clare, not for him.

"I wish I had prepared a few profound words to say about Clare, but I hadn't expected to be the one speaking here. But now that I am, I suppose I'd better say something."

In all, I spoke for nearly ten minutes.

I talked at length about our childhood and the bonds of being twins, about our teenage years and us both wanting to be jockeys, about Clare's success in her career, and how we had all thought she had so much to live for.

My mother sobbed.

Finally, I turned to face the wooden box that contained the broken mortal remains of my dear twin.

"Clare, we loved you and we failed you. We should have prevented this and we are so sorry. I hope you are somewhere in a better place and you can forgive us."

I went back to my seat and sat down with a heavy heart.

Nicholas patted me on the back. He was crying. Brendan next to him was crying. In fact, there was crying going on all around me.

I noticed that even my father was now in tears. Maybe it hadn't simply been anger but guilt that had made him behave so strangely.

The minister completed the committal, and the electrically

operated curtains closed around the casket, masking it from our sight.

"Well done," Nicholas said to me as we stood up. "You were right."

"But what is wrong with you all?" I said to him in frustration. "Was that really the best the collective minds of the Shillingford family could come up with?"

"There's no such thing as collective minds in our family," he replied. "You should know that by now. The truth is that no one did anything because we were all terrified of upsetting someone else, so, in the end, nothing got done at all. This funeral wasn't planned, it simply drifted into existence."

Geoff Grubb came over to me. "I thought there would have been more people here."

"It was for immediate family only," I said.

"Oh. Sorry. I didn't realize."

"It doesn't matter," I said. "I'm pleased you came."

"She was a nice girl." He, too, seemed close to tears. "I'll miss her." He turned away from me and wiped his eyes, clearly embarrassed by his crying. "She was like immediate family to me. Looked after me, she did, since my Gloria passed away last year. We had no kids of our own."

I was quite surprised by his show of emotion, as well as by the thought of Clare in any way looking after him. Everyone thought of Geoff Grubb as a training machine with a heart of stone. But I still didn't think he could possibly have been the elusive secret boyfriend.

Geoff and I walked out of the crematorium chapel together into the watery sunshine. My father was standing there.

"Dad," I said, "this is Geoff Grubb, who Clare rode for. He also owns Stable Cottage where she lived."

My father shook Geoff's offered hand and thankfully resisted the urge to ask him why he was here.

"Well spoken, Mark," he said instead, looking me in the eye.

"Thank you, Dad," I said, looking straight back at him.

It was the first time I could remember in my whole life that my father had praised me for anything. He held out his hand to me and I shook it warmly.

"Excuse me," said a voice on my right, breaking the moment.

I turned to find the elderly couple who had been standing at the back. My father faced the opposite direction, away from them, and walked off. I actually thought he was crying again.

"Hello, Mark," said the man, holding out his hand.

"Hello." I shook his hand. "And you are?"

"You must remember us," the lady said.

I looked at them more closely.

"Mr. and Mrs. Yates," I said, smiling broadly. "How lovely to see you again."

"Fred and Emma," Mr. Yates said. "It is good to see you again, too, Mark, but it's a shame about the circumstances. Clare was such a sweet girl."

Fred and Emma Yates had been our regular babysitters when Clare and I had been kids, always coming to the house together, and even staying over if our parents were away. I hadn't seen them for nearly twenty years.

"We've always followed Clare's riding," Fred said.

"And you on the television," added his wife. "Really proud of both of you, aren't we, Fred?"

"Thank you," I said, meaning it.

The two young women who knew Clare from school were hovering to my right. I, meanwhile, was trying to look over them to see where my father had gone.

"Hello," I said, turning my eyes to the women. "Sorry about my father. He can be rather rude at times."

"We know," said the taller of the two, "from our school days."

"I'm sorry," I said, "but I don't remember you from school."

"We were in the tennis team with Clare. I'm Hanna and this is Sally."

We shook hands. "I'm Mark."

"We know," said Sally, smiling. "We always watch the racing on the telly. Mostly because of Clare. We loved it when she won. We even went to Ascot this year with some other friends just to see her ride. We were in the Silver Ring, wearing our fancy hats. We stood by the rail and cheered every time she came past. And she waved to us on the way to the start for every race." She paused. "We loved Clare."

Fred and Emma Yates, Hanna and Sally, Geoff Grubb: how many other people had loved Clare? How many were proud of her and had admired her achievements?

But what about the race fixing? Would they be proud of her for that as well?

As far as I was aware, I was the only person who knew about the seven definite cases and the four possible ones that I had found on the database.

I must use that knowledge with care. The last thing I wanted to do was to blacken people's memory of my sister.

TOBY WOODLEY spoke to me outside the chapel, coming up as I was guiding my mother back to the cars.

"Can you give me a quote?" he asked in his squeaky voice.

"I've said all I wanted to, thank you."

"You should be nice to me," he whined. "I've been good to you."

"And how is that exactly?" I replied, my voice heavy with irony.

"I was going to write all about you in last Monday's paper."

"What about?" I asked.

"Never you mind," he said. "But, luckily for you, my editor's better nature convinced me not to kick a man when he's down."

"Well, that would make a change. I didn't realize your editor had a better nature. Now, please go away." I was doing my best to keep my temper and to remain polite.

"I wish now he hadn't been so kind," he sneered, "but he said it wouldn't make us any friends, not being so soon after your sister and all. Said it would be too tough on the family."

"Death is always tough on the families," I replied, not really knowing what he was talking about.

"Suicide, you mean. Why do you think she did it?"

I ignored him and settled my weeping mother into the front seat of my father's old Jaguar.

"Any ideas?" he persisted, coming up close to my side.

I thought about pushing him away, but, knowing the Daily Gazette, there'd be a photographer watching every move. Instead, I tried to ignore him.

"Come on, Mark," he whined, prodding my arm, "you must have some idea why she killed herself. You don't just jump off a hotel balcony for no reason."

I was sure he was goading me into a reaction. So I looked around for a camera and, sure enough, a man was standing half hidden in the gardens of remembrance with a telephoto lens at the ready. His editor's better nature obviously hadn't prevailed for very long.

"Sorry, Toby, you little creep," I said, unable to keep the anger out of my voice any longer, "I can't help you. Now, piss off, and leave my family alone to grieve in peace."

He didn't, of course, asking more questions of my brothers. But he didn't really know who they were and they gave him short shrift anyway. When he asked Brendan for directions to my parents' house, he was told in no uncertain terms that he wouldn't be welcome at the family home—or anywhere else, for that matter.

At one point I thought Brendan was actually going to hit him, but thankfully, with the photographer in mind, good sense prevailed, and we all drove away, leaving Toby standing alone in the crematorium parking lot.

ONLY THE FAMILY returned to my parents' house, Geoff Grubb declining my invitation, while Mr. and Mrs. Yates, plus Hanna and Sally, had obviously thought better of it.

But so little planning had gone into Clare's funeral that no provision had been made for any refreshments afterward.

"Surely there's some drink in the house?" I said to Stephen incredulously.

"I doubt it," he said. "Dad's been knocking it back all week. I bet there's nothing left."

"I'll go and get some wine. You see if you can find some glasses. I'll try to organize some food as well."

I cleaned a local filling station out of its remaining sandwiches and also bought four bottles each of red and white wine, none of which would have won any prizes for taste, but it would have to do.

Nicholas and I stood side by side in the kitchen, cutting up the sandwiches and opening the bottles of wine.

"Will you still be coming to Tatiana's eighteenth on Friday?" he asked with a sigh.

"Of course." Tatiana was Nicholas and Angela's only child, my niece, and also my goddaughter. "Why? What's wrong?"

"Your father says he and your mom won't be coming now. He says it's too soon after all this and that we should cancel or postpone. But I think that life has to go on, and we've made all the arrangements and paid for them too. The bloody tent costs a fortune, and don't even talk to me about the caterers. I can't afford to cancel and then do it all again later. And Tatiana is so looking forward to it. All her chums from school are coming. I don't really know what to do."

"I am sure Clare would not have wanted you to cancel. Anyway, I've been writing my godfatherly speech in readiness." I smiled at him.

"But are you sure it's all right to go ahead?"

"Certain. Take no notice of Dad. I'll try and have a word with him and change his mind about coming."

"He's been very quiet since the service."

"Silly old bugger," I said. "I wonder why he gets so angry all the time."

"It's because he feels challenged by you."

I looked at him. "Don't be silly."

"I'm not," he said. "You and Clare, but especially you, you're the only ones in this family who don't do what he tells you to. Angela is all for canceling Tatiana's party simply because he says we should. But then you tell me to take no notice of him. So, you see, you are the only one who doesn't do as he says. And, what's more, you never have."

"But why does that challenge him?"

"He's the eldest male member of the family and he believes it is his role to decide on family matters and that everyone else should agree with his decisions without question. But I think he knows deep down that you are likely to make better decisions than him, and that if you feel he's wrong, to not follow his orders."

"Damn right," I said.

"That is why you should have been here this week helping him make the right decisions for the funeral. All week he's been trying to second-guess what you would have said."

"But we would have fought. It would have all ended in a shouting match and I would have walked out. Better that I kept away."

"You think that service was better for you keeping away?" His voice was full of sarcasm.

"No. I suppose not."

"No? Then you and your father will have to learn how to make compromises without fighting and to make yourselves heard without shouting."

"You should be a counselor," I said.

"I am."

"Are you really?" I asked.

"Yes," he said, smiling. "But don't tell your father. He thinks I'm a merchant banker in the City. And I do work for a bank, but I don't deal with the money. I'm the company counselor."

"Doing what exactly?"

"Counseling the staff. It is one of their inclusive company benefits."

"Counseling them on what?"

"Anything they like, but marital problems mostly. They all work so bloody hard and for such long hours, trying to earn the tons of money they need to pay their huge mortgages, and only because they think their families will be happier living in enormous houses with indoor swimming pools. The families, however, would much rather live somewhere smaller and see more of Daddy. By the time these guys get to fifty-five and are ready to give it all up to live on their accumulated millions, their wives and kids have had enough of being on their own, have left them, taken half their money, and gone to live with someone else. It's all rather sad."

"So what do you tell them to do?"

"Go home earlier and stay out of the office at weekends."

"And do they listen?"

"Not often," he said with a laugh. "In the City, money equates to testosterone. All of them are driven to get more and more of it, irrespective of the human cost."

I knew some people in racing who were just like that, people for whom winning was like a Class A drug, and they were addicted.

I took a tray of sandwiches and offered them around to the miserable bunch of my relatives who were sitting in the drawing room. Conversation topics, it seemed, were minimal, and the food provided some relief, something to talk about. Nicholas followed me with the wine that I hoped might lighten the gloom.

I went back to the kitchen to find Brendan helping himself to a large glass of red.

"Just what I need," he said, taking a sizable slug. "Perhaps I shouldn't have brought the kids. They're quite distressed by it all. Their first funeral."

"How old are they now?" I asked, not really that interested.

"Christopher is sixteen and Patrick will be fourteen next week."

"Mmm," I said, "maybe they are still a bit young." Nicholas and Angela hadn't brought Tatiana, and she was older than both of Brendan's boys.

"But the boys were so eager to come." He laughed. "Probably just to get a day off school. But I think they might be regretting it now though. There's not much fun in this family."

I poured myself a large glass of red as well.

"How often did Clare ride for you?" I asked. I was thinking of one of the definites I had found in the database, the race when she had stopped Brendan's horse, Jasmine Pearls, in the Chester City Plate.

"Not that often," he replied. "Most of mine are ridden by Dennis Wilson, and Clare was always riding for Grubby."

"Don't I remember her riding one for you at Chester back in July?"

"Jasmine Pearls," he said, nodding. "She should have won too. I don't think Clare was at her best that day. She went to the front too soon, and the horse stopped itself. Pearly obviously didn't like being in front. Some horses don't. She's won since, though, at Leicester, having been held up to the last moment."

"Did Clare ride her then?"

"No. Dennis. And he should also have been riding her at

Chester, but he'd been thrown the previous day and hurt his ankle."

"So how many times did she ride for you altogether?"

"Maybe a dozen or fifteen over the years. Perhaps more. She last rode for me a couple of weeks ago at Doncaster on a difficult sod of a colt called Cotton House Boy. He always seems to go better with a girl up. Strange, that."

He took one of the cheese-and-pickle sandwiches off the tray I was still holding.

"Suppose I'd better get these kids back home," he said with his mouth full.

"I went to the hotel yesterday," I said.

"Hotel?"

"The London Hilton, on Park Lane."

"Oh?" he said. "And?"

"It seems that Clare met two men in her room before she died, and one of them might even have been there when she fell."

"Any idea who?"

"No," I said, "but I certainly intend to find out. The police took away some of the hotel CCTV video. I've asked them if I can have a look, but the detective in charge is on leave this week and, unbelievably, no one else seems to know anything about it. I'll just have to wait until he comes back, but it's bloody frustrating."

"Would it make any difference if you knew who the men were?"

I sighed. "I suppose not, but I'd like to understand why she did it. And I'd like to know if one of the visitors was her mystery boyfriend. Maybe they'd had a tiff, or perhaps it was something else to do with him that was troubling her."

Or, I thought, had she jumped because of what I had seen at Lingfield and because of what I'd said to her at dinner?

Oh God, I hoped not.

Perhaps I was desperate to find some other reason for her death just to relieve the burden of guilt that weighed so heavily on my chest.

9

On Tuesday morning I went back to work again, this time properly. Life, it seemed, had to continue, and Clare's death was last week's news. The world, and racing, went on regardless without her.

I was due to be the racetrack commentator at the jumps meeting at Stratford-upon-Avon, so I left my apartment early and drove clockwise around the London orbital, then up the freeway to Warwickshire. I spent the journey thinking back to the previous afternoon and, in particular, my rather strange encounter with my father at the conclusion of the proceedings.

With Nicholas's wise words still fresh in my memory, and also with his troubles over the on/off nature of Tatiana's birthday party, I had sought out my father for a quiet chat.

At first I hadn't been able to find him anywhere, but eventually I discovered him sitting in his high-backed desk chair in his study, in the quiet, facing the window.

"Hi, Dad," I said. "You OK?"

He'd swiveled slowly around to face me.

"Not really. You?"

"No. Not at all."

"I've been a fool," he said. He rotated the chair back so that he was again looking out at the garden and he sat silently for some time.

"In what way?" I asked finally. But he'd been a fool in all sorts of ways.

"Please leave me," he replied. "I'd rather be alone."

I could tell from his voice that he'd been close to tears.

"No, Dad. Talk to me."

"I can't." His whole body was shaking with sobs.

Not only had that day been a first for him ever praising me, it was also the first time I had ever seen my father cry. He had always believed, and had stated loudly and often through my childhood, that crying was a sign of weakness. Yet there he was, sobbing like a baby.

I didn't really know what to do. I was sure that he was embarrassed. Perhaps I should have left him alone to recover. Instead, I grabbed the back of his chair and spun him around to face me.

"Talk to me," I almost shouted at him. "We never communicate. We just argue."

"She didn't say good-bye," he said suddenly.

"What?"

"Clare. She never said good-bye to me."

"Dad, she was hardly likely to ring you up to say good-bye before she killed herself."

"No, not that," he said, now openly crying. "I mean, she never said good-bye to me when she left here that evening. We had argued. We always seem to, these days. I can't even remember what it was about. Something about the house, or the garden. She kept telling me I was getting too old to look after it. Anyway, it doesn't matter what we argued about—suffice to say, we did. And I told her that she was an insufferable spoiled brat who should know better than to speak to her parent like that."

I could imagine the exchange. I'd had them myself with the old git.

"She just walked out without another word," he said miserably. "She didn't even say good-bye to your mother. I followed her outside, telling her not to be so bloody stupid, but she didn't reply. She didn't even look at me. She got in her car and drove away without a backward glance." He sobbed again. "I feel so guilty."

Join the club, I thought.

IT WAS ONLY about twelve o'clock when I turned in through the gates of Stratford racetrack and parked in one of the spaces reserved for the race officials. Terence Feynman, the judge for the day, pulled in beside me.

"Hello, Terence," I said, climbing out of my car.

"Hi, Mark. I'm so sorry about Clare."

"Yeah," I said. "Not great."

"No. And just as she had made the breakthrough into the big time. Funny old world."

I didn't feel like laughing.

"Are you commentating or presenting?"

"Commentating."

"See you later then up top." He rushed away across the

parking lot as if he were late even though nearly two hours remained before the first race.

The judge's booth was alongside the commentator position at the top of the grandstand, his being directly in line with the winning post to enable him to accurately call the winner, assisted if necessary by the photo-finish camera that sat immediately above him.

Prior to 1949 there were no such cameras, and the judge was the sole arbiter of who had won and who hadn't.

Infamously, in the 1913 running of the 2,000 Guineas, the judge, Charlie Robinson, announced a horse called Louvois as the winner when every single other person at Newmarket that day believed Craganour had passed the post in front and won easily by a length.

Nevertheless, Louvois was declared the winner because the judge said so.

There was speculation and rumor at the time that Robinson had been influenced by the fact that he'd had friends who had died on the *Titanic* the previous year. Craganour was owned by C. Bower Ismay, younger brother of J. Bruce Ismay, chairman of the White Star Line, the company that had owned the *Titanic*. And it had been widely reported at the time, albeit wrongly, that J. Bruce Ismay had saved himself by securing a place in one of *Titanic*'s lifeboats by disguising himself as a woman.

But whatever anyone else might have thought, the judge's decision was final, and Louvois remained the official winner, and his name is still in the record books.

Not until 1983 were photo-finish cameras used at all British racetracks, and the first colored images were not available until 1989.

And it hasn't been just the judge's role that has changed due to modern technology.

The very first racetrack commentary in England was at Goodwood on July 29, 1952. For the previous eight hundred years, since the first documented racetrack at Smithfield in London in the twelfth century, races had been run in silence, the only sounds being the thudding of the horses' hooves on the turf and the cheering of the crowd.

Even as late as 1996, races at Keeneland, a premier racetrack in Lexington, Kentucky, were run without any public address other than a bell being rung when the race began. At Ascot, they still ring a bell to alert the crowd when the runners enter the finishing stretch even though there has been race commentary at the track since the mid-1950s.

I walked into Stratford racetrack through the main entrance only to come face-to-face with Toby Woodley from the *Daily Gazette*.

"Have you seen my piece today?" he asked in a loathsomely self-satisfied manner.

"No," I replied. "I never read your rag."

"You ought to," he sneered. "You might learn something. Especially today."

He walked off toward the bar, and I watched him go. I wondered if he could have been Clare's secret boyfriend. No, surely that was impossible.

I walked around behind the stands to the press room, which fortunately was deserted long before the first. In common with most racetracks, Stratford looked after members of the press pretty well, providing them with tea and coffee, a tray of sandwiches, and occasionally hot soup. However, I was in search of the newspapers that they regularly left in a stack by the door. In particular, I was looking for a copy of the *Daily Gazette*, which I spread out on one of the wooden desks.

My blood ran cold.

CLARE SHILLINGFORD WAS A RACE FIXER, ran the headline in bold type across the back page.

However, the story beneath was speculative at best and related to a race the previous April when Clare had ridden a horse called Brain of Brixham into second place on the all-weather Polytrack at Wolverhampton. It had been at an evening meeting under lights, and Clare claimed she had mistakenly thought that a pole used to support a TV camera on a wire had been the winning post. Hence she had stopped riding hard some twenty yards short of the finish and had been subsequently overtaken and beaten by another horse right on the line.

I'd seen the video of the race at the time and I remember thinking that Clare had been rather foolish, but it had definitely not been like the others I had found. As far as I could recall, it had been just a silly, but genuine, error.

But could I be totally sure?

The stewards at Wolverhampton had accepted Clare's explanation that it had been accidental and they had given her a fourteen-day suspension for careless riding. Now Toby Woodley was claiming that she had done it on purpose and been paid handsomely by a betting syndicate for her trouble.

I heard the door open behind me.

"So she wasn't such an angel after all," said Woodley with his distinctive squeak.

I spun around. "You're a bloody liar!" I shouted. "That race was simply an error of judgment and you know it."

"How about the betting syndicate?" he said. "They made a fortune laying that horse."

"Says who?" I demanded. "This rubbish doesn't name anyone." I waved my hand at the spread-out paper.

"Sources," he said, tapping the side of his nose with his finger. "I have my sources."

"Your imagination, more like it. You've made the whole thing up."

"You may think so," he sneered, "but this story will run and run."

"I'll sue," I said.

"On what grounds?"

"Libel."

"Don't you know?" He grinned, showing me his nicotine-stained teeth. "Under English law, you can't libel the dead." He laughed. "You should have spoken to me yesterday at her funeral. I was treated like dirt."

So was that the story? Was he simply piqued by being shouted at by my father and brushed off by me?

"Not treated like dirt," I said. "More like shit."

"You'll regret that."

I picked up the newspaper and waved it at him. "And is this what you meant by saying yesterday that you'd been good to me. Ha! Don't make me laugh. You don't know what being good means."

He was about to say something further when the door opened and Jim Metcalf walked in. Jim was the senior racing correspondent for *UK Today*, one of the country's best-selling national newspapers, which prided itself on its coverage of horseracing.

"Hi, Mark," said the newcomer. "Welcome back."

"Thanks, Jim," I said, meaning it. "And thank you for your note last week."

"No problem," he said. "We're all going to miss Clare. She was a lovely girl." He shook his head slightly, as if not knowing what else to say. Instead, he turned to Toby Woodley. "What do you want, you little runt? I thought we'd made it clear you weren't welcome in the press rooms."

"I have as much right to be here as you do," Toby whined.

"Right, maybe," said Jim. "But we don't want you here, understand? You make the place smell. Now, clear off."

I thought for a moment that Toby was going to stand his ground, but Jim was even taller than my six-foot-two and he'd once been a Royal Marine Commando. Toby, at about five-foot-six, would have been no match.

"Good riddance," Jim said, smiling, as the door closed. "He's a nasty piece of work."

"Have you seen his piece today in the *Gazette*?" I handed it to him.

"Is it true?" Jim asked after reading it.

"No," I said with certainty.

"Are you sure?"

"Of course I'm sure," I said.

But was I really sure? After what I'd seen on the films, could I be sure of anything concerning Clare's riding?

"What can I do about it?" I asked. "I can't sue him because it seems you can't libel the dead."

"That's right," Jim said, nodding. "But you could call him a liar on the air. Then he'd have to sue you or else be laughed out of his job. You'd then get your day in court. He'd have to prove he wasn't lying and that the facts of the story were accurate. But, sadly, even if you won, you wouldn't get any damages from the little weasel, and you might not get your costs because he'd be sure to claim it was fair comment even if the story wasn't true."

"Do you do the legal work for *UK Today* as well as the racing?" I asked with a smile.

"Not if I can help it." He smiled back. "But if you want my advice, I would say nothing and do nothing. Everyone knows that the *Gazette* is just a rumor mill. No one believes what it says even when it's true."

"But the *Daily Gazette* sells millions of copies."

"I know they do," he said. "But millions also watch soap operas on the telly and they don't really believe those either."

I wasn't so sure. I knew people who believed all sorts of crazy things.

I left Jim Metcalf tucking in to a ham-and-mustard sandwich while I went out to wander around the parade ring and the enclosures. It was still an hour before the first, but the crowd was beginning to fill the bars and restaurants, encouraged out from their houses by the warm late-September sunshine.

It was good to be back on a racetrack. The last week had seemed to drag on forever. Things might never be the same again without Clare, but at least today, at a jumping meeting, I could get my life back on track. Clare wouldn't have been here today even if she were still alive.

I WAS UP in my commentator position well before the first race. I liked commentating at Stratford not least because it was one of the minority of racetracks with the parade ring in front of the grandstands. That gave me more opportunity to study the colors.

I used my binoculars to scrutinize the horses as they walked around and around. I habitually used the race cards printed in the *Racing Post*, with their colored diagrams of the jockeys' silks. Now I made notes in black felt-tip pen of which horses had white marks on their faces, or had sheepskin nosebands, or blinkers, or visors, or white bridles, or breast girths, or anything else that might help me recognize them if I couldn't distinguish the colors, something that was not unknown if the track was very muddy.

Not that that would be an issue today, I thought, not on a fine September afternoon when the problem for the racetrack had been too little water, not too much. Indeed, the dry conditions and the firmness of the track meant that the number of declared runners in each race was small. It made my life easy, but it wasn't good for racing in general.

I watched as the jockeys came out of the weighing room and into the paddock. I couldn't help but think back to the last time I'd seen Clare doing the same thing at Lingfield. If only, I thought for the umpteenth time, if only I had known then what would happen later. I surely could have prevented it.

Suddenly the horses were coming out onto the racetrack, and I had been daydreaming instead of learning the colors. Get a grip, I told myself.

Fortunately there were only eight runners in the novice hurdle and many of them I knew well from having seen them run before. It would be an easy reintroduction to commentary for me. It seemed like longer than just the eleven days since I'd last done it at Lingfield.

I switched on my microphone and described the horses as they made their way to the two-mile start on the far side of the course.

"*Hi, Mark,*" said Derek's voice through the headphones. "*Coming to you in one minute.*"

Derek, sitting in the blacked-out RacingTV scanner truck, was at Chepstow racetrack, some seventy miles away to the southwest in Wales. He would be watching the same pictures that I had on the monitor in front of me, pictures that showed the eight runners here at Stratford circling while they had their girths tightened by the starter's assistant.

"*Ten seconds,*" said his voice into my ears. "*Five, four, three . . .*" He fell silent.

"The starter is moving to his rostrum," I said into the live microphone. "They're under starters orders. They're off."

The race was uneventful, with the eight horses well strung out even by the time they passed the stands for the first time. On the second circuit, three of them pulled up and the other five finished in an extended line astern with not a moment's excitement between them.

I tried my best to sound upbeat about the winner, as he strode away after the last hurdle to win by twenty lengths, but the crowd didn't seem to mind. He'd been a well-backed favorite, and most of the punters were happy.

"*Thanks, Mark,*" said Derek. "*Back with you for the next.*"

I sighed. The fun suddenly seemed to have gone out of my job.

I stayed in the commentary booth between the first two races and thought about what Toby Woodley had written in the *Gazette.* Was he just trying to get even for being humiliated by my father or was there more to his story? Did he really have his sources and knowledge of a betting syndicate or had he made up the whole thing?

If so, he was a bit too close to the mark for my liking.

I decided that perhaps I shouldn't make too much of a fuss about it. The last thing I wanted was to attract any unwelcome scrutiny of Clare's recent riding. I just hoped that the story was a one-day wonder that would quickly fade away to nothing and that everybody would soon forget about it.

Fat chance of that.

THANKFULLY, the second race was more exciting than the first, this time with seven runners battling it out over fences in a two-and-half-mile Beginners' Steeplechase.

"Beginners" were horses that had never won a steeplechase before, either on a racetrack proper or at a recognized point-to-point meeting, and it showed, with two of the seven falling at the first fence. However, the remaining five put up more of a contest, with three of them still with a chance at the last and fighting out a tight finish all the way to the wire.

That was more like it, I thought, smiling as I clicked off my microphone.

"First number, one, Ed Online," Terence the judge called over the public address from his booth next door. "Second number, three; third number, six. The fourth horse was number two. Distances were a neck and half a length."

"*Well done, Mark,*" said Derek through my headphones. "*That was more like it. Back with you for the next.*"

"OK," I replied, pushing the right button on my control box. "I'll be here."

There was a thirty-five-minute gap between the second and third races, which gave me about twenty minutes until I was needed back in my position, so I decided to go down to the weighing room for a cup of tea. However, I was intercepted by

Harry Jacobs, my leisurely friend whom I'd last seen at Lingfield the day Clare had died.

"Hello, Mark," he said, shaking my hand warmly. "You must come and have a drink."

"I'm working," I said.

"I know," he replied with a smile. "I've been listening to your dulcet tones over the loudspeakers. But surely you've got time for a quick one?"

I looked at my watch. "All right," I said, smiling back. "But it will have to be quick."

"But they can't start the race without you anyway," he said, chuckling.

"Oh yes they can," I assured him. "The race will start on time, with or without the commentary."

"We'd better be quick, then."

He put his hand on my shoulder and guided me around behind the stands toward the pre–parade ring. "I've got a box," he said as we climbed a metal staircase. "In here." He opened a door, and we went into a room full to overflowing with people who all seemed to be talking at once. The noise was almost overwhelming.

"Are all these your guests?" I asked him, shouting.

"Yes!" he shouted back. "Stratford's my local course, so I've asked along a few chums from home. Plus a few others I've sort of picked up since we arrived." He grinned broadly at me. "Now, what will you have?"

"Do you have a Diet Coke?" I asked.

His face showed that he didn't approve of any of his guests drinking nonalcoholic beverages. "Are you sure you won't have champagne?"

"Oh all right, then," I said with a laugh. "I'll force it down."

A waiter miraculously moved through the throng and delivered two slender glasses of bubbles into our hands.

"Cheers," I said, raising mine to my lips.

We were still standing close to the door, and Harry decided to dive deeper into the room. "Come on," he said, reaching out his hand and grabbing my jacket.

I didn't have much choice, so I followed him.

We struggled through and out onto the balcony on the far side, overlooking the parade ring.

"That's better," Harry said. "More air out here." He looked over my shoulder. "Hi, Richard," he shouted, and dived back into the melee, leaving me alone.

I turned to my right just as the lady behind me turned to her left so that the two of us ended up standing face-to-face, crammed together by the crowd.

"Hello, Sarah," I said.

Her irate husband, Mitchell Stacey, stood behind her, looking at me, and I swear I could see steam emanating from his ears.

I turned away from him and left, forcing my way through the mob without much finesse or consideration for toes, and I didn't look back to see if he was following. I almost ran down the metal stairs and then back to the commentary booth, where I remained holed up for the rest of the afternoon.

I LEFT IMMEDIATELY after the last race and hurried out to the parking lot, but Stacey was ahead of me, waiting at my car. I stopped ten yards away.

"I told you to stay away from my wife," he hissed at me through clenched teeth. "I warned you."

I decided to say nothing. I could have tried to explain to him that Sarah and I had come together by accident, that I hadn't even known she was at Stratford until we had ended up, nose to nose, on Harry Jacobs's balcony. But I didn't think it would help. Saying nothing was surely the best policy. Allow the volcano to subside, I thought. Don't go poking it with a stick.

He'd told me at Newmarket that he would have had my legs broken, but he could hardly do it on his own. For a start, I was half his age. I was also a good four or five inches taller than he and I kept myself fairly fit, not least by climbing stairs to the commentary booths at the top of all the racetrack grandstands.

If he was going to break my legs, he'd need help.

I glanced around, but there were no Stacey henchman lurking in the shadows. Rather, there was a group of inebriated racegoers making its unsteady way toward a row of buses.

"I warned you," he said again.

He suddenly strode toward me, so I moved quickly to the side to put a car between us but he didn't follow. He simply marched past where I'd been standing and continued in a straight line back toward the racetrack enclosures.

I breathed a huge sigh of relief. The confrontation was over for now, but I would be naïve if I thought it would be over forever.

10

Toby Woodley's story didn't fade away. Quite the opposite.

Wednesday morning's *Daily Gazette* had upgraded it from the back page to the front with an "Exclusive" tag beneath a two-inch-high headline in bold capital letters: RACE FIXING.

The article beneath reiterated the allegation that Clare had stopped Brain of Brixham in the race at Wolverhampton, even providing details about the amount of money that had supposedly been won by those laying the horse on the Internet betting exchanges.

It must have been a slow news day, I thought, and Toby Woodley's imagination had obviously been running in overdrive to fill the gap.

But there was also an underlying tone to the piece that vaguely implied that Clare's ride on Brain of Brixham might not have been an isolated incident but rather part of a pattern.

Watch this space, it said at the end, *for further revelations tomorrow. And not only about Clare Shillingford, but also about her brother, Mark.*

I stared at it. What revelations about me was Toby Woodley going to make up now? He's told me I'd regret saying at Stratford that he'd been treated at Clare's funeral not like dirt but like shit. Now the little bastard would make me pay. Unlike Clare, I *would* be able to take him to court if he lied.

And this wasn't the first time that the *Daily Gazette* had made accusations about race fixing either. It had done so the previous May, but not on the front page. On that occasion the whole thing had quickly died away to nothing as the paper had been unable to produce any firm evidence and had declined to name any individuals, probably for fear of being sued.

Even the *Racing Post,* which should have known better, had a report following up on the *Gazette*'s story, demanding answers and challenging Toby Woodley to reveal the identity of members of the betting syndicate "for the good of racing." The *Post*'s tenor may have been more "put up or shut up," but it wouldn't help to reduce the speculation. At least Jim Metcalf in *UK Today* had refused to join the chorus.

OTHER THAN READING the newspapers, I spent most of Wednesday morning studying the brochures for the eight houses I had looked at on the Internet. The various realtors had been most efficient in sending details, each brochure arriving with a cover letter telling me, each in a slightly different way, that now was the ideal time to buy a house.

I was sure that every realtor always thought it was an ideal time to buy a house. They were hardly likely to say it wasn't, now were they?

I was particularly interested in a house in a North Oxfordshire village. I'd often thought that Edenbridge in Kent was far from being the ideal place to live for someone with my job. Lingfield Park was certainly handy, and Brighton, Plumpton, and Folkestone were pretty close as well. It was also not bad for Fontwell, Goodwood, and the London courses, but I spent much of my time at the tracks in the Midlands and the North and they were all a long way off. It was no wonder that the odometer on my old Ford had been around the dial twice.

Oxfordshire, I thought, was a good central location, one where I could get to and from almost all the English racetracks in a single day, although there were none in the county itself.

I sat and looked at the glossy pictures and wondered if I was doing the right thing. In particular, was it sensible to move away from my parents at a stage in their lives when they soon would be needing more help?

That alone, I decided, was one very good reason why I should move. As things stood, I could see that it was going to fall to me alone to look after them, as had indeed become the case in recent months. If I lived in Oxfordshire rather than just five miles down the road, my elder siblings might start believing that they also had some responsibility for their parents, especially as they would all then be living closer to them than I.

Perhaps I should call the realtor and made an appointment to go see the house. Maybe I'd do it tomorrow.

———

MIDWEEK RACING under the lights at Kempton Park on the all-weather Polytrack has become standard fare for punters, although during the winter months the "crowd," if that is the right term for the sparse gathering of the faithful, wisely spend most of their time inside the glass-fronted bars and restaurants.

However, in late September the weather gods had been kind, and England was enjoying an Indian summer, with hot days and balmy evenings. So much so that I left my overcoat in my car, which I parked in the track parking lot.

I generally liked commentating on racing under lights.

I had first been night racing at Happy Valley racetrack in Hong Kong as a nineteen-year-old. It probably had been the strange environment as much as anything, but I'd found the whole experience so exciting, and part of that excitement remains every time I see jockeys' silks shining vividly in the bright glow of artificial light.

But that would have to wait. The first race was at twenty minutes to six, and the sun was still well up in the sky as the ten runners were loaded into the starting gate at the one-mile start on the far side of the oval track.

"They're off in the Crane Park Limited Maiden Stakes," I said into my microphone. "Quarterback Sneak breaks well and is quickly into stride on the nearside. He goes into an early lead, with Waimarima a close second. Popeye's Girl is next, in the pink jacket and sheepskin noseband, with Apache Pilot alongside in the dark green. Next is Banker's Joy, with the yellow crossbelts, and then Marker Pen in the hoops, with Kitbo now making some headway on the outside in the white cap."

The race unfolded, and I continued to describe the action as they swung right-handed into the stretch as a closely bunched group, the horses spreading across the track as their jockeys searched for a clear run to the line.

And every one of the jockeys looked to me just like Clare.

I almost lost it completely, but I forced myself to concentrate on the horses and pulled myself back from the brink.

"Quarterback Sneak is still just in front, but here comes Apache Pilot, with Popeye's Girl going very well on the wide outside. Just between these three, as they enter the final hundred yards. Quarterback Sneak seems unable to quicken, and Popeye's Girl goes on to win easily from Apache Pilot, with Kitbo a fast-finishing third. Next comes Quarterback Sneak, then Marker Pen and Banker's Joy together, followed by Waimarima, who faded badly in the closing stages."

I went through the rest of the field and then clicked off my mike.

I leaned back wearily against the wall of the commentary booth and wiped a bead of sweat from my clammy forehead. I felt wretched, and wondered if I would ever again be able to commentate on a race like that without seeing Clare as one, or all, of the jockeys.

Throughout her career, and particularly in the early years, Clare had ridden often at the all-weather tracks, especially during the winter months when there was no turf flat racing in Great Britain. It was how up-and-coming jockeys nowadays learned their trade, taking rides in January and February while many of their more established colleagues were sunning themselves on Caribbean beaches or riding winners in the warmth of Australia, Dubai, or Hong Kong.

I sat down on the stool in the commentary booth and looked out across the racetrack, the lights of the aircraft landing at Heathrow now shining brightly in the darkening sky.

I told myself that the reason I didn't feel like going down to the weighing room was I didn't want to meet anyone who had read the *Daily Gazette* or who might ask me difficult questions after seeing the *Racing Post*. But, in reality, it was because I felt I had to psych myself up for the next race.

I realized that commentating hadn't been a problem the previous day because Clare had never ridden at Stratford, and never would have, since they staged just hurdle races and steeplechases. Only tonight, here at Kempton, was I suddenly struck by her absence from the track.

Staying in the booth, however, wasn't the ideal preparation for the next race, as I couldn't see the runners in the parade ring, which at Kempton was situated right behind the main grandstand.

I studied the race program and tried to memorize the colors, but there was nothing like actually seeing the jockeys wearing the silks. All too often, the pigment of the inks used in the printing bore little or no resemblance to the actual dyes used in the material.

I went out of the commentary booth and turned left.

As was the case at many racetracks, the commentary booth at Kempton was high above and behind the grandstand seating but still under its large cantilevered roof. It was one of a number of separate booths opening off a long corridor that ran behind them to a metal staircase at one end.

During the races, the various booths contained not only the course race caller but also the judge, the race stewards, television cameramen, as well as the photo-finish technicians, who were on a higher level still immediately above the judge's booth, accessed by a second metal staircase at the far end.

It was a strange world that the public never saw, with multiple cables running along the tops of the undecorated walls, each essential for carrying the pictures and sound to the racetrack crowd and beyond.

I went to the end of the corridor and climbed the staircase to the photo-finish booth. Opposite was a door that opened out onto the grandstand roof. I unlocked the door and stepped out.

The Kempton grandstand had been built in 1997, and, like many similar projects of the time, much of its structural support was gained from a tubular steel framework that sat above the roof like a series of gigantic wire coat hangers.

There were a number of intersecting walkways that allowed access to the various air-conditioning units and the multitude of electronic aerials and satellite dishes, which were spread out all over the place. Each of the walkways had a metal grille floor and railings down either side to prevent anyone straying off them onto the roof itself.

I knew from experience that it was possible to see the parade ring from one of the walkways. I'd used it before, the previous year, when I'd twisted my ankle and didn't fancy going all the way down to ground level to see the horses.

I now spent a few moments checking the jockeys' silks. It was rare, but not unknown, for the printing in the paper to be wrong—for example, if a horse had been sold the night before a race and was running in the new owner's colors, something that was not that uncommon in the Grand National.

But on this occasion I was satisfied that all were attired as expected and I made my way back down to the commentary booth in time to describe them to the crowd as they cantered around the end of the track to the seven-eighths-of-a-mile start point on the far side of the course.

This time when the horses spread out as they entered the stretch, I was ready for the "Clare moment," as I decided to call it, when all the jockeys were facing me and each one of them reminded me of her. This time, in some strange way, I felt somewhat comforted by it rather than being overcome.

Far from trying to put Clare out of my mind in case it was too upsetting, I wanted to remember her every day, and this would be the way I would do it.

Suddenly I was more at ease with life, and I realized that, as for my father, feelings of guilt over Clare's death had overshadowed and distorted my grief. From that moment on, I told myself, I was going to rejoice in the memory of her brief existence and do my best to protect it.

Not that I didn't still feel terrible guilt over not answering the telephone calls from Clare that night. I did. And I lay awake for hours most nights rehearsing to myself what I could have done better to prevent the disaster.

But Jim Metcalf's advice to say nothing and to do nothing was for the old indecisive me. The new resolute and well-focused me would call Toby Woodley's bluff and make him prove what he was claiming was true or else admit that he couldn't.

I DID GO DOWN to the weighing room after the second race and instead of avoiding people who might ask me questions about the front page of the *Daily Gazette* or the piece in the *Racing Post* I started every conversation by saying how ridiculous it was and how Toby Woodley was just a little insect that needed stamping on.

"A worm is more like it," said Jack Laver, the racetrack broadcast technician who had made me the tea at Lingfield. "Nasty piece of work, that one. He was here earlier. Always tries to snoop round the weighing room to see if there's any gossip he can use or make up. The Clerk threw him out."

The Clerk of the Scales presided in the weighing room like a judge in a courtroom, sitting behind a desk and ensuring that everything was done correctly, including keeping the press out.

His primary role was to ensure that all the jockeys "weighed out" for each race at the correct weight and also that the winner and those who placed "weighed in" again afterward, together with any other jockeys that the Clerk may choose at his sole discretion. He also had to ensure that each jockey was wearing the correct colors and had the right equipment, such as blinkers or a visor, which the horse may have been declared as wearing.

And all the jockeys called him sir.

Not that they weren't averse to trying to fool him—usually because they were having trouble getting down to the required weight.

"Cheating Boots" have been around almost since racing first began—ultralight, paper-thin riding boots used only for weighing out, which the wearer then illegally exchanges for a more substantial pair back in the jockeys' room well out of sight of the Clerk. Weighing back in is not a problem as riders are allowed up to two extra pounds to provide for rain-soaked clothes or accumulated mud thrown up from the track.

These days, a jockey's racing helmet is not included in his riding weight, unlike his saddle which is. However, the colored cap that is worn over the helmet is included, but there are always those who will try to place the cap down on the Clerk's table while weighing out.

Every little bit helps.

In truth, it was all a bit of a game, and just like the schoolteacher and his miscreant pupils, the Clerks of the Scales were wise to jockeys' schemes and almost always won, but that didn't stop them from trying.

"Everything all right up top?" Jack asked. "Monitor OK?"

"Fine," I said, "as long as I can turn down the brightness a bit now that it's getting dark."

"There are some buttons on the side," Jack said. "Click the menu button twice, then use the down button on the brightness. Or do you need me to do it?"

"I'm sure I'll manage," I said. "I'll come back after the next if I can't."

I went out to the parade ring, keeping a careful watch out for Toby Woodley. I really didn't want to come face-to-face with him tonight. I wasn't at all sure I could restrain myself from hitting him and that surely wouldn't have helped the situation.

I stood and watched the horses for the third race walking around and around, noting on my race program that two of them were wearing sheepskin nosebands. Some trainers ran all their horses in nosebands. They thought it made them easier to spot, which was true as long as everyone didn't do it.

THE LAST of the eight races was not until after nine o'clock and by then many of the crowd had made their way home, not least because the evening had cooled considerably.

As my commentary of the race echoed around the deserted

grandstands, I wondered if anyone at the course was actually listening to me, although I hoped that some at home might be via their televisions.

"*Thanks, Mark,*" said a voice into my headphones as I switched off the microphone for the last time.

"Pleasure, Gordon," I replied, pushing the right button. Gordon was another of the RacingTV producers. "See you at Warwick tomorrow?"

"*No,*" he replied. "*Derek will be back doing Warwick. I'm in the studio tomorrow, then I'll be at Haydock Friday and Saturday. You?*"

"I'm presenting for Channel 4 on Saturday at Newmarket. Friday's a rare day off for me."

"*Have fun. Bye, now.*"

There was a click in my ears, and the system went dead. It was time to go home.

I packed my binoculars, colored pens, and race programs into my bag, went down to ground level, and followed the last remaining punters out past the parade ring in the direction of the parking lots.

By that time of night, there was a definite chill in the air, and I wished I'd brought my coat with me after all. But it was only a hundred and fifty yards or so to my car and I hurried along toward it.

I never got there.

TOBY WOODLEY was in the parking lot, standing beside a white van.

If I'd seen him sooner, I'd have made a detour to avoid him, but as it was I came around the back of the van and there he was only about six feet away. I stopped.

"What the bloody hell do you want?" I asked him.

He didn't answer but rolled his head toward me. He was actually leaning against the side of the van with his head back against the metal.

"Are you all right?" I asked.

He didn't reply.

I stepped forward toward him just as he slithered sideways down the side of the van, catching him just before he landed facedown. Even in the relatively dim glow of the parking lot lighting, a bright red streak of blood was clearly visible on the van's white panel.

"Help!" I shouted as loudly as I could. "Help! Somebody call an ambulance."

I turned Toby on his back and looked into his face as I struggled to remove my cell phone from my pocket. His eyes had an air of mild surprise in them. I thought he was trying to say something, but it was just the sound of his rasping breath. There were flecks of bright scarlet blood in the froth coming from his mouth.

"Help!" I shouted again. "Get an ambulance."

A man came running over toward me as I finally managed to extract my phone. "Call an ambulance," I said, tossing it to him.

"What's wrong with him?" the man asked.

"I think he's been stabbed," I said. "There's lots of blood."

The man glanced at the side of the van and pushed 999 on my phone.

I looked back at Toby's face. The air of surprise seemed to have gone. Now he was just staring, but his eyes didn't see. The rasping breath was no more.

"I think he's dead," I said to the man. "He's stopped breathing."

"Has he got a pulse?"

I tried to feel his wrist, but the only beat I could detect was from my own heart thumping away.

"I don't know," I said.

"Give him mouth-to-mouth," said the man. "The ambulance is on its way."

Not surprisingly, kissing Toby Woodley had not been on my planned agenda for the day, but nevertheless I tilted his head back, put my lips over his, and breathed into him. There was no noticeable movement of his chest, so I tilted his head back farther and repeated the drill.

"Keep going," said the man. "I'll do chest compressions."

The man knelt down next to me and started vigorously pumping with his hands up and down on Toby's breastbone as I breathed into Toby's mouth.

We went on like that for a good five minutes.

"Bloody hell," said the man, pausing for a moment, "this is hard work."

"Do you want to swap?" I said.

"No," he replied. "Keep going as we are."

"Does he have a pulse now?" I asked between breaths.

"Just keep going," said the man, resuming his chest compressions.

So we kept going for what seemed like at least another five minutes until an array of bright blue flashing lights announced the arrival of an ambulance and two green-clad paramedics came running over to us followed by a sizable group of onlookers, some of them with camera phones held high.

One of the paramedics bared Toby's chest and attached some sticky patches to his skin while the other connected leads to the patches and also to a yellow box with a small screen on the front. Even I could tell that the trace on the screen was flat and lifeless.

One of the paramedics pulled another box from his large green bag and soon had two metal plates placed on either side of Toby's chest.

"All clear," he called, making sure no one was touching Toby. "Shocking!"

Toby's body convulsed for a moment, then lay motionless again. The line on the screen, meanwhile, stayed completely flat.

"All clear again," called the paramedic. "Shocking!"

He repeated the process another three times while his colleague injected something into Toby's arm. That wouldn't do much good, I thought, not without any circulation. For all their effort, the trace on the screen never even flickered.

The paramedics took over the mouth-to-mouth and chest compressions, and they went on for far longer than I would have expected, each time they stopped, the line on the screen remaining stubbornly flat. They shocked Toby yet again and shone a flashlight in his eyes.

"No pressure," said one. "No vital signs. CPR terminated at . . ."—he looked at his watch—"nine forty-five." He began to pack up his equipment.

"What happened?" the other paramedic asked me, all urgency having suddenly evaporated.

"He's been stabbed," I said.

"What with?" he asked while pulling Toby's shirt wider and looking down his abdomen. "And where?"

"There's blood on his back," I said. And, I suddenly realized, I was kneeling in the stuff. A great pool of it surrounded Toby's body. All those chest compressions, I thought, had done nothing more than pump the blood out of him.

The police arrived in force, and suddenly the atmosphere changed again. It was no longer just a racetrack parking lot. It had become a murder scene.

11

Now, Mr. Shillingford, are you absolutely sure that Mr. Woodley was alive when you first saw him in the parking lot?"

"Yes," I said. "Quite sure. He was leaning against the white van, and he moved his head round to look at me when I spoke to him."

I was sitting in a cubicle in a mobile police incident room that had been parked in a corner of the Kempton Park racetrack parking lot, well away from the square white tent that now stood over the spot where Toby Woodley had died.

And I was cold.

"Can't you get me something warmer?" I asked the detective who was asking the questions. "I'm freezing in this." I fingered the white nylon coveralls I had been given to put on when my clothes had been removed and bagged for forensic purposes. Ignominiously, I had been made to stand in my underwear, shivering, as a masked forensic officer, also dressed from head to foot in white nylon, had examined my skin, hair, fingernails, and mouth for any clues.

"There's a tracksuit on its way from the station," said the detective, "and a pair of training shoes." He gesticulated at another policeman, who had been sitting quietly listening to our conversation. The second man stood up and went out of the cubicle, closing the door behind him.

If the rest of me was cold, my feet were like blocks of ice, resting as they were on the freezing metal floor of the glorified van.

"Did Mr. Woodley say anything to you?" the detective asked once again.

"No," I repeated. "I told you, he just slid down the side of the van and died."

"So why did you tell the paramedic that Mr. Woodley had been stabbed?"

"Because of the blood on the van," I said patiently. "I just presumed he'd been stabbed."

"I see," he said, making a note.

"And was he?" I asked.

"Was he what?"

"Stabbed?"

"The autopsy will determine that, sir," the detective said formally.

The second policeman came back into the cubicle and sat down again on the same upright chair as before. He shook his head, and I took that to mean the tracksuit and training shoes were not yet here. I went on shivering.

"When can I go home?" I asked the detective.

"That will be up to my superintendent," he replied unhelpfully.

I looked at my watch. It was well past eleven o'clock and nearly two hours since Toby Woodley's life had expired.

"Look," I said, "could you please tell your superintendent that I need to go home now. I've got to be up tomorrow in time to go to work."

"And what is your work, sir?" the detective asked.

"I've already told you." My patience was beginning to run rather thin. "I'm a race caller and TV presenter. I was commentating here tonight, and I found Mr. Woodley in the parking lot as I was leaving. I tried to help him, but I couldn't. He died in spite of another man and me giving him artificial respiration. That's all I can tell you. And now," I said, standing up, "I'd like to go home."

The detective, who remained seated in his chair, looked up at me.

"Mr. Shillingford," he said, "have you read today's *Daily Gazette*?"

I stood there looking back at him. "Am I under arrest?" I asked.

"No, of course not," the detective said, smiling. "We just need you to remain here a while longer to help us with our inquiries."

"And how about if I say I'm going home anyway?"

"That wouldn't be wise," he said.

No. Then I probably would be arrested.

I thought back over the interview.

"You haven't asked me why I think Mr. Woodley was attacked."

"No, sir," said the detective without elaborating.

"Why not?" I asked.

"All in good time, sir," he replied.

We sat in silence for a while, and I wondered what the police were doing that took so long. Looking for a knife, I supposed. That's it, I thought, they couldn't arrest me for stabbing Toby unless they could find the knife because otherwise there was no way I could have done it.

And maybe they wouldn't ask me why I thought Toby had been stabbed until they knew whether I could have done it. Perhaps it would affect how they asked their questions.

I sat there hoping the killer had taken the murder weapon away with him. Knowing my luck, he'd have thrown it away under my car.

Someone came into the cubicle carrying a folded tracksuit and a pair of training shoes. Thank goodness, I thought. My feet had lost all feeling.

I was left alone briefly to change, but the detective and his sidekick soon returned, accompanied this time by another man who was clearly their boss—the superintendent.

"Mr. Shillingford," he said. "Detective Superintendent Cullen." He held out his hand toward me and I shook it. "I'm sorry you have been asked to stay here for so long. I hope my boys have been looking after you?" He smiled.

No knife, I thought.

"They have been charming," I said, smiling back. Two could play at this game. "And thank you for the tracksuit and shoes." We both smiled again.

Another chair was brought in, and we all sat down, although the cubicle was hardly big enough for the four of us.

"Can you think of any reason why Mr. Woodley would be murdered?" the superintendent asked.

"Other than because of today's front page of the *Daily Ga-zette*?" I said. There was little point in not mentioning it, and I thought it would be better if I did so first.

"Exactly. Other than that."

"Lots of them," I said.

"I beg your pardon?"

"I can think of lots of reasons why someone might want to murder Toby Woodley. He was a horrible little man who preyed on other people's weaknesses." I paused briefly. "I'd have happily stuck a knife into his back."

"And did you?" he asked seriously.

"No," I said. "Someone else seems to have done it for me."

"Is that an admission of a conspiracy?"

"No, of course not," I said. "But if you're expecting me to grieve over Toby Woodley, you'll be disappointed. I hated the little creep."

"I understand," he said slowly, "that you have been telling people here this evening that he was nothing more than an insect that needed stamping on. Is that right?"

"Quite right," I said. "Because he's been trashing my late sister's reputation with his lies and I couldn't do anything about it."

"Someone may have."

"Well, it was not me."

"What were the revelations about you that Mr. Woodley was going to write about?"

"I have absolutely no idea," I said. "I was rude to him at Stratford races yesterday, and I expect he was planning to make up some nonsense about me out of revenge."

"How were you rude to him?"

"I basically told him he was a little shit," I said. "Because he was."

Superintendent Cullen looked down at his notebook, then up at me.

"Are you happy he's dead?"

I sat there and looked at each of the three policemen in turn.

"I tried to save his life, didn't I? I put my mouth over his—over the mouth of someone I hated and despised—and I breathed into him." I instinctively wiped my mouth with the sleeve of the tracksuit. "Of course I'm not happy he's dead. But, equally, I'm not especially sad about it either."

THEY FINALLY let me go at about half past midnight after I had agreed to and signed a full account of the incident as I remembered it. But they kept my clothes, my shoes, and, much to my annoyance, my car.

"I need my car," I said.

"None of the cars close to the white van can be moved," the superintendent said to me. "We need to search the area again properly in the daylight, and I'm not prepared to compromise any forensic evidence present by moving anything."

"But how am I going to get home?" I asked. "Especially at this time of night?"

"I'll get a car to take you."

"Thank you. How about my clothes?" I asked. "And my shoes?"

I was rather fond of those shoes.

"You'll get them back in due course."

I didn't like to ask how long "in due course" might be.

Years, probably, particularly if they provided evidence that was pertinent to a prosecution.

"I'll need my car tomorrow morning," I said. "I've got to get to Warwick races."

"Don't push your luck, Mr. Shillingford," the superintendent said, but with a smile. "You're lucky to be getting a ride home. I could always change my mind. Ever heard of trains? Leave your car keys and your phone number with my sergeant and he'll contact you when you can retrieve your car."

I didn't push my luck. I gave my car keys to the sergeant.

"Thank you," he said.

I was driven in an unmarked police car by a driver who didn't say a word to me all the way from Kempton to Edenbridge. He dropped me outside my front door, still silent, and drove off.

I let myself in and then sat in my sitting room–cum–kitchen–cum–dining room–cum–office with a stiff whisky. I didn't often drink spirits, but I didn't often have someone die with his head in my lap.

Who would have wanted to kill Toby Woodley?

Sure, there were lots of people, myself included, who might rejoice at his passing, but I couldn't imagine that anyone would actually kill him over something he had written in the paper. As Jim Metcalf had said, everyone knew the *Daily Gazette* was nothing more than a glorified rumor mill and no one really believed any of it.

So why was Toby Woodley dead? And did his death have anything to do with his pieces in the paper about Clare? Or was it totally unrelated? Indeed, were the deaths of Toby Woodley and Clare Shillingford entirely isolated incidents for which the only common factor was me?

I sat for a while pondering such questions but without coming up with any useful answers.

I knocked back the rest of my whisky and went to bed.

What I needed most was someone to talk to, someone to bounce some ideas off. In the past that would have been either Clare or Sarah.

I lay in the darkness, missing both of them hugely.

ON THURSDAY MORNING I caught a train from Edenbridge to London, and then another from London to Warwick.

I usually went everywhere by car, and it was quite a change for me to just sit and watch the world go by the window.

I bought a stack of newspapers at Edenbridge station and mostly spent the journey reading everything I could find about the murder of Toby Woodley in the Kempton parking lot. There was precious little that I didn't know already.

Only the *Racing Post* named me as one of the two men who had tried to save Toby's life. I wondered how much flak I would get from my colleagues for that.

The *Daily Gazette*, in contrast, named me as someone who was helping the police with their inquiries, which I suppose had been true at the time the paper had gone to press late the previous evening. The paper also speculated as to why one of its "star reporters"—their words—had been so cruelly cut down in the prime of life. Was it something to do with the *Daily Gazette*'s ongoing investigation into race fixing? Without actually saying so directly, they used the obvious association of the Shillingford names to imply that it must have been me who had killed Toby Woodley to shut him up.

Perhaps I should contact my solicitor and sue them. But I

knew of others who had sued the *Daily Gazette*, and even though a few of them had won sizable damages, they always lost in the end. Newspapers in general were relentless and vindictive, and the *Gazette* led the way on both counts, hounding its detractors forever, with every misdemeanor, however slight, every speeding ticket, every marital indiscretion, every faux pas, splashed across its front page in big bold type.

I took a taxi from Warwick station to the racetrack.

I was early.

I climbed up the stairs to the commentary booth and sat silently looking out across the track. There was a good hour and a half to go before the first race, but I needed to think. In particular, I needed to think once again about why Clare might have killed herself. And also why anyone would murder Toby Woodley.

The phone vibrated in my pocket. It was Superintendent Cullen's sergeant.

"Mr. Shillingford," he said, "did Mr. Woodley have a black leather briefcase with him last night when you first saw him in the racetrack's parking lot?"

"I didn't really notice," I said. "Why?"

"Mr. Woodley was seen with it earlier in the track's press area, but now it's missing."

"So was it a robbery that went too far?" I asked.

"Possibly," the sergeant replied. "We are trying to determine if the theft of the briefcase was the reason for the attack on Mr. Woodley or whether it was taken afterward by a third party."

"I'm afraid I can't help you. I don't remember seeing any briefcase."

He thanked me anyway and then told me that my car was

now ready to pick up and that the keys would be at the Kempton Park office, which was open late as they were racing that
evening.

"Thanks," I said, not really meaning it. The sergeant
hung up.

Not having my car was a bore. I'd better look up the return
train times from Warwick to London.

So the meeting at Kempton tonight was going ahead. Just as
it had been with Clare's, Toby Woodley's demise had been but
a minor blip in the ever-moving symphony of life that plays on
regardless. Are we each so insignificant, I thought, that our
death would mean nothing more to most people than a slight
inconvenience collecting a car?

Clare's death certainly meant more to me than that.

I still couldn't believe she had gone forever.

I yet again listed in my head the only reasons I could muster
to explain why she would have killed herself and yet again came
up with precious few.

She must have been depressed. Surely people who kill themselves must be depressed. But depressed about what?

I kept coming back to the question of the elusive boyfriend.
She had definitely been seeing someone—more than that, she'd
been sleeping with him. I thought back to our conversation at
that last dinner: *What a lover!* she had said, and she'd grinned
like the cat who'd got the cream. But she'd refused point-blank
to say who it was, and I felt she'd become quite aggressive about
it when I'd pressed her.

So who was Clare's great lover and was he one of the two
men that Carlos, the bellman, had seen go to her room?

But why hadn't he come forward to grieve with the family?

He might be married, I thought. Or perhaps the affair had

finished sometime between dinner and eleven-thirty that night. Was that the reason she had jumped?

Or had it been to do with her riding?

Had someone else spotted what I had seen in the race at Lingfield? Maybe somebody had threatened to tell the racing authorities. I thought back again to something else Clare had said that night: *I can't imagine a time when I couldn't ride anymore. I wouldn't want to go on living.*

And how about Toby Woodley?

Were his death and Clare's connected? Had someone killed him to shut him up? Had there been more truth to his articles than I'd given him credit for? Was there indeed a betting syndicate that had made a fortune laying Brain of Brixham in April?

I didn't think there could be. For a start, the Internet exchanges would have told the British Horseracing Authority if there had been any unusual betting patterns on that race, particularly as Clare had been suspended for riding carelessly in it.

Perhaps Toby Woodley hadn't got the details completely right, but nevertheless someone had thought he'd been close enough.

Overall, I was frustrated by my lack of information. I hoped that the Hilton Hotel's CCTV film or the guest list from the Injured Jockeys Fund gala might give me some clues.

Provided I could get hold of them.

I COLLECTED MY CAR from Kempton at eight o'clock that evening, having cadged a ride from Warwick with a south-coast trainer who didn't mind a brief detour off the London orbital freeway.

"It's the least I could do," he said. "I was very fond of Clare."

He dropped me at the gates of the Kempton parking lot, and I walked through to the racetrack office. The only signs of the previous day's murder were the white tent still covering the spot where Toby had died and a very large number of police officers, standing around, holding clipboards.

"Excuse me, sir," called one of them as I emerged from the office with my car keys. "Were you here yesterday evening?"

"Yes, I was," I said. "I'm collecting my car, which was kept here. I was interviewed last night by Superintendent Cullen."

He still wrote down my name and address on his clipboard. "Is there anything else you've remembered since you were interviewed that might be useful to us?"

"No," I said. "Sorry."

He let me go, and I walked toward my car, which someone had moved over to the fence near the exit.

I felt slightly uneasy.

Less than twenty-four hours ago someone had been murdered in this parking lot. Stabbed in the back. While now there was easily enough light to see the cars, there were plenty of dark shadows in which someone could be hiding. The hairs on the back of my neck stood upright, and I spun around to check.

There was nobody there.

I laughed at myself. Of course there was nobody there.

Even a psychopath would surely think twice about murdering someone here with this many police about.

But I did walk right around my old Ford before I opened it, and I also checked the backseat to make sure no one was lurking there with intent.

They weren't. Not this time.

12

On Friday morning I packed a suitcase and drove myself to Newmarket.

My original plan had been to come there after racing at Warwick the previous day and stay for a couple of nights with Clare. But that plan had changed even before Clare's death. About a month ago we had both sort of decided during a phone call that two nights was one night too many given the current belligerent atmosphere between us.

But Clare had then laughed and promised to hide all the kitchen knives during my stay. At least, I thought, we hadn't gone too far down an irreversible path that we were unable to see the funny side and laugh at ourselves. But then the disastrous event in Park Lane had overtaken us.

Oh, how I longed again for her still to be alive. It was like an ache that wouldn't go away. Painkillers had absolutely no effect. I'd tried.

I parked next to Clare's cottage and collected the key from

Geoff Grubb's stable yard office. There must have been another key in Clare's handbag, and I presumed the police had that. I would have to ask Detective Sergeant Sharp for it on Monday. Would they also have her car? I would ask the detective about that as well.

The rent's paid for the rest of the month, Geoff had said to me at Windsor races when I'd seen him just two days after Clare had died. Well, today was the last day of the month, so I had better get on doing something about clearing out her stuff.

I let myself in and stood in her sitting room. It was only eight days since I'd last been there, but so much seemed to have happened since. Somehow, though, I felt it was a little easier being there this time.

I took my things up the narrow staircase to the spare bedroom, hanging my dinner jacket in the wardrobe.

Clare and I had planned to go to Tatiana's eighteenth birthday party together, and I had a slight emotional wobble as I recalled Clare's surprise at being asked.

"I hardly know the girl," she had said. "You're her godparent, not me."

"But you can't really blame her. If you had a celebrity aunt, you'd also invite her to your party."

"Celebrity, my arse," she replied with a laugh. "You're the celebrity. That's what being on TV does for you."

But Clare *had* indeed been quite a celebrity, as the abundant column inches of obituary that had appeared in *The Times* and the *Daily Telegraph* had proved. All the more reason why I should endeavor to defend her reputation from the slurs in the *Daily Gazette*. And, I thought, all the more reason for ensuring that I told no one of her irregular riding practices on Bangkok Flyer and the like.

I sighed. I didn't feel like going to an eighteenth birthday party. I could have done without all that noise for a start, not to mention a late night before I was due to appear on *The Morning Line* for Channel 4. But I had agreed ages ago to make the birthday speech, so I had to be there. And I wanted to support Nicholas, my brother-in-law, who was still worrying himself sick over whether or not he should have postponed the whole thing.

He and Angela had asked me if I would like to be Tatiana's godfather when I'd been only fourteen. I'd been really flattered, but, to be honest, I probably hadn't been the most conscientious of godfathers. I had no idea about her faith, but I'd always sent Christmas and birthday presents, which is what I reckoned were my main duties.

Nicholas and Angela lived near Royston, about twenty miles southwest of Newmarket, and the party was in a tent in their garden. According to the invitation, it started at eight o'clock, so I decided that I should leave at about seven forty-five in order to arrive suitably early but without appearing to be too prompt. I reckoned that if I was there pretty much at the beginning, I could get away well before the end.

I looked at my watch. It was just after twelve, midday. So I had nearly seven hours for sorting and packing before I needed to get ready. But where did I start? I wasn't even sure how much of the furniture had belonged to Clare and how much had been rented with the cottage.

I decided to deal with her clothes first. I went out to my car to collect some large blue bags and some cardboard boxes that I had brought with me just for that purpose.

I started with the overly full drawers of frilly black lace underwear, which filled up one of the blue bags to overflowing. It made me sad that Clare had invested so much in something that almost no one saw. But I suppose it must have given her pleasure.

I managed to pack the rest of her clothes into four more of the bags, with shoes and boots filling two of the cardboard boxes. I took the bags and boxes down the stairs and stacked them in the space underneath.

Next I turned my attention to the desk in the corner of the sitting room. Her phone bill was where I'd put it down last time and then forgotten to collect it. I now folded it carefully and put it in my pocket.

I sat down on the chair and started to look through Clare's papers. I wasn't sure what I was really looking for, if anything, but I couldn't just throw stuff away without going through it first. There might be share certificates or other important documents. I hoped there might even be a will.

The desk had three drawers on each side of a central knee-hole, and the top two drawers on the left-hand side were full to overflowing with payment advice slips from Weatherbys, the company that administers racing's finances. They detailed all of Clare's rides, showing the riding fees paid to her bank account, along with any percentage of prize money she'd been entitled to, and she had clearly been stuffing them into the drawers for some time.

The bottom drawer on the left contained her bank statements and these were in better order. I picked up the top one, which was for the previous month.

I thought it unlikely that Clare had killed herself due to any money worries. According to the statement, just two and a half weeks before she died, her current account balance had been on the plus side of twenty thousand pounds.

I skimmed through the credits for the previous four months. Almost all were direct transfers from Weatherbys, with only a couple of small amounts paid in by checks. There were certainly no unexplained credits that matched the dates of the seven definites and four possibles, although any payment for her riding of Bangkok Flyer would not yet have appeared on a statement.

I filled another cardboard box with the statements and the payment slips and turned my attention to the drawers on the right.

The top one contained all her office supplies: a stapler, pens, notepads, stamps, and paper clips. There were also several checkbook stubs, held together with a red rubber band, and two pairs of sunglasses, one with a broken arm.

In the second drawer there were various documents, including Clare's birth certificate, her passport, her jockey's license, and a stack of investment portfolio valuations, all of which showed that Clare had been sensibly providing for her future after riding. A future that would now never be.

At the very back of the drawer, behind the investment valuations, I found a sealed white envelope.

I opened it.

The envelope contained two thousand pounds in cash, all of it in twenty-pound notes in packs of a thousand, each pack held together with an inch-wide paper band.

I didn't immediately assume that the cash was in any way irregular or sinister. Lots of people I know keep a supply of cash in case of emergencies, although two thousand pounds was rather on the high side. However, the thing that did raise some doubts in my mind was that the bands around the cash had "Barclays Bank" printed on them, while I knew from her bank statements that Clare banked with HSBC. It was not easy to get that amount of cash from a bank where you didn't have an account.

And my suspicions were raised a further fifty or so notches by what was written on the front of the envelope in capital letters: *AS AGREED, A.*

Had Clare been paid a couple of thousand pounds for not winning? And who was A.?

I leaned back in her chair and wondered if she had fully understood what she had become involved in. It wasn't just a game, it was full-blown criminal fraud for gain, and discovery would have resulted in not just the loss of her career but likely the loss of her freedom.

I was suddenly very angry with Clare.

How could she have been so stupid? And why had she told me it was all about power and control when, at the same time, she was accepting a couple of grand from someone? It didn't make sense. All I could think was that she hadn't thought the money important. After all, her bank balance and her investment portfolios were very healthy, and the cash had still been in a sealed envelope as if she hadn't even bothered to count it.

I wondered if there were any fingerprints on the envelope that might help identify who had given it to Clare. Or maybe DNA, if someone had licked the envelope to seal it shut. The problem was, however, that I would have to go back to the police with my suspicions in order for them to investigate and did I really want to do that? Yes I did if it was pertinent to Clare's death, but no otherwise. The difficulty was knowing which was the case.

I put the cash back in the envelope, carefully holding it by the edges, then placed the envelope in one of the cardboard boxes along with other stuff.

That left only the bottom drawer on the right, and it was full of press clippings. I looked through the lot. All but two of them were about Clare herself, stretching back over four years. I was pleasantly surprised to find that one of the other two was about me, a background piece done by a national daily a year or so previously. But it was the final clipping that was the most intriguing.

It was the two-page spread run in the *Daily Gazette* the previous May about race fixing and it had been written by Toby Woodley.

I had heard about the story at the time, but I hadn't seen the original article, so I now read through it from start to finish. There was no mention of Clare or of any of the horses she had later ridden in any of my eleven suspect races. The piece was actually more speculative than factual, as was usually the case with the *Daily Gazette*, but it did seem to firmly imply that a well-known trainer was betting to lose on his own horses.

Betting to lose was strictly against the Rules of Racing for certain individuals, in particular the owner and trainer of the horse. And not only were they banned from doing it directly, they were also banned from instructing others to do so on their behalf or from receiving any proceeds from such activity.

But Toby Woodley had stated categorically that he knew of

a racehorse trainer who regularly layed his horses on the Internet and then ensured that the horses didn't win. Needless to say, he hadn't mentioned the trainer by name.

I was intrigued not so much by the article's content, which I only half believed anyway, but why Clare had chosen to keep this clipping with all the others.

Perhaps she had known it was true.

I ARRIVED at Tatiana's party at twenty past eight to find that I was one of the last to get there. Nowadays, it seemed, the young arrived at parties bang on time, just as soon as the caterers started pouring the drinks.

Getting ready in Clare's cottage as the day had faded into night had been very difficult. Evenings had always been the best times at Stable Cottage, with lots of parties and dinners. Even on quiet nights, there had always been open bottles of Pinot Grigio and Cabernet Sauvignon, even though Clare herself rarely had more than a single glass.

The whole place had seemed very quiet and lonely as I had showered and dressed in my tuxedo, so much so that I realized I'd made a big mistake staying there. I should have accepted one of the other offers of a bed that I'd received from Newmarket friends. I wasn't particularly relishing the thought of going back to Stable Cottage alone later, but it was too late now.

"Hello, Mark." Angela greeted me at their front door. "Coat in the dining room, then go on through. We're in a big tent in the garden. Nick's out there with Brendan."

I did as I was told, placing my overcoat on the pile in the dining room and then walking through the sitting room and out of the French doors.

I was astonished at how big the tent was. Even though I'd been here quite a few times before, I was amazed that the garden was large enough to hold such a structure.

"Incredible, isn't it?" Brendan said, standing just inside the tent with a glass of red wine in his hand. "It apparently occupies the whole place. The guylines are even secured over the fences in the neighbors' gardens."

I could see that there were flower beds down each side of the tent, and a small tree appeared to grow right through the middle of the black-and-white dance floor.

"Amazing," I agreed.

"Had any luck with finding out what happened at the hotel on the night Clare died?" Brendan asked.

"None," I said. "I can't believe the police. Someone goes away on holiday for a week and the whole investigation comes to a complete halt. It's bloody ridiculous. Thankfully the detective is back on Monday."

"Let me know how you get on," he said, draining his glass. "I'm off to find a refill."

Brendan went over toward a waiter holding a tray just as Nicholas walked over to greet me.

"It's fabulous," I said to him. "Absolutely fabulous."

He beamed at me. "Yes, it is rather good, isn't it?"

We stood for a moment surveying the scene.

"So where's the birthday girl?" I asked.

"Over there somewhere," Nicholas said, pointing at a large crowd of youngsters propping up the bar at the far end of the tent. "She's eighteen and exercising her legal right to drink alcohol." He rolled his eyes. "Not that she hasn't been drinking alcohol for ages. I know she has. They all do. And I fear I'm going to be the villain tonight by closing the bar every so often to give them a rest. I don't want them all to get so drunk they ruin everything, not until after dinner and the speeches anyway. I've taken two bottles of vodka off a girl who I happen to know is only seventeen, and her breath smelled like she'd already drunk a third. And Brendan's boys are hitting it pretty bad behind their mother's back, and Patrick's not even fourteen until Sunday."

"At least they are their parents' responsibility, not yours."

He laughed. "Brendan and Gillian seem to be well ahead of them. They've been here since seven, as they're staying the night with us, and Brendan in particular is getting stuck in the red wine."

"I've seen," I said.

Nick waved his hand toward the group of scantily dressed girls at the bar. "But it's these other young things I'm really worried about. They seem determined to get hammered, and quickly. And they *are* my responsibility."

"Good luck," I said with a laugh.

"I'm going to need it," he said. "Especially when your mom and dad get here."

"They are coming, then?" I was surprised.

"They said so, but they aren't here yet, which is slightly ominous. They finally agreed to come only yesterday and that was thanks to you."

"Don't thank me just yet," I said with a laugh. "You know how Dad can be a nightmare."

"To tell you the truth, I was half hoping they wouldn't come, but Angie is delighted that they are so I'm trying to be pleased too."

As if on cue, Angela came through the French doors of the sitting room into the tent with our mother and father.

"Hi, Mom," I said, giving her a kiss on the cheek. "Lovely, isn't it?"

She looked around her as if in a bit of a daze. "I wish Clare had been here to see it." I could tell that she was very close to tears.

"Yes," I said, "you're right, Mom, so do I. But tonight is Tatiana's big moment, and we have to be happy for her."

My mother smiled at me wanly. "Yes, Mark," she said, "I know. I'll be fine."

"Evening, Mark," my father said brusquely.

I had been quite forceful in telling him that Nicholas and Angela couldn't afford to postpone Tatiana's party and that he should give his blessing for it to proceed. But I hadn't expected him actually to attend the event, and, unless he cheered up a bit, it might have been better if he hadn't.

"Evening, Dad," I said. "Doesn't it all look wonderful?"

"I suppose so," he grunted. But the tent did look wonderful, with a dozen round tables set for dinner and surrounded by white ladder-back chairs.

"Let me get you all a drink," Nicholas said, sensing the tension. He waved vigorously at one of the waiters, who brought over a tray of glasses.

I took an orange juice from the tray, and Nicholas raised his eyebrows.

"I've a speech to make," I said, "and I'm driving. I might have a glass of wine with dinner."

"You're making the toast, remember, and we have champagne for that."

"I won't forget," I assured him.

I went over to the bar to give Tatiana a kiss and wish her a happy birthday.

"You look gorgeous, darling," I said to her, although in truth I thought her skirt six inches too short and her heels four inches too high.

"Your speech is not going to be too embarrassing, is it?" she asked.

"Probably," I said.

"Oh God. It's bad enough with Mom insisting on putting these dreadful pictures on all the tables. They're so crass."

I looked at the one nearest to me. It showed Tatiana as a baby, sitting naked in the bath. I could understand how she felt uncomfortable having a picture of herself like that for all her school friends to see. But, equally, I could appreciate how Angela would have found it rather amusing.

"Don't worry," I said, "I won't be as embarrassing as that."

She smiled at me. "I'm so glad. Now, come and meet my friends."

AT DINNER, I found myself sitting between Angela and a girl called Emily Lowther. I say a girl, but she was about my age, dark-haired, slim, and beautiful. She was wearing a low-cut black dress that displayed just the right amount of bosom, and almost the first thing she told me was that she was a childless divorcée and one of Angela's best friends from the local gym.

I detected a barefaced attempt by my sister to matchmake and I told her so in a fierce whisper.

"So what?" Angela said, unabashed. "Emily needs a husband, and you need a wife. And she is gorgeous, isn't she? And frighteningly bright as well."

She certainly was gorgeous, but did I really need a wife? Was I not happy enough as a bachelor?

It was certainly true that the ending of my affair with Sarah had made me rather glum, but I'd been so depressed anyway because of Clare that a little more misery didn't seem to matter much.

And I kept telling myself that I missed Sarah only because some of the excitement had gone out of my life rather than for the loss of any undying love I might have had for her. In fact, I wondered if the possibility of being found out had been the most arousing aspect of our affair. So would I find the same thrill in a relationship that I could be open and honest about?

"What happened to her husband?" I asked Angela quietly as Emily talked to my father, who was sitting on her other side.

"Stupid man decided after four years of marriage that he preferred boys. I ask you. Left our gorgeous Emily for some French hairdresser called Pierre. The man must be a raving lunatic."

Emily put her hand on my arm. "Mark, I'm so sorry about Clare."

"Thank you," I said, turning toward her but not removing her hand. "It has been a very difficult couple of weeks."

Was it really only two weeks? How the time had dragged.

"It must have been," Emily said. She moved her hand forward and placed it on the back of mine, squeezing it a little. "Do say if there's anything I can do to help you. Anything at all."

"Thank you," I said, looking her directly in the eyes, "I will."

Was I mistaken or had I just been propositioned for sex?

13

And finally, will you all stand up and raise your glasses to join me in a toast to my favorite goddaughter—happy eighteenth birthday, Tatiana."

"Happy birthday, Tatiana," chorused the assembled guests.

We all sang "Happy birthday to you . . ." as a magnificent cake with two rows of flaming candles was brought out by Nicholas. To rapturous cheers from her school friends, Tatiana blew out the eighteen candles, cut the cake, then made a short speech of thanks to her parents, with every second word being "amazing."

"Yours was a great speech. Well done," said Emily, again squeezing my hand.

"Thanks."

"I hate speaking in public," she said. "I get so nervous."

"I do it for a living," I replied. "You get used to it."

"Yes, I know. I've seen you on television. But don't you get one of those autocue things to read?"

"Never," I said. "You only get those in a studio and I work exclusively at racetracks."

At that moment the DJ decided to turn up the volume of the music from loud to earsplitting, making further conversation difficult if not impossible. I looked at my watch. It was already almost eleven o'clock.

"Do you want to dance?" Emily shouted into my ear.

"Not really," I replied, fortissimo, in hers. "I need to go fairly soon. I've got an early start."

"I could come with you," she said, looking straight into my eyes. "If you want."

Did I want?

"I'm sorry, but not tonight," I said in her ear. "I am staying at my dead sister's cottage. I think I'd rather be there alone. But thank you."

"We could go to my place."

Was she being a tad too desperate?

"I need to be at Newmarket racetrack at seven a.m. for *The Morning Line* and it's just a mile from my sister's cottage. That's why I'm staying there."

"I'll take that as a no, then."

"Look, I'm sorry. It's not that I don't want to. It's just that . . ."

"You don't need to explain," she said quickly. "It's fine." But I could see from her expression that it wasn't really.

"I think I'd better go now." I leaned forward and gave her a brief kiss on the cheek. "It's been lovely meeting you." It was a totally inadequate thing to say, and both of us knew it.

I stood up to go but turned back to her.

"Do you have a number?" I asked. "Perhaps I could call you?"

She produced a pen from her handbag and wrote down a number on a scrap of paper, which she then handed to me.

"Call me in the morning, after the program," she said. "I'll be watching."

"OK. I will."

Was I being a fool? I'd already bemoaned to myself how lonely Clare's cottage had seemed when I'd dressed there earlier and here I was turning down the perfect opportunity not to have to spend the night there. But did I actually want to jump into bed with someone I'd only just met. Mind you, it wouldn't have been the first time, not by a long shot. But . . .

"Go on, go!" Emily shouted over the music. It was as if she knew what I was thinking. "Call me tomorrow."

I went to find Angela and Nicholas to thank them for a lovely party. Angela was in the house, where thankfully it was much quieter.

"Do you really have to go so soon?" she asked.

"I'm on *The Morning Line*," I said by way of explanation.

"But what about Emily?" she asked, looking over my shoulder.

"She's been very nice," I said.

"But isn't she going with you?"

"No," I said.

"Oh," she said, clearly disappointed.

"Nice try, sis," I said, giving her a kiss. "Enjoy the rest of the party. Where's Nick?"

"Trying to close the bar, I think. At least for a bit. Some of those girls are getting very drunk."

I personally thought they'd been very drunk for ages. Long legs, short skirts, and tipsy—some of the boys clearly thought that Christmas had come early this year, if only they themselves hadn't drunk too much to make the most of the situation. I was quite glad that none of them were my concern.

"Will you say good-bye to him for me?" I said, collecting my coat. "And to Tatiana and the rest of the family. I don't want to be a party pooper by telling them I'm going so soon. I'll call you tomorrow, but not too early."

"Early as you like," Angela said with a smile. "We've got fifty or so of Tat's friends sleeping in the tent tonight and we want them all out and gone by lunchtime."

"You must be mad," I said, opening the front door.

"Totally. But thank God she's eighteen only once."

"It'll be her twenty-first next."

"Nope," she said. "This is the only one. She had the choice."

"Well, it's a wonderful party, but I hope you have understanding neighbors."

"Both sides are here as guests. And Tatiana has been to all the houses in the street to tell them. The music will decrease in volume at one o'clock and stop completely by two."

I gave Angela another kiss. "Tatiana's a very lucky girl."

"Tell me about it." I could hear her laughing as she closed the door.

The music sounded significantly louder outside than in, and, I thought, it wasn't just this street Tatiana had needed to visit. The whole neighborhood could hear it.

I walked across and down the road to my car, which I'd parked about forty yards away.

Dammit, I thought. This was the first time for about six weeks I had been asked to be on *The Morning Line* and it would just have to be the day after I wanted to stay out and play—or even stay in and play. There was no doubt that Emily had been willing, eager even. Had I made the wrong decision?

But I knew that I had to have some decent sleep if I was to be any good in the morning. Last year I'd been out late and had a few drinks the night before I was on and I thought I'd been rubbish. Television is very unforgiving of puffy eyes and a pallid complexion. I knew of an ex-colleague who had arrived for a show slightly late and rather hungover and he had never been invited on again. There are always those like Iain Ferguson standing in the wings, waiting to take over when your star wanes, and I had no intention of giving anyone an easy ride into my seat.

I had started my old Ford and was reaching for the gearshift when something was thrown over my head and tightened around my neck. I grabbed at it, but whoever was pulling it was much too quick for me to get any fingers between the ligature and my skin.

My head was snapped back hard against the headrest. I tried to cry out but nothing happened. I couldn't breathe, neither in nor out.

I began to panic and dig my fingers into my neck, trying to get them behind whatever was strangling me. But the harder I tried, the harder the person behind me pulled.

I reached back over my head, but I couldn't get my hands down far enough owing to the headrest.

I was dying. And I knew it.

I could feel my heart thumping extra fast, trying its best to pump blood to my ever-dulling brain. But the blood wasn't getting there. There was a blockage at the neck.

My lungs were filling with carbon dioxide, and they were bursting to breathe, but there was no way out for the poison gas and no way in for life-giving oxygen.

I thrashed around behind me with my hands, but there was nothing to grab.

This was it. I was going. Unconsciousness and death were but seconds away.

I didn't want to die.

I banged the steering wheel with my fist in anger and frustration, and I could hear the car horn sounding over the ringing in my ears.

The ignition must be on, I thought. Of course it was—I'd started the engine.

I reached forward with my left hand and, using the very tips of my fingers, I pushed the lever into first gear. Next I released the brake, then I positively stamped on the accelerator, released the clutch, and hoped the car wouldn't stall.

I couldn't see—my vision had gone completely—but I felt the car lurch forward. I didn't know where we were going, but I didn't care either, and I kept my right foot hard down on the gas right to the floor.

It seemed an age before we hit anything, but it was probably not more than a couple of seconds. There were two almighty crashes and another loud bang inside the car as the driver's air bag deployed. Then everything went quiet, save for the music from the party.

But, best of all, the pressure on my neck eased, and I gasped in a huge gulp of night air. I leaned forward against the steering wheel, holding my throbbing neck and trying to breathe in shallow breaths to reduce the excruciating pain.

Things began to return to normal in my brain.

My sight came back suddenly with a rush, but all I could see was white. I realized my head was up against the now deflated air bag, so I lifted it and looked through the windshield.

We had bounced off another car and then hit Nicholas and

Angela's stone gatepost pillar full on. The whole hood was crumpled. My dear old Ford looked to be mortally wounded, but it had clearly accelerated as well as any sports car.

I put my head back down again on the steering wheel. It was more comfortable like that, but part of my reoxygenated brain was suddenly screaming at me.

Danger! Danger!

The rest of my brain began to listen.

Someone was trying to kill me and he might still be here.

I quickly turned in the seat and looked behind me.

The back door on the driver's side was open. Whoever had been there, whoever had tried to kill me, had now fled.

My sudden turning movement had resulted in a severe bout of dizziness, so I rested my head once more on the wheel.

That was better.

In the distance, I could hear a wailing siren getting closer and closer.

"HE MUST BE DRUNK," I heard a voice say. "Look at his suit. He's been to that party."

I wasn't drunk. I'd only had a small glass of red wine with dinner and a sip of champagne for the toast. I tried to say so but nothing came out. Instead, my neck went on hurting like hell, and I was having difficulty swallowing.

I opened my eyes and lifted my head a little. A uniformed policeman was crouching in the open driver's door.

"Are you all right, sir?" he asked.

I tried to say no, I wasn't all right, but the words wouldn't form in my throat. So I just shook my head slowly from side to side.

"Sam, we need an ambulance," the policeman said.

"It's already on its way." Sam's voice, out of my vision.

"Oh my God, that's Mark's car," I heard Nicholas say. "Is he all right?" Nicholas's face appeared briefly at the car door.

"Thank you, sir," said the policeman. "Now, please stand back."

"But he's my brother-in-law," Nicholas said, disappearing from the door and climbing into the car through the open back door. "Are you all right, Mark?" he asked from somewhere near my left ear.

I started to turn my head around.

"Keep still," ordered the policeman. "You can make neck or back injuries worse if you move."

I kept still.

"Has he been at this party?" the policeman asked Nicholas.

"Yes. It's my daughter's party. Mark here made a speech."

"Has he been drinking?"

"No, I don't think so. I mean, I don't really know. I wasn't sitting with him at dinner."

Oh thanks, Nick, I thought. That's just what I need.

"Can I help?" Brendan had now climbed into the back alongside Nicholas.

The policeman looked at him. "We're trying to determine if this man has been drinking."

"Can't help you," Brendan said with a nervous laugh. "I know I have."

"I'm not drunk," I tried to say, but nothing but a croak came out.

"It's all right, sir," said the policeman, looking back at me. "You rest now, the ambulance is on its way."

I didn't want to rest. I wanted to tell them that I wasn't drunk, that someone had tried to kill me, that I'd been strangled, but my voice box and my mouth wouldn't do what my brain was asking of them.

"He must be drunk to have driven straight across the road into this gatepost at that speed," said the other policeman, Sam, the one I couldn't see. "Blind drunk, I shouldn't wonder. Is he well enough to do a breath test?"

I nodded at the policeman in the door, but he didn't immediately say anything. He just stared into my eyes. Then he shone a flashlight right in my face.

"I don't like the look of him."

I thought that was quite personal.

"In what way?" asked Nicholas.

"He's got red spots on the whites of his eyes." I didn't like the sound of that. "And there are some more on his face."

More flashing lights and another siren signaled the arrival of the ambulance, and a paramedic soon joined the policeman at the car door.

"He seems unable to speak," the policeman said to the new arrival, "and I don't like the look of his eyes."

I looked at them both as they looked at me.

"He may have had a stroke," said the paramedic.

I shook my head at them and made a gesture indicating I wanted to write something. The policeman removed a notebook from his pocket and passed it over with a pen.

I've been strangled, I wrote. *Somebody tried to kill me.* I handed the notebook back.

They both looked at what I had written and then up at my face.

I could tell from his expression that the policeman didn't believe me.

"They could be petechia," said the paramedic.

"What could?" said the policeman.

"The red spots. They could be petechia. It's the bursting of tiny blood vessels just under the skin and in the eyes. It can be brought on by asphyxia. He may well have been strangled." He gently tilted my head back and looked at my neck. "And there's definitely some bruising round the larynx. That might be why he can't speak."

"Bloody hell," said the policeman, "it's a crime scene. Sam, get everyone back. You two," he said, pointing at Nicholas and Brendan over my head, "out of the car. Now!"

IT SEEMED LIKE at least another half hour before they lifted me out of the car, by which time some semblance of my voice had returned.

One of the paramedics insisted on going behind me to attach a large plastic brace around my neck in spite of me complaining that it hurt my windpipe in front. Then they placed a board along my spine and strapped me to it. By this time the fire department had also arrived and they proceeded to remove the whole roof of the car.

Meanwhile, in little more than a croak I assured them that I was fine apart from my neck, which still hurt like hell.

"You can't be too careful," said one of the paramedics, although I believed they were being just that, a sentiment clearly shared by the plainclothes detective who had been summoned to the scene by his uniformed colleagues.

He'd already tried to talk to me twice but had been sent away on both occasions by the paramedics as they had fit me first with an oxygen mask over my nose and mouth and then with a saline drip needle in my hand.

"The extra fluid keeps your blood pressure up," one paramedic had explained, "and that helps deliver more oxygen to your brain."

Finally, they were ready, and I was lifted from the car and laid flat on a stretcher. I wouldn't have minded so much if there hadn't been such a large audience of young, scantily clad partygoers, together with most of my family, including my mother and my father, all of them standing on the sidewalk, shivering in the cool of the night.

I waved at them with my non-needled hand, much to the disapproval of the paramedic, who told me in no uncertain terms to lie perfectly still.

"I'm all right," I said very croakily through the mask. "I really think I could walk."

"No chance," he replied. "Asphyxia patients can die hours later even if they seem wide awake and well. You stay put."

I stayed put.

I was carried into the ambulance, and the detective tried to climb in with me, but the medics were having none of it.

"You can speak to him at the hospital," one of them said, "once he's stable."

"Which hospital?"

"Addenbrooke's, in Cambridge."

One of the paramedics drove while the other connected me to blood pressure and heart monitors.

"I feel fine now," I said. "It's only my throat that hurts."

"Nevertheless, it's better to get you checked out," he said, sticking wired pads on my chest. "Don't want you dropping down dead on us, now do we?"

No, I thought, we didn't.

"You just relax and let us do the worrying."

I wasn't particularly worried, not about my health anyway. I was far more worried about who would want to kill me and why.

"SO DID YOU see who attacked you?" asked the plainclothes policeman, who had introduced himself as Detective Chief Inspector Perry.

"No," I replied in my now familiar croak.

We were in a curtained-off cubicle of the emergency room at Addenbrooke's hospital, me lying on an examination table and him sitting next to it on a chair.

"Was the car locked when you arrived at it?"

"I think so," I said, "but I suppose I don't really know. I remember the car's indicator lights flashing when I pushed the unlock button on the key, but it's an old car and does that whether it's locked or not. I know because I've left it unlocked outside my apartment before."

"But you definitely had the keys with you?"

"Yes," I said. "They were in my coat pocket."

"And was the person already in the car before you got in?"

I tried to think back.

"I would say so, yes. I don't remember hearing any of the other doors open." But, in truth, my memory of the incident was hazy in places. The hospital doctor had said it might be. Oxygen starvation, it seemed, caused funny effects in the brain. It was why he wouldn't let me go home yet.

So much for my relatively early night.

I was wide awake at two o'clock in the morning, still dressed in my party gear, minus jacket and tie, answering endless questions.

"Why do you think someone would want to kill you?"

"I have absolutely no idea," I replied. It was the question I had been asking myself for the past three hours and I hadn't yet come up with any sensible answers. Was it something to do with Clare's suicide or with Toby Woodley's murder? Or had it merely been a botched attempt to steal my car?

Somehow, I doubted that.

For a start, my Ford was very old and hardly worth stealing, and strangling the driver just to steal a car seemed rather excessive.

"Did you find a rope?" I asked.

"So it was a rope?" he said.

"I'm not sure." I felt my neck. "It may have been some sort of material. Did you find anything?"

"My men are searching the area, I haven't heard yet what they found." He wrote something in his notebook. "Do you have any enemies?" he asked, looking up at me.

"No," I said, "not really."

But I thought of Mitchell Stacey. He was an enemy. And he knew my car.

The policeman must have read something in my face.

"Yes?" he asked. "Who is it?"

"Someone did threaten me, that's all."

"In what way?"

"He told me that if I didn't stay away from his wife, he'd kill me. But I don't really believe that he meant he would actually kill me. It was just a figure of speech."

"And when was this?"

I worked it out. "Eight days ago, at Newmarket."

"And have you stayed away from his wife since then?" asked the policeman in a deadpan voice.

"Yes," I said. "Well . . . I bumped into her on Tuesday, but it was an accident. We didn't do anything, if that's what you mean. We hardly even spoke."

"And does the lady's husband know you saw her on Tuesday?"

I thought back to my encounter with Mitchell in the Stratford races parking lot. "Yes. He knows, all right. He was there."

"I'll need his name, sir."

"I'm sure he wouldn't have done it," I said. But someone had. My throat still had the bruises to prove it.

"His name?" The chief inspector persisted.

"Mitchell Stacey," I said. "He's a racehorse trainer. He and his wife live in East Ilsley, near Newbury."

I gave him the full address and he wrote it down in his notebook.

"And is he the only irate husband who has threatened you recently?"

"There's no need for irony, Chief Inspector," I said. "And, yes, he's the only one."

"I also need your full name and address. For the record."

"Mark Joseph Shillingford," I said, and I gave him the address of my apartment in Edenbridge. He wrote it down.

"Shillingford?" he said. "Unusual name. Not related to that girl that killed herself, are you?"

"She was my sister," I said. "My twin sister."

"Oh," he said. "I'm sorry."

"Do you follow horse racing at all, Chief Inspector?"

"Not really my thing," he said, shaking his head. "I'm a football man myself. Hornets fan."

"Hornets?"

"Watford," he said.

We were interrupted by a nurse, who came into the cubicle to take my pulse and my blood pressure and also look into my eyes with a flashlight.

"When can I go home?" I croaked at her.

"The doctor will do his round soon," she said. "You can ask him then."

The nurse went out again.

"Right," said the chief inspector, closing his notebook and standing up. "I'm going home to my bed."

"Is that it?" I asked, surprised.

"You'll have to give a full witness statement, of course, but that can be done in the morning. Call me round ten to fix it." He handed me a printed card with his details.

"How about Mitchell Stacey?"

"I'll interview Mr. Stacey after you've done your witness statement and after the forensic boys have examined your car. That will also take place in the morning."

"But what if he tries again?" I asked.

"Do you think he might?"

"I'm not sure it was even him," I said. "But don't I get police protection, or something, just in case?"

"I think you should be safe enough in here," he said rather dismissively.

"But how about if I go home?"

"Then I'd advise you not to get into a car without first checking the backseat."

"Oh thanks a lot," I said sarcastically. "Why do I get the impression you're not taking me seriously?"

"I am taking you seriously, Mr. Shillingford, very seriously, but I simply don't have the resources to provide you with a personal bodyguard. Anyway, I believe that the person who tried to kill you is long gone. And I doubt that they'll try again. I've studied a few criminals in my time, and I think it's highly likely that this was a one-off attack and the perpetrator will have second thoughts before trying anything like it again."

A policeman who fancied himself as an amateur criminal psychologist was all I needed.

"No," he said, "I think you'll be perfectly safe from now on. I reckon if he'd really wanted to kill you, then you'd have been in a morgue, not a hospital."

I damn near had been.

14

I had just closed my eyes and drifted off to sleep when I was awakened again by the nurse to do her half-hourly check.

"There are two people outside in the waiting room who want to see you," the nurse said as she listed the latest results on a chart. "That policeman said we weren't to let anyone in, but they've been here for ages, and they say they absolutely won't go home without seeing you first."

"Who are they?" I asked.

"Two women," said the nurse. "One of them says she's your sister."

Clare, I immediately thought. But of course it couldn't be Clare. It had to be Angela.

"Would you please ask them to come in," I said, smiling at her. "I don't think that policeman meant to keep my family out."

"If you're sure," she said.

"Perfectly sure," I replied. "And I won't tell him if you don't."

She smiled back at me. "All right, then. I'll go and get them."

Indeed, it was Angela, and she had Emily with her, both of them looking worried and tired.

"You should both still be at Tatiana's party," I said to them in my croaky voice.

"That finished hours ago," said Angela. "In fact, it pretty much finished when you hit the gatepost."

"I'm so sorry," I croaked.

"Don't be." Angela laughed. "At least it stopped everyone drinking."

"I wasn't drunk," I said. And that was now official. I'd been Breathalyzered when I'd first arrived at the hospital and had passed with ease.

"So what happened?" asked Emily. "Nick told us something about you being strangled." I could tell from the tone of her voice that she clearly thought that Nick had been mistaken.

I wondered how much I should tell them. And how much they would believe. Attempted murders in rural Hertfordshire were hardly common, but I couldn't really lie to them, especially as I assumed the police would soon be around asking them questions.

"There was someone waiting for me in the car," I said, "in the backseat. He tried to strangle me."

The two women looked suitably shocked.

"Was he trying to rob you?" Angela asked.

"Maybe," I said. "Although it was a funny way to do it if he was. I actually think he was trying to kill me."

"But why would anyone want to do that?" Emily asked.

I decided against mentioning anything to them about Mitchell Stacey or my affair with his wife. Clare had been the only member of the Shillingford family privy to that information, and I rather hoped to keep it that way.

"I've no idea," I said. "The police are investigating. They told me they'll search my car for fingerprints."

"It was all wrapped up in blue plastic," Angela said, nodding. "And then it was taken away on a truck. It took them ages, and it didn't please the caterers, I can tell you that." She smiled. "They couldn't get their van out of the driveway. There was a flaming row between them and the police."

"So what happens now?" Emily asked. "How much longer are you going to be stuck here?"

"I don't really know. I'm waiting for the doctor to do his round."

"I'll go and find someone," Emily said, and she disappeared through the curtains.

"God, you gave us all such a fright," said Angela, taking my hand. "I couldn't bear to lose you as well." She was crying, and she wiped her eyes on the sleeve of her jacket. "I'm sorry."

"Don't be," I said.

Clare's death was still very raw for all of us. Our emotions were on knife-edge. One minute we could weep or laugh, the next minute fly into a rage.

Emily returned with the doctor. I knew from personal experience that saying no to Emily was difficult, I now fervently wished I'd said yes to her. It might have saved all this bother.

"How are you feeling?" asked the doctor.

"Fine," I answered. "Apart from a sore neck and a croaky voice."

"Your vitals are good and stable," he said, looking at the

chart. He came forward and examined my neck. "You were very lucky. Your larynx is only bruised and not fractured. I see no reason why you can't go home, but you shouldn't be left alone for the next twelve hours or so. Asphyxia patients can sometimes develop cerebral edemas, and they are very dangerous."

"What's a cerebral edema?" Angela asked him.

"A fluid buildup that causes the brain to swell in the skull. It's very nasty, and often the last person to realize he has one is the patient. But I don't think you'll have a problem. I would have expected to see something by now if you did."

"We'll look after him," Emily said, holding my hand.

"Fine," said the doctor. "I'll get the discharge papers. But get him back here immediately if he starts to act strangely or slurs his words."

The doctor went out of the cubicle, and I swung my legs over the side of the table. I looked at my watch. It was a quarter past three.

"Come on," I said, "let's get out of here."

"WHERE TO?" Angela asked as we sat in her Volvo in the hospital parking lot. She was in front while Emily and I were sitting together in the back, and, yes, I had checked the car for potential stranglers before we'd opened the doors.

"You can't come back to our house. We're full with Brendan and Gillian and their boys. Not unless you want to sleep in the tent with Tatiana and her friends."

"We'll go to my place," Emily said decisively. "I'll look after him."

I could see Angela giggling in the rearview mirror. I suspected that this had been a rehearsed exchange.

"Where is your place?" I asked Emily.

"In Royston," she said. "About a mile from Nick and Angela."

"I need to be at Newmarket racetrack in under four hours, and Royston's in totally the wrong direction."

"But surely you're not going to do the show now," said Angela.

"Why not?" I said. "As long as my voice doesn't get any worse, I'll be fine."

"But someone has just tried to kill you."

"All the more reason for going on."

"You're crazy."

"Maybe I am," I said. "But I'll be damned if I am going to sit back and do nothing. Someone tried to kill me tonight and I'm bloody well going to find out who it was." I yawned, which I discovered was not very pleasant when one had a sore windpipe. "Please take me to Clare's cottage. I'll try and get some sleep, and I'll order a taxi to collect me in the morning. I need to change my clothes anyway. I can hardly go on *The Morning Line* wearing this."

I saw Angela look at Emily in the mirror. Their little plan was falling apart, and I could tell that they didn't particularly like it.

"Look," I said, "I am not trying to be evasive, I promise. I would more than happily go to Emily's place under different circumstances, but right now I'd like to go to Clare's cottage."

"One of us would have to stay with you," Angela said. "The doctor was pretty insistent."

"It had better be me who stays with Mark," Emily said. "Nick will be wondering where you are already." She laughed. "He's probably in the tent trying to keep those drunken, randy boys away from Tatiana."

"Don't even joke about it," Angela said. "All right, Mark, you win. Clare's cottage it is."

She started the Volvo and pointed it toward Newmarket.

IN THE END, all three of us stayed at Clare's cottage, Angela having been assured by Nicholas on the telephone that all was well, both at the house and in the tent, where Tatiana was safely cocooned amongst her girlfriends.

Angela and Emily slept together in the guest room while I settled down on the sofa in the sitting room downstairs. I suppose it would have been all right to use Clare's bed, but I sensed an air of collective relief when I had volunteered to be on the sofa.

Even though it was almost four o'clock by the time I turned out the light, I found it difficult to sleep. My mind was racing with too many unanswered questions, the uppermost being who had tried to kill me and why?

I had told DCI Perry about Mitchell Stacey, but did I really believe he could be responsible? He had certainly shown the ugly side of his nature in the parking lots at Newmarket and at Stratford, but he was a bull in a china shop who would surely confront me man-to-man rather than sneaking up anonymously and trying to strangle me.

But what other suspects did I have?

None.

And what could anyone else gain by killing me?

Surely Iain Ferguson didn't imagine that his career would advance more quickly if I was quite literally taken out of the picture?

I MUST HAVE drifted off to sleep eventually because the next thing I knew I was wide awake and listening hard for the noise that had awakened me.

There had been a metallic clank. Or had I dreamed it?

I lay in the dark, listening. There it was again, and it was outside.

I quietly stood up from the sofa and went over to the window, my heart again pounding hard inside my chest.

I pulled back the heavy curtains to find that it was daylight and people were already up and about. Racing folk start work early, and the metallic clanks had been the sound of Geoffrey Grubb's stable staff fetching metal buckets of water for the horses.

I laughed at myself. I must be getting paranoid.

I looked at my watch. It was half past six, I'd been asleep for only about two hours. But it was high time I got myself moving if I wasn't going to be late.

I went into the kitchen and made myself a cup of instant coffee, which went some way to waking me up properly. Then I made two more cups and took them up to the guest bedroom.

Angela and Emily were both still fast asleep, and it took me about a minute of gentle prodding to wake Angela.

"Go away," she said, putting her head under the pillow.

"I need to go in ten minutes," I said. "Shall I take your car? I could be back by ten past nine."

"Do what you like," she murmured.

I collected some clothes and my electric razor from my suitcase and went into the bathroom to shave, shower, and dress.

The lumps in my throat that had persisted all the previous night had finally begun to ease, and my voice seemed a little more normal. And the little reds spots in my eyes and on my face had almost faded away to nothing.

I emerged from the bathroom to find Emily standing there wrapped in a sheet, hopping from foot to foot.

"We're both coming with you," she said. "Though God knows why. Angela's said something about dropping you off and then going home."

"But I need to go right now."

"So do I. I'm bursting." She grinned, pushed past me, and closed the bathroom door.

I laughed. I decided I could get to like Emily, maybe to like her a lot. Just as long as someone didn't succeed in killing me first.

"**WHAT DO YOU MEAN,** someone tried to murder you? That's the worst excuse I've ever heard for someone being late."

"It's not an excuse," I said. "It's true."

I could tell that Lisa, *The Morning Line*'s producer, didn't believe a word I'd said, and she clearly was not happy. I'd been only five minutes late, but there was another crisis going on with the program's main guest, who was going to be much later.

"Someone really did try to strangle me last night," I said, "and I wonder if it has anything to do with the murder of Toby Woodley at Kempton on Wednesday."

That shut her up, but only briefly.

"And does it?" she asked.

"I don't know."

"So where's the story in that?" she asked flatly. "You could at least have arrived with a smoking gun or a knife with Toby Woodley's blood on it."

"How about a bruised neck?" I asked. "And a croaky voice?"

"Not visual enough. But the voice may be a problem. We'll have to say you've got a cold."

"Why not tell the truth?"

"Too complicated," she said. "Now, have you done your homework on the two-year-olds?"

The big race at Newmarket that afternoon was the Millions Trophy, the richest contest for two-year-old horses in Europe.

"Of course I have," I replied, knowing full well that I hadn't really done enough. But I knew all the horses well from having seen them run previously.

"Good, because you might have to talk about them for much longer than planned if that bloody Austin Reynolds doesn't turn up."

"Austin Reynolds?" I said, surprised. "I thought the guest was Paul James."

"Paul had a fall last night at Wolverhampton and has cried off. Austin agreed to step in, but now he's called to say his car won't start and he'll be late."

"But he only lives in the town," I said. "Can't someone go and fetch him?"

"Seems he's coming up from London." She didn't sound pleased.

Austin Reynolds, the "nearly man" of British racing, was the trainer of Tortola Beach, one of the runners in that afternoon's big race.

Tortola Beach had been one of the definites that I'd found

in the RacingTV database. Clare had purposely ridden him to lose in a race at Doncaster the previous August.

And Austin Reynolds also trained Bangkok Flyer.

"*Thirty minutes to air time, everybody,*" shouted Matthew, the floor manager.

"I must get back to the scanner," Lisa said and hurried off.

TO THE UNTRAINED EYE, the next twenty-five or so minutes may have looked a bit chaotic, but, in fact, they were precisely choreographed.

Cameras moved from side to side, then back and forth, rehearsing, all under the control of the program director, who was sitting out in the scanner and communicating with the cameramen via their headphones.

"*Fifteen minutes to on-air,*" Matthew shouted.

The presenters were wired up with microphones and earpieces, each of us rehearsing what we would say for sound levels and then checking with Lisa that we could all hear the talk-back and that she could also hear us.

Then we sat in our positions for final checks on camera angles while someone applied dabs of powder to those parts of our faces that were shining too much under the powerful lights.

"*Five minutes to on-air.*"

And still there was no sign of Austin Reynolds.

"*Four minutes.*"

I went over in my head once again what I planned to say about each of the horses in the big race.

"*Three minutes.*"

"Mark," Lisa said into my ear, "*we'll come straight to you after the weekly roundup to discuss the fillies' race and also the Scoop6 Cup at Ascot. We'll have to hope that Austin is here by the first commercial break, and we'll do the Millions Trophy after that.*"

"OK," I said, shuffling madly through my copy of the *Racing Post* to find the relevant pages.

"*Two minutes.*"

One of the staff placed a *Morning Line*–branded cup full of coffee in front of each of the presenters.

"*One minute.*"

There was nothing quite like live television to raise the pulse.

Nothing, that is, except being strangled.

AUSTIN REYNOLDS finally arrived on the set just before the second commercial break, by which time there was less than ten minutes left to the program. I could imagine Lisa pulling her hair out in the scanner.

"*Get him in during the break,*" she said in all our ears.

Fortunately it was Lisa's practice always to have far more content available than we could ever have fit into the allotted time. Most weeks we ran well behind the printed schedule, and things at the end had to be either dropped or postponed until another week.

This time we were glad of it to fill in missing interview time with Austin, which had been expected to last about fifteen minutes but would now be less than five.

"*Five minutes to shut-up,*" said the production assistant into my ear.

"So, Austin," I said, "how do you rate your chances this afternoon with Tortola Beach in the big race?"

"He should run well," Austin said, smiling. "Let's just say I'm hopeful."

"So you think he'll stay the seven-eighths-of-a-mile trip?" I asked. "Let's have a look at his last run at Doncaster seven weeks ago. And remember, that was over only three-quarters."

"Cue VT," Lisa said on the talk-back.

The now familiar film of Tortola Beach running at Doncaster in August appeared on the screen in front of us. I continued to speak over the images. "Tortola Beach seemed certain to win from here, but he fades badly in the last two hundred yards to be third." I didn't need to watch the film again to know what happened in the race. Instead, I watched Austin's face closely for any reaction to it.

"That's true," Austin said. "But that run was inconsistent with his work at home, where he's shown good stamina even over a mile."

"Three minutes to shut-up."

The VT ended.

"Cue Mark. Camera two."

The on-air light on the camera in front of me glowed red.

"Did my sister, Clare, who was riding him there, say anything to you after the race which might have explained why he faded so badly?"

"No," Austin said. "She had no explanation for it at all. As I said, it was contrary to what he's done elsewhere. And it's not that he doesn't like to be in front. He's usually a natural front-runner. I think it must have been a one-off. Perhaps he was just having a bad day."

"Two minutes to shut-up."

"OK, Mark," Lisa said into my earpiece. *"Wind up the interview, and also close the show."*

"Well, let's hope he proves you right this afternoon," I said, smiling at Austin. "Tortola Beach is currently fourth favorite, quoted by most bookmakers at nine-to-one, and my money will certainly be on his nose to win."

"One minute to shut-up," said the voice in my ear.

"I think you'll get a good run for your money," said Austin. "And I'd like to say how sorry I am that Clare will not be riding him today. I can't believe she's gone. She's a great loss to our sport."

"Thirty seconds."

"Thank you very much, Austin," I said. "I think we all miss her. I know I certainly do."

"Twenty seconds."

"And good luck to you this afternoon with Tortola Beach."

"Ten seconds, nine, eight . . ."

I turned to face camera two as the countdown continued in my ears. "I hope you will join us this afternoon for seven races here on Channel 4 from both Newmarket and Ascot, as well as a special bonus, the Two Year Old Trophy from Redcar. And it all starts at one fifty-five. See you then. Bye, bye."

". . . two, one, shut up," said the production assistant on the talk-back just as the red light on the camera in front of me went out and the program credits appeared on the screen.

"Well done, everybody," said Lisa. *"A bit disjointed, but we had no choice. Mark, tell that bloody Austin Reynolds to get a new car."*

"Will do," I replied. "Austin, Lisa the producer says thank you so much for coming. She's still down in the production van." And I could hear her laughing in my ear over the talk-back.

An audio technician came over and relieved me of my microphone and earpiece, and then he removed Austin's microphone as well. One should always assume a microphone was live—a lesson that some politicians never seem to learn.

Austin started to get up, but I asked him to stay with me just for a minute or two. So we sat next to each other on the sofa while the rest of the crew began dismantling the lights and packing away the cameras and other equipment around us.

"How often did Clare ride for you?" I asked.

"Oh, quite often," Austin replied. "When she was up at the northern tracks and not riding for Geoff Grubb. These days, I tend to run most of mine on the Yorkshire circuits, as many of my owners are from there. I always liked Clare to ride my horses, if she could. She rode lots of winners for me."

"Yes," I said quietly. "But how often did she *stop* them winning for you?"

15

W hat did you say?" Austin Reynolds said.

"I asked how often Clare stopped horses for you."

"I don't know what you're talking about."

"Oh yes, I think you do," I said.

I had watched him intently as the VT of the race had been shown and there had been a distinct smirk of satisfaction on his face.

I was in no doubt whatsoever that Austin Reynolds had known exactly what would happen to Tortola Beach in that race at Doncaster and that he had been delighted by the outcome.

"Did you lay Tortola Beach to lose?" I asked.

"No. I told you, I don't know what you're talking about," he said, but he looked worried and sweat had appeared on his brow.

I thought back to what had been written on that white envelope in Clare's desk: AS AGREED, A.

Had the A. stood for Austin?

"And did you pay Clare two thousand pounds for stopping him?"

That shocked him. I could tell from his eyes.

It had been a bit of a guess on my part but I had clearly hit the bull's-eye.

"You can't prove anything," he hissed.

"You think so, do you?" I said. "I wonder if the police can get fingerprints from twenty-pound notes. Or DNA from the envelope they were handed over in."

He went quite pale.

"And were you also sleeping with her?"

"What?"

"Were you having an affair with my sister?"

"Don't be ridiculous. Of course I wasn't."

I was tempted to believe him on this point. He had been genuinely surprised by the question, and I didn't really think that he was Clare's type in spite of the fact that she tended to fall for older men. But Austin Reynolds was very much older, some twenty-five years, and he didn't much give the impression of being a great Lothario.

"What are you going to do now?" Austin asked miserably.

"Nothing," I said. "At least nothing just yet."

"So what should I do?" he said.

"Whatever you like," I said. "Running all your horses to win might be a good start."

He looked at me with uncertainty in his eyes, mixed with a touch of hate and contempt.

"But what about the money?" he asked.

"What about it? You surely don't want it back?"

"Not that money," he said, "the other money."

"What other money?"

"Look, stop playing games with me." I thought he was close to tears. "I'm talking about the ten thousand you've asked for."

"I haven't asked you for anything," I said. "I was aware that Clare had purposely stopped Tortola Beach from winning, but I only realized that you also knew when I watched you looking at the race just now."

"Oh God," Austin said, "then who is it?"

"Who is what?" I asked.

"Who is blackmailing me?"

At that point, rather inconveniently, Lisa arrived from the scanner and walked over toward us.

"Aren't you both coming for breakfast?" she asked.

"We'll be there in a minute," I said. "Austin and I are just discussing the running of his horses."

She looked at Austin. "Did Mark tell you that I said you should get a new car?"

"I'm sorry I was late."

"Yeah, you're a bloody nuisance," Lisa said.

She had a well-earned reputation for believing that it was she who was doing the favor for the guests who agreed to come on her program rather than the other way around. And she wasn't against giving them a hard time if they didn't do as they were told.

"I said to be here by seven-thirty, not twenty to nine."

"I couldn't help it," he whined, "the battery was flat. I had to wait for the Automobile Association. I got here as soon as I could."

I bet he was now wishing he hadn't bothered to make it here at all.

—————

AUSTIN MANAGED to escape from my attentions by saying he was going to the gents' on our way to breakfast and then disappearing altogether.

I didn't mind too much. I knew where to find him. For a start, he would be with Tortola Beach in the parade ring before the third race later that afternoon.

"So how come you got yourself strangled?" Lisa asked as we tucked in to bacon and eggs in one of the grandstand restaurants. "Whoever did it couldn't have been much cop if you're still here to tell the tale."

"Oh thanks a lot," I said. "I tell you, I'm damn lucky not to have been murdered."

I explained to her in detail how I had crashed my car in order to survive and how I'd spent half the night in Addenbrooke's hospital.

At last, Lisa started to take me seriously. "Have you any idea who it was?"

"None," I said. "And I've no idea why either."

I decided not to mention anything to her about Mitchell Stacey. The more I thought about it, the less likely it seemed that he had been involved. Strangulation from behind just didn't seem to be his sort of thing. But I suppose I couldn't be sure.

"Were you serious when you said it might have something to do with the murder of Toby Woodley?"

"I really don't know," I said. "Was it just coincidence that there were two 'racing' attacks only two days apart and I was present at both of them?"

"Coincidences do happen, you know," Lisa said. "And Toby

Woodley was such an awful little creep that there must have been a shedload of people queuing up to kill him. Me, for one."

"He may have been an awful little creep, but his death was still horrible. And no one deserves to be stabbed in the back."

"Oh please," she mocked, "don't make me cry. Toby Woodley deserved everything he got."

"You're a hard woman, Lisa. You might think differently if he'd died in your lap."

"Why, did he die in yours?"

"As a matter of fact he did."

She was surprised. "I'd heard a rumor that you'd helped to give him CPR, but I didn't really believe it."

"All true, I'm afraid," I said. "Guilty as charged. Not that it did him any good. He bled to death, and quickly too. Very nasty."

"Do the police have any idea who did it?"

"Not that I'm aware of," I said, "but they'd hardly tell me anyway."

"Probably someone who got fed up with his bloody sniping. I don't believe that man ever wrote a single word of truth in that rag of his."

"Do you remember that piece he did in the summer about a trainer laying his horses on the Internet and then ensuring they lost?"

"Remember it?" Lisa said with irritation. "We did a segment about it on the show. Even had Woodley on as a guest because he promised me he'd reveal who it was on the air."

"And did he?" I couldn't remember it, but I'd been abroad on holiday in late May.

"Did he, hell! It was a total waste of time. One of my worst-ever shows. Little creep just sat there grinning like the Cheshire

Cat, making promises he never kept. I reckon he simply made it all up. Load of old tosh. The bastard made me look like a fool."

So that was why Lisa hated him so much.

"And, madam, what were you doing on Wednesday evening last at nine o'clock?" I mimicked a policeman holding a notebook.

"Ha, ha," she said, forcing a smile. "I was at home, Officer, watching *The Apprentice* on television, and I have witnesses to prove it."

I thought about Austin Reynolds. Had he been the trainer in the story? Had Toby Woodley in fact been much closer to the truth than Lisa, or anyone else, had imagined?

"You don't think that story had anything to do with his death, then?" I asked.

"Do you?"

I could hardly say yes without backing it up with some sort of evidence and I didn't really want to do that. Lisa had an uncanny ability for smelling out a story, and the last thing I wanted was to put her on the scent of Clare and race fixing.

"I don't know," I said tamely, "but there must have been some motive. People don't just stab someone for no reason."

"Don't they?" she said. "Haven't you watched the news recently?"

Lisa lost interest in our conversation and started talking to the show's director on her other side.

I sat there thinking about Austin Reynolds and what he had said about being blackmailed. Someone else must have known about his involvement with race fixing.

Had it been Toby Woodley? Was that why he'd been killed? Where, I wondered, had Austin Reynolds been at nine o'clock last Wednesday evening? Could he have been in the parking lot at Kempton races, murdering Toby to save having to pay his blackmail demands?

But that didn't make any sense. Not half an hour ago when I'd confronted him, Austin had clearly thought that it must have been *me* who was blackmailing him. So why would he think that if he'd believed Toby was responsible, and to the point of murdering him?

No. There had to be a fourth party involved. At least. And that was assuming Toby's death had indeed been something to do with the race fixing story in the first place, something that was by no means certain.

I USED my cell phone to call Detective Chief Inspector Perry at ten o'clock, as he'd requested.

"How are you feeling?" he asked.

"Tired," I said. "I didn't get to bed until four, and I was up again at six-thirty."

"I heard from the hospital that they sent you home. Where are you now?"

"Newmarket racetrack," I said. "I'm working here, and will be for the rest of the day."

"Doing what?" he asked.

"I present racing on television. We're covering Newmarket this afternoon."

"Is that why you asked me last night if I followed racing?"

"Yes," I said. "I thought you might have seen me if you did."

"Sorry, no." He didn't sound very sorry. "Is your voice better?"

"It's a lot better now than last night, thank you." But I was glad I wasn't commentating. "Did you find any fingerprints in my car?"

"Masses of them," he said. "We now have to find out if any of them belong to our strangler. We'll do a computerized criminal records comparison first, but we may need to eliminate anyone who's recently been in the back of your car."

I thought about Nicholas and Brendan, and also the paramedic. All three of them had been in the back after the attack, to say nothing of the firemen who'd cut off the roof.

"How about the rope?"

"A search of the area revealed nothing. He must have taken it with him. Maybe it was a scarf or something."

"You said you wanted a witness statement," I said.

"Yes, please," he replied. "I'll send my sergeant over to take it now."

"How long will it take?" I asked.

"That depends, Mr. Shillingford, on how much you have to say."

"How much to do want me to say?"

"Everything that is relevant. Especially what you can remember after going out to your car."

"I have a production meeting here at eleven o'clock, and I'm going to be pretty busy after that until we go off the air at four-twenty. Can't I just write out a statement rather than have your sergeant take it down? I could do it now on my laptop and e-mail it to you."

"Could you print it out and sign it? And also have your signature witnessed? My sergeant will then collect it in about an hour."

"No problem," I said. "I'll leave it at the racetrack office."

"Right. Do that. If I need anything further, I'll leave a message at this number."

"What about my car?" I said. "What happens to that now?"

"The forensic boys are still going over it. They're apparently now looking for material fibers."

I laughed. "I don't think the inside of that car has been cleaned out since I've had it and that's about eight years. There must be handfuls of fibers present, and dog hair, candy wrappers, and God knows what else."

"Forensics will bag everything just in case it's needed later."

"Then what?" I asked.

"I suppose it's then yours to take away, but it's rather badly bashed in at the front and it has no roof. I saw it this morning at the police compound. It would cost more to repair than a car of that age is worth, and you know what insurance companies are like, it would be better for them to write it off completely."

But not, of course, better for me. I would end up with a paltry sum from the insurers and no car. I sighed. Was it time to get a new car as well as a new house? How about a new girlfriend?

Next I called the number that Emily had given me at the party. She answered on the second ring.

"I thought you might be asleep," I said.

"I should be," she replied.

"Did you watch the show?"

"I only saw the last bit of it. I now wish I'd stayed with you instead of coming back here with Angela. But I think she was glad I did."

"And how are all the sweet young things this morning?"

"Hungover, mostly. The party may have ended prematurely,

thanks to you, but if Angela thought that had stopped them drinking she was much mistaken. They must have had bottles stashed away somewhere. Half of them are still incapable of walking properly."

"That's because of their high heels."

She laughed. I liked that.

"What are you doing for the rest of the day?" I asked.

"What would you like me to do?"

"How about coming to the races?"

"Love to," she said.

I was suddenly very excited.

"Great," I said. "Can you be here at twelve-thirty? I'll meet you outside, where you drive in. Just follow the signs."

"OK, I'll be there. See you later."

"Oh, Emily?" I said.

"Yes."

"One more thing." I paused.

"Yes?" she encouraged.

"If you like," I said nervously, "you could bring an overnight bag."

"OK," she said slowly. "I would like that. Very much."

I WENT to the press room with my computer to type my witness statement for Chief Inspector Perry. Not surprisingly, with almost four hours to go until the first race, I was the only member of the press there.

It took me about forty minutes to complete the statement, reliving the horrors of the previous night and expressing them in words. But try as I might, I couldn't recall anything at all that I thought would help in identifying the strangler. I even closed my eyes and tried to evoke his smell, but there was nothing.

I could remember far better what had happened *after* I'd sat down in my car than before. I suppose that was bound to be the case, as before had been rather mundane while after had obviously not, if one could possibly describe being propositioned by a beautiful woman for sex as mundane.

I remembered that, all right, and it made me smile in anticipation. But I decided against putting it in my witness statement, although it was perhaps the real reason I hadn't even considered my safety as I'd gone to my car. Suffice to say, my mind had been elsewhere.

I used the printer in the press room to print out the statement and was about to go in search of someone to witness my signature when Jim Metcalf walked in.

"Hi, Jim," I said. "What brings *UK Today*'s star reporter here so early?"

"Boredom," he said. "I got fed up waiting at the hotel. I stayed up here last night. I'm doing a feature on Peter Williams, and I was out on the Heath with his string at seven this morning."

"Clare reckoned his colt Reading Glass is a good prospect for next year's Guineas."

"Possibly," said Jim, "but he still needs to grow a bit behind. And Peter's got some other good young colts that will certainly shine next year as three-year-olds. He's so good at not over-racing them at two and burning them out. That's what I'll be writing about."

"I'll look forward to reading it."

"It'll be in the paper next Saturday," he said. "To coincide with Future Champions Day."

I still had my witness statement in my hand.

"Jim, could you do me a favor?" I asked. "I need someone to witness my signature on something."

"Sure," he said. "Is it your will?"

"No," I said, laughing. "It's a witness statement for the police."

"What did you witness?" he asked.

I was suddenly not at all sure that this had been a good idea. But I'd already told Lisa, so it was hardly a secret.

"Someone tried to kill me last night," I said.

"Not Mitchell Stacey?"

I was stunned. I just stood there with my mouth hanging open.

"How . . ."

"Come on, Mark, I've known about you and Sarah Stacey for ages. Worst-kept secret in racing. You've hardly been that discreet, going out openly to pubs and restaurants and the like. I know for a fact that you went to the theater in London together in August to see that revival of *Oklahoma!* while Mitchell was up at the sales in Doncaster. I have my contacts." He tapped the side of his nose, just as Toby Woodley had done at Stratford.

I was quite surprised that my private life should have been of such interest to him. And I didn't much like the thought that I'd clearly been watched without my knowledge.

"Did Toby Woodley also know about us?"

"I don't know, but any racing journalist worth his salt should have been able to find out."

"But Woodley never wrote anything about us in the *Gazette*."

But was that what he'd been going on about at Clare's funeral? Had he actually known about Sarah and me, but his editor had prevented the story being published in the paper so soon after Clare's death?

"Maybe he didn't know, then," said Jim, "but I'd be surprised. Most of what he wrote was rubbish and speculation, but there was usually a glimmer of truth in there somewhere, and he did have an amazing knack for sniffing out real stories."

"Yes," I said, "and how exactly did he manage that?"

"I expect he used good old-fashioned journalistic techniques like the rest of us—hiding in the undergrowth with a powerful telephoto lens, paying the police for information, and of course hacking into people's phone messages."

"Isn't hacking illegal?"

He looked at me as if I were an idiot. "Of course it is. And so is speeding on the freeway. But we all do it. At least we did before all the fuss."

"Is that how you found out about me and Sarah?" I asked.

"No. As a matter of fact, it wasn't."

"So how did you, then?" I pressed.

"You don't want to know," he said slowly.

"Yes I bloody do."

He didn't say anything.

"Come on, tell me," I said aggressively. "How did you find out?"

"Clare told me."

"Clare?" I said, surprised. "She can't have. She wouldn't have."

"Well, she did," Jim said.

"When?"

"A long time ago. I don't think she meant to tell me. It just sort of slipped out. She swore me to secrecy."

"How come she was even speaking to you in the first place? I thought she despised all journalists."

"She didn't despise me."

I wondered if Jim had been one of the string of unsuitable older men that Clare had bedded.

"Were you sleeping with her?" I asked.

"That's none of your business," he replied.

"I think it is," I said, staring him in the eye.

"OK, I was," he said. "But it was a couple of years ago now, and it only lasted a month or two." He laughed. "Only until Clare realized the error of her ways and dumped me."

So Jim Metcalf wasn't the "new man" that Clare had been so flattering about at our last dinner.

"But I still loved her enough," he went on, "to keep her confidences about you and Sarah Stacey. But it amused me to watch you both."

"Well, for your further amusement and information," I said, "Mrs. Stacey and I are no longer an item. It's over, finished. I've moved on."

"But was it Mitchell who tried to kill you? I hear through the press's grapevine that he'd found out about your affair, and I, for one, wouldn't want to be on the wrong end of that temper."

"No, you're probably very wise," I said, remembering my encounters with Mitchell in the parking lots. "I don't know if it was him, but I doubt it. Whoever it was went to great lengths to remain hidden and that doesn't smack of Mitchell's methods. He's more of a confrontational sort of guy."

"So how did this person try to kill you?"

"On the record or off?" I asked.

"Either way," he said. "You choose."

I handed him my witness statement and he read it through from start to finish.

"Blimey," he said, "it really was attempted murder."

"It sure was," I agreed.

"I never realized being a racing journalist could be so dangerous, what with that creep Woodley getting himself murdered."

"The police seem to think that might have been a robbery that went too far."

"What was stolen?" Jim asked.

"It seems his briefcase is missing."

"Ah, the famous Woodley briefcase."

"What's famous about it?" I asked.

"Don't you know? He'd always go berserk if anyone went near it in the press room. That's partly why he was so unpopular with the rest of the racing press. He treated that briefcase as if it was a bloody baby. He was obsessed by it."

"What was in it?" I asked.

"God knows," said Jim. "Probably just his sandwiches."

"Somebody must have thought it was valuable if they killed him for it."

"I can't imagine why," said Jim, laughing. "I'd have happily killed him for nothing."

"I wouldn't say that if the police can hear you." I thought back to my interview with Superintendent Cullen. I hadn't done myself any favors telling him that I hadn't liked the victim.

I looked at the clock on the wall. I was late for the production meeting.

"Jim, could you witness my signature? The police will be here soon to collect it."

I signed the paper at the bottom, and Jim added his signature alongside as witness.

"So can I use any of this?" he asked, pointing at my statement.

"Why not?" I said. "It can't do any harm."

16

I went out to meet Emily immediately after the production meeting just in case she was early.

I realized that I had no idea what type of car she drove, so I stood next to the entry road, staring intently at the driver of every vehicle that passed me, in case I might miss her. But I needn't have worried. Bang on time, at precisely twelve-thirty, she arrived flashing her lights and sounding her horn as soon as she saw me.

And I should have guessed her choice of car. She drove a metallic red Mercedes SLK sports roadster, and she had the roof down.

I was laughing as I climbed in beside her, in the sure knowledge there was no strangler lurking in a backseat because there was no backseat.

"Hello, gorgeous," I said, leaning over and giving her a brief kiss.

"Where to?" she asked, grinning broadly.

"Straight on down to the end," I said. "We'll park in the press lot, it's nearer to the entrance than the one for the public."

What was it that Jim Metcalf had said about me not being very discreet in my private life? Well, there was nothing in the slightest bit discreet about Emily's and my arrival in the Newmarket racetrack's press parking lot.

For a start, not many members of the press drive Mercedes sports cars, and even fewer arrive for a race meeting in October with the roof down. Then there was the spin of the rear wheels on the gravel by the entrance, and the slight drift of the back end on the damp grass as Emily turned sharply into the parking space.

Next came the dramatic closing of the electric roof, and, as if there were not enough of the press watching already, there was Emily's loud squeal of delight as she came around the back of the car, enveloped me in her arms, and kissed me passionately full on the mouth.

Perhaps, I thought, the public parking lot would have been better after all. But at least this might kill off any belief lingering amongst the Fourth Estate that I was still romantically involved with Sarah Stacey.

We went through the entrance to the racetrack, and I took her around to the fenced-off compound where the Channel 4 scanner and the other broadcast vehicles were parked. There was still over an hour until we went on the air, but I had to do the voice-over recordings for some of the VTs that would be shown later during the live transmission.

I also had some script notes I wanted to write out in preparation for what was likely to be a busy afternoon, with races from both Ascot and Redcar on the program, as well as three from

Newmarket. The more material we had prepared and were ready to transmit at the touch of a button, the better we would be able to cope with any unexpected problems that might arise, as they surely would.

It was very much a case of the nine Ps: *Proper prior planning prevents piss-poor program presenter performance.*

Emily sat in the scanner and watched while I recorded the voice-over for a host of video clips of previous races, highlighting the running of some of the horses that were in action again today. The whole VT would be used as part of the introduction for the afternoon.

"It's fascinating," she said when I'd finished. "It all seems so seamless when you watch on a Saturday."

"Ah, the magic of live television," I said. "Never believe anything you see on the TV. It's all done with smoke and mirrors."

"Don't tease me," she said.

"I'm not," I said. "I mean it. We will show eight races from three different racetracks hundreds of miles apart all within the span of two and a half hours, and the viewers believe that the whole thing is sequential and under our control, which it isn't. Now, that's what I call magic."

"Does it ever go wrong?" she asked.

"Often," I said. "And the real trick is to carry on regardless and make out that everything is proceeding exactly as we had expected it to, and to stop talking only when you drop down dead or the program finishes, whichever comes first."

"You're crazy." She laughed.

"Bonkers," I said, laughing back.

It was the first time I'd felt even the slightest bit happy since Clare had died. Emily was clearly good for me.

———

"GOOD LUCK, EVERYBODY." Neville, the producer, was speaking over the talk-back in our earpieces and headphones as the production assistant counted down to zero to the start of transmission.

The familiar theme music played, and I watched the opening sequence on the monitor in front of me.

"Cue Mark."

I took a deep breath and looked straight into the lens of the camera being held in front of my face. "Good afternoon, everyone, and welcome to *Channel 4 Racing* on the day of Europe's richest race for two-year-olds, the Millions Trophy, which is amongst the three races we're covering from here at Newmarket, as well as four from Ascot, including the Scoop6 Cup, and, as a special bonus, one of the premier northern races for the youngsters, the Two Year Old Trophy from Redcar at four o'clock."

"Cue VT," said the director, and the video clips played that I had previously voiced over.

The program was up and running.

I could almost feel the injection of adrenaline into my bloodstream that the countdown to the start had produced. And I loved it. I was an adrenaline-rush junkie and was hopelessly hooked.

I waved and smiled at Emily, who was standing about five yards away, out of picture. We were both in the Newmarket parade ring, close to the winner's enclosure. It is where I would stay for the duration of the program, watching all the races on the monitor set up in front of me.

The VT was coming to an end. *"Cue Mark,"* said the director into my ear.

"So let's go straight over to join Iain Ferguson for the first of our three Group races from Ascot. Good afternoon, Iain."

The red light on the camera in front of me went off to indicate I was no longer live on air. I could relax a little as the first race from Ascot was being broadcast. I went over to Emily and gave her a cuddle.

"I hope you're not too cold," I said. She had no coat and was wearing what I thought was far too thin a dress for being outdoors in October in spite of the unseasonably warm weather we had been enjoying. However, it did hug her alluring figure superbly, and that also did wonders for my adrenaline level.

"I'm absolutely fine," she said. "But aren't you meant to be saying something? I thought you told me that you mustn't stop talking."

"The presenter at Ascot is speaking now. The first race we're showing is being run there, so I reckon I've got about another eight minutes before I'm back on."

But, nevertheless, my brain would still be on the alert for the word *Mark* just in case things didn't go as planned and I had to step in. It was something you got used to: carrying on a conversation with a third party while listening for your name being spoken in your ear by the producer or director. The rest of the talk-back could float over me without really registering, but I would be brought to full awareness by the first *mmm* of Mark.

The afternoon progressed without any major problem—that is, until the third race at Ascot was badly delayed due to a horse getting loose on the way down to the start and galloping on its own right around the racetrack.

I could imagine the panic going on in the scanner as it was realized that the Ascot race would now coincide with the buildup for the big race of the afternoon at Newmarket. The pitch of the voices over the talk-back rose a notch with tension.

"If that damn nag at Ascot isn't caught soon, the two races will be run at the same time," said Neville into my ear.

It was his worst nightmare. One of the golden rules in horse race broadcasting was that no races were to be shown recorded, they had to go out live.

Once upon a time, delaying a race broadcast by a bit wouldn't have been too much of a problem, but now with Internet gambling, especially the growing popularity of betting on horses during the actual running of the race, being *live* was absolutely essential.

"Matthew," Neville called over the talk-back to the floor manager in the Newmarket parade ring, *"see if Newmarket will hold for a couple of minutes if it looks like there'll be a clash. Otherwise we'll have to use a split screen."*

I watched as Matthew ran over to the weighing room to speak to the stewards. But delaying the race wasn't usually that simple. The meeting was also being broadcast live on the radio and any change in time, even by a couple of minutes, could badly disrupt the schedules.

"Two minutes max," said Matthew. *"On your call."*

"Great, thanks," replied Neville. *"Tell Kevin to get down to the start right now."* Kevin was the program runner, literally, and he already would be rushing down to the course to relay the producer's message to the starter should it became necessary.

"OK. Listen up, everyone," said Neville in everybody's ears. *"We continue with the big race buildup here at Newmarket, with Ascot*

shown, mute, picture-in-picture. We stay with Newmarket but go over to Ascot for their race live, if and when they're ready. We'll only hold the Newmarket race for the two minutes if it looks like there's going to be a clash. We might even need to take Newmarket before Ascot. If we have to use a split screen, we'll take the commentary of whichever race starts first, then switch when it finishes."

And just when you thought things couldn't get any worse, the director reminded everyone that we had to fit in a three-minute commercial break before Newmarket's race. It was part of our contract with the broadcaster.

The loose horse was finally caught and subsequently withdrawn from the Ascot race, which started ten minutes late but just in time for the Newmarket race to go off as scheduled immediately after it. And the commercial break was somehow shoehorned in before both of them.

Heart rates all around returned to normal levels, and the talk-back profanity count reverted to more acceptable proportions. It was a running joke in broadcasting that recording the talk-back was a sackable offense.

Tortola Beach won Newmarket's big race easily by three lengths and was led triumphantly into the winner's enclosure by a beaming Austin Reynolds.

"Mark, get a quick interview with Austin—now!" Neville demanded in my ear. *"It will be a good follow-up to your conversation with him on* The Morning Line.*"*

Little did Neville know what else had been said in our conversation after *The Morning Line* had gone off the air.

The cameraman and I stepped forward boldly, me with a handheld microphone at the ready like a gun. We gave Austin Reynolds no chance to say no.

"Cue Mark."

"Congratulations, Austin Reynolds, trainer of Tortola Beach. A great run."

I pushed the microphone toward his mouth.

"Yes," he said. "Very pleasing."

"You said on *The Morning Line* earlier today that you were confident he would stay the seven-eighths-of-a-mile trip and so it has turned out. Do you think this confirms that his last run at Doncaster when he faded so badly near the finish was just a one-off anomaly?"

He looked at me with a certain degree of loathing in his eyes.

"Yes," he said. "I'm sure it was."

"So will he run in the Two Thousand Guineas next year?"

"Quoted at twelve-to-one for the Guineas by Coral's," Neville said into my ear.

"That's the plan," said Austin.

"I hear he's currently being quoted at twelve-to-one for the Guineas by Coral's," I said. "Do you think that's a fair price?"

"A bit short, I'd have said. He only started at tens today."

Yes, I thought. And I wondered if part of the reason for stopping the horse at Doncaster had been to get his starting price nice and long for this race.

"Mark, OK, wrap the interview. Link to Iain for Ascot presentations."

"Thank you, Austin," I said, turning away from him and back to the camera. "And now over to Iain Ferguson at Ascot for the presentations for their third race."

"Cue Iain," said the director, and the camera's red light in front of me went out.

I would have loved to ask Austin Reynolds right there and then who he thought might be blackmailing him and why, but

I didn't particularly want everyone else in the country to over-hear his answer.

I decided to have a word with him later after the transmis-sion was over, and after my microphone had been removed.

The program went to another commercial break while the cameraman covered the Newmarket trophy presentation, which was recorded in the scanner.

"Mark," Neville said, *"on return, discuss the Two Thousand Guineas ante-post market caption, and then we'll go to the VT of our trophy presentation. Coming back to you in five, four, three, two, one . . . cue Mark."*

I looked into the lens. "Welcome back to Newmarket, where the place is still buzzing from that spectacular win by Tortola Beach. So let us look at the ante-post market for the Two Thou-sand Guineas next May." The graphic appeared on the screen, and I went through the list, Tortola Beach now being quoted as joint sixth favorite. The graphic disappeared, and I looked back into the camera lens. "And now we have the Millions Trophy presentation to the connections of Tortola Beach."

"Cue VT."

The recently recorded footage of the trophy presentation was broadcast as I voiced over it live while, at the same time, I had the director and producer wittering away in my ear. *"Mark, Scoop6 update, please—after four legs, there are only twenty-six tickets still left in. Then hand over to Iain at Ascot. Back to you in picture in five, four, three, two, one . . . cue Mark."*

And so it went on, relentlessly, right through until twenty past four, when the production assistant said *"Shut up"* and we could all relax.

"Well done, everybody," said Neville. *"Good job. See you all back here next week for Future Champions Day."*

"Wow!" said Emily when I went over to her. "I had no idea." The sound engineer had wired her up and she'd been listening to the chatter on the talk-back. "It's amazing."

"It certainly is," I agreed. "Those Hollywood film stars have no idea how easy they have it, doing multiple takes until they get it right and having breaks between scenes to learn their lines. I tell you, there's nothing quite like live television to concentrate the mind."

"I could concentrate your mind," Emily said seductively.

WE WENT TO CLARE'S COTTAGE.

I didn't think Clare would have minded as she was always telling me to get a proper girlfriend. And Emily's place at Royston was simply too far away. We were both more eager than that.

I had intended seeking out Austin Reynolds to ask him more about the blackmailer, but that, too, had been postponed due to the urgency of our more basic human urges.

We hardly made it up the stairs to the guest bedroom, but, in the end, our lovemaking was gentle and tender, though not without passion and hunger.

For both of us, it was a journey of exploration, a trip into new territory, and I for one found the experience hugely satisfying.

"Wow!" Emily said again, lying back on the bed. "A day full of surprises."

"Good surprises?" I asked.

"Absolutely," she said with a smile. "Wonderful surprises." She suddenly sat up straight. "Do you have any wine? I've never been to the races before and not had a drink."

I laughed. "I'll go and see."

I picked up my shirt and boxers from where they had fallen on the landing and put them back on. Somehow it didn't seem quite right for me to be wandering around this house without any clothes on.

"Red or white?" I called.

"How about champagne?"

"I'll check."

I went downstairs and looked in Clare's fridge for some cold bubbles.

There were plenty of things that were out-of-date, and even some that were growing a nice covering of mold, but there were no bottles of champagne. I did find one, however, in her drinks cupboard in the sitting room, a nice bottle of Bolinger Special Cuvée, but it was decidedly warm.

"Do you mind if the champagne's warm?" I shouted up the stairs.

"Isn't there an ice bucket?" came the reply.

There was, a silver one, sitting on the mantelpiece along with Clare's other trophies.

I took the bucket back to the kitchen and looked in the freezer. It was one of those American-style refrigerators with an internal ice maker. The hopper was only half full, so I lifted it out and poured the contents into the bucket.

I was returning the empty hopper to the freezer when I noticed a flat plastic case stuck to the inside with some tape.

I pulled the case away and opened it.

It contained a DVD and a folded sheet of ordinary white copier paper.

I sat on a stool at Clare's breakfast bar and carefully unfolded the paper. There were three lines of printed text across the middle:

I KNOW YOU DID THIS ON PURPOSE.

A CONTRIBUTION OF JUST £200 WILL MAKE THE STORY
  GO AWAY.

GET THE CASH READY. PAYMENT INSTRUCTIONS WILL FOLLOW.

I sat there staring at the words, turning the DVD over and over in my fingers.

So it wasn't only Austin Reynolds who had been black-mailed.

17

Are you going to sit there all day? I'm thirsty."

I turned around to find Emily standing provocatively in the kitchen doorway, and, unlike me, she obviously had no qualms about being naked in this house.

She walked over and ran her fingers through my hair. "Are you coming back to bed or do I have to go and play with myself?"

"Sorry," I said. "I'm just coming."

"What are you looking at anyway?"

"Oh, nothing," I said, starting to fold the sheet of paper, but Emily was already reading it over my shoulder.

"Oh my God!" she screamed. "It's a blackmail note. Who sent you that?"

"No one," I said.

"And what was it that you did on purpose?"

"It wasn't sent to me," I said. "I found it in the freezer."

"In the freezer? Where?"

"In amongst the ice. It was taped to the inside of the hopper with this DVD. Clare must have hidden them in there."

"Were they sent to her?"

"I assume so."

"Who by?" Emily asked. "And what was it that she did?"

"It can't have been very much, not if two hundred pounds is all the blackmailer asked for. Perhaps the DVD will give us a clue."

"Oh yes," she said breathlessly. "How exciting."

Excitement wasn't the first thing that came to my mind, but I was intrigued nonetheless.

"There's a DVD player in the sitting room," I said. "Let's go and see."

Emily ran upstairs and then quickly reappeared wearing one of Clare's dressing gowns while I loaded the disk.

I was a bit apprehensive as I pushed the play button. Did I really want to know what Clare had been up to? And, in particular, did I want Emily to find out as well? But it was too late to stop now. I had to see, and there was no way I was going to get Emily to go back upstairs and wait for me in the bedroom while I had a quick look at the DVD on my own. She was perched on the edge of the sofa in eager anticipation, bouncing up and down gently like a child waiting for a Christmas present.

I thought it quite likely that the DVD would contain a recording of a race, but I was really surprised that it was the one at Wolverhampton the previous April when Clare had ridden Brain of Brixham into second place while mistaking the camera support pole for the winning post.

"What's so special about that?" Emily asked, obviously disappointed not to have seen some salacious footage.

"Nothing," I said.

"So what's she supposed to have done on purpose?"

"I presume it was that she didn't win."

I played the film through again and explained to Emily what had happened.

"But how can you blackmail someone for making a silly mistake?"

"That's a very good question."

I went up the stairs a little to retrieve my shoes and pants from where they had been discarded earlier.

"Where are you going?"

"I need my laptop. It's in your car."

I went out to get it, and then logged on the *Racing Post* website to see who trained Brain of Brixham.

Why was I not surprised to discover that it was Austin Reynolds?

Time for me to go and ask him some more questions, I thought.

IN SPITE OF my protestations, Emily came with me.

"For a start," she said, "I need to drive my car. You're not insured for it."

I thought I probably was through my own insurance, but I could see that there was no way I was going to convince her not to come.

She drove through Newmarket, then out on the Bury Road toward Austin Reynolds's training establishment, where she parked on the gravel driveway in front of his mock-Georgian mansion.

"Please wait in the car," I said to Emily firmly. "It will be difficult enough to get him to talk to me alone. He certainly won't do so with someone else listening."

Grudgingly, she agreed, and sat there rigidly holding the steering wheel while I went to ring the front doorbell.

"I don't want to talk to you," Austin said, carelessly opening the door before he saw who it was. "Leave me alone."

He tried to close the door again, but I had my foot against it.

"I only want to ask you a few questions."

"I haven't got time," he said. "We've got the Ingrams staying, and we're having a small celebration here this evening. In fact, I thought you were the caterers arriving. Come back tomorrow."

Mr. and Mrs. Joshua Ingram were the owners of Tortola Beach.

"Perhaps the Ingrams might be interested to know why their horse didn't win at Doncaster in August."

"I thought you said you weren't blackmailing me."

"I'm not," I said.

"That sounded like blackmail to me."

"It will only take a few minutes."

He thought for a moment. "Go round to my office. Down the side." He pointed to his right. "I'll come and let you in there."

Reluctantly, I removed my foot from his door and he closed it.

"Down the side," I shouted to Emily, and she drove behind me as I crunched over the gravel.

Austin Reynolds's office was attached to the back of his house, looking out toward the stable yard beyond, and he was already standing at the door, holding it open.

"Who's in the car?" he asked.

"Just a friend." I was suddenly very glad that Emily was with me. This felt a bit like walking into the lion's den.

I followed Austin into his office. There was not a lion to be seen.

"What do you want?" he asked, sitting down behind his large oak desk.

"I want to know who is blackmailing you."

"So do I."

"But you must have some idea."

"None," he said. "All I received were notes."

I removed from my pocket the sheet of paper that I'd found in Clare's freezer and laid it out flat on the desk in front of him.

"Were they like this?" I asked.

He looked at it briefly and nodded. "Pretty much, except mine accused me of laying horses to lose."

"Did they arrive with DVDs?"

"The first one did."

"How many have you received?" I asked.

"Three."

"And what did you do about them?"

"Paid up," he said. "At least I did for the first two. Whoever it was didn't ask for very much, so I paid."

I was amazed.

"Except now," he said, "I've been asked for more and I don't like it."

"What do you mean?"

He looked at his watch and stood up. "I've got to go and get changed."

"Not yet," I said forcefully, pointing a finger at him. "Answer my questions first." He sat down again heavily. "What did you mean by being asked for more?"

"It was that bloody race at Wolverhampton," he said angrily. "I wish I'd never run the damn horse."

"Brain of Brixham?"

"Yes."

"But surely that was a genuine error on Clare's part?"

"Yes, it was."

"So why are you being blackmailed over it? Why didn't you just go to the police?"

"Clare wanted to," he said.

"So why didn't you?" I asked. He said nothing but just sat looking down at his desk. "Was it because you had indeed layed the horse to lose?"

He looked up at me. "Not a lot," he said. "I'd thought old Brainy would run really well, so I had a big bet on him to win. Too big, really. Then I started to have cold feet, especially when he seemed a bit off-color on the morning of the race."

"So you layed him on the Internet?"

"Yes," he said. "Though not using my own name, of course. And just to limit my losses if he didn't win."

Austin and I both knew that trainers laying their own horses was strictly against the Rules of Racing and would be punished by a lengthy ban from the sport.

"I didn't lay the full amount. I still stood to lose a lot if Brainy didn't win."

That probably wouldn't have made much difference to an inquiry.

"It was very stupid," he said. "I know that."

"But not as stupid as arranging with Clare to stop Tortola Beach at Doncaster."

"That was all her idea," he said. "When she found out I'd layed Brainy at Wolverhampton, she said there was a much better way of stopping a horse winning, one that nobody would ever discover."

Except me, that is.

"So did Clare pay the two hundred pounds?" I said, pointing at the note.

"I paid it for her to stop her going to the police," Austin said miserably, "along with two hundred from me. That bloody mistake of Clare's has cost me a fortune, what with the loss of prize money and my big bet, not to mention the blackmail."

"How about the second note? When did that come?"

"About six weeks ago."

"Asking for the same amount?" I asked.

"No, it was a thousand that time."

"Did Clare get another one too?"

"Yes," Austin said. "Also for a thousand."

"And did you pay that for her as well?"

"No," he said. "I told her to pay it out of the money I'd given her for losing on Tortola Beach."

She obviously hadn't done that, not if the two thousand I'd found in her desk had been the same money. I wondered if she'd paid it at all.

"But you paid?"

"Yes," he said gloomily.

"And you still didn't go to the police?"

"I couldn't, could I? Not when I'd paid up once before."

"And not when you'd also layed Tortola Beach to lose."

"That was only a bit," he said. "I couldn't do too much or it would have been suspicious."

"But why on earth would you stop a horse if you weren't making much from it?"

He looked the picture of abject misery, a stark contrast to

when he had led his victorious horse into the winner's enclosure earlier that afternoon.

"Clare was adamant that we should do it. She seemed to act like it was a game. I told her not to be so bloody silly, but she said that she would give it a go anyway whether I wanted her to or not."

"So you agreed?"

"Yes."

"But why then did you pay her two thousand pounds if you didn't make much out of it?"

"It was like a bet between us. I told her she could have half what I made if she pulled it off without there even being a stewards' inquiry. She claimed it was easy and that she'd done it before, but I didn't believe her. I really didn't think she could do it, but, boy, did she prove me wrong. It was brilliant. I've never seen anything like it in my life."

My stupid, brilliant sister, I thought, competitive to the end. It hadn't been the money that had been important, it had been winning her bet with Austin.

"You said you've now been asked for more."

"Yes," he said. "I had another note yesterday morning demanding ten thousand." He again looked close to tears. "I can't afford that sort of money."

"Show me the note," I said.

He opened the top left-hand drawer of the desk and removed a single sheet of paper, placing it down in front of me.

TIME TO PAY A LITTLE MORE.

A PAYMENT OF JUST £10000 IS NEEDED FOR ME TO
    REMAIN SILENT.

GET THE CASH READY. PAYMENT INSTRUCTIONS WILL FOLLOW.

It did look remarkably like the one I'd found in Clare's freezer, but it had one very significant difference. The amount of ten thousand pounds had had the last zero added by hand. When it had been printed, it had read just one thousand. The blackmailer had obviously decided at the last minute to seriously up the stakes.

"If it had been for just a thousand like last time," Austin said, "I'd probably pay it. But ten grand is completely out of order."

I thought that even one thousand was out of order.

"When did you say this arrived?"

"Yesterday morning," he said, "in the mail."

"Where's the envelope it came in?"

He took an envelope out of the drawer and placed it on the desk. It had been addressed in the same printed small capital letters as the note, and the postmark showed that it had been mailed on Thursday even though I couldn't read from where.

"Have you had the payment instructions?" I asked.

"Not yet."

"How did you hand the money over before?"

"I was told I had to place used twenties in a brown envelope and then leave it under my car in the owners and trainers parking lot at Doncaster races, against the inside of the offside rear wheel."

"Didn't you watch to see who collected it?"

"No," he said, "I was told not to. Anyway, I had a runner in the first and had to go and saddle it."

"You could have got someone else to watch."

He stared at me in disbelief. "Oh yeah! Tell me, who was I going to get to watch the package without telling him exactly why?"

"How did you get the instructions?"

"They also came in the mail," he said. "They arrived the day before I had to leave the cash."

"Did Clare get the same instructions?"

"I don't know," he said. "The first time, I just put a note in with my payment to say that I was including hers."

Crazy, I thought.

"And was it the same drop method both times?"

"Yes," he said. "Except the second time was at York, not Doncaster."

"And you've heard nothing else?" I asked.

"Not until yesterday morning, although there were those bloody pieces in the *Gazette* this week. I nearly shit myself when I saw that headline on Tuesday."

"Why? Did you think it was written about you?"

"What would you think?" he said.

"But it didn't say anything about the horse's trainer being involved."

"It did last May when there was that piece about a trainer laying his horses on the Internet."

"Was that you?" I asked.

"I've no idea," he said. "But it was still much too close for comfort."

"Was the article printed in the paper before or after you paid the first two hundred?"

"After," he said definitely. "I remember clearly that the first note arrived on my birthday, the twenty-fifth of April. It wasn't much of a birthday present, I can tell you."

At that point a neat little woman opened the office door and put her head through the gap.

"Austin," she said in a cross tone, "will you *please* come and look after our guests."

"Just coming, dear," Austin said, standing up.

The neat little woman removed her head and closed the door.

"Please go now," he was almost pleading with me.

"OK," I said. "But let me know when you receive the payment instructions." I smiled at him. "Then we can try and catch the bastard, and without involving the police or the racing authorities."

"Why are you doing this?" he asked. "What have you got to gain?"

"I'm trying to find out why my sister died. Your secrets are safe with me as long as Clare Shillingford's good reputation remains intact."

EMILY WAS still waiting for me in her car.

"I was about to send in the cavalry," she said as I climbed in beside her. "You've been ages."

I looked at my watch. I'd actually been in Austin's office for only half an hour. Somehow it had seemed longer.

"Sorry," I said. "It was important."

"How important?" she asked. "Is that man the blackmailer?"

"No," I said, "he isn't."

"Then who is?"

I sighed. "I wish I knew."

Dammit, I thought. I'd been so busy asking Austin about the blackmail notes that I'd forgotten to ask him about the running of Bangkok Flyer at Lingfield on the day Clare had died.

That race had been the start of all of this. Would Clare have died, I wondered, if I hadn't witnessed that race and confronted her at Haxted Mill?

Why oh why hadn't I answered my telephone that night?

Emily started the car engine. "Where to now?" she said.

"I like you being my driver," I said with a forced laugh, trying to put my guilt and self-pity back in their boxes.

"I can think of better things I'd rather be of yours."

"Good," I said, smiling genuinely. "Let's go back to Clare's cottage."

"Great idea," she said. "That champagne will be nice and cold by now."

"**TELL ME ALL ABOUT IT,**" Emily said as we snuggled down together on Clare's sofa with the bottle of chilled champagne.

"About what?" I asked.

"About why your sister was being blackmailed and why finding that note suddenly meant we had to go and see that man."

"Austin Reynolds," I said.

"That's the one."

How much did I want to tell her? How much could I trust her? I hadn't even known her yet for twenty-four hours. But she had seen Clare's blackmail note. Was it not better to tell her something rather than have her ask other people?

"It's all nonsense, really," I said. "Clare was being blackmailed for something she hadn't even done."

"In that race?"

"Yes," I said. "All Clare did was confuse the position of the winning post. It was a genuine mistake, but someone thinks she did it on purpose."

"So what's the problem?" Emily said. "'Publish and be damned.' If she did nothing wrong, I can't understand how she was being blackmailed."

Nor could I, but things weren't that simple.

"And anyway," Emily said, "it surely can't matter anymore now that she's dead."

"The man I went to see is also being blackmailed and he's very much alive."

Her eyes opened wider in delight. "It's just like something on the television."

Yes, I thought, but who's writing the script.

"So what has the man done?" Emily asked eagerly. "He can't be being blackmailed for the same mistake that Clare made."

"No, he's not. But he did do something that was wrong," I said. "He's the trainer of the horse and he placed a bet that it wouldn't win that race."

"So? What's wrong with that? I thought that betting on horses was not only legal, it was almost compulsory."

"Racehorse trainers are allowed to bet that their horses will *win* a race but not that they will *lose* it. It would be too easy for them to make sure a horse didn't win by simply not training it properly or giving it too hard a gallop too close to the race."

"But surely that's not serious enough to be blackmailed over."

"The maximum penalty for a trainer betting on his own horse to lose is a ban from all racing for ten years. It is a very serious offense."

"Well, then the man's an idiot," Emily said. "And perhaps he deserves it."

There was a lot of sense in what she said, but the whole story would come out, and Clare was bound to be implicated. And, after the *Daily Gazette* articles on Tuesday and Wednesday, her memory would be tainted forever.

"Are you going to inform the racing authorities?"

"No," I said, "not if I can help it."

"Why not?"

I refilled our glasses while I thought through my answer.

"My sole aim is to discover why Clare died. Everything else is irrelevant. I couldn't care less whether Austin Reynolds loses his training license, his reputation, and his big house. He's been a fool, but I don't think he's a real crook."

I paused and sipped my champagne.

"But I really do care that Clare was driven to kill herself, and, quite possibly, the blackmailer might have been doing the driving. So I want to know who is demanding money from Austin Reynolds, and me going to the racing authorities and telling them what a naughty boy Austin's been will not help. The blackmailer would simply walk away."

"He can't be much of a blackmailer anyway," Emily said.

"Why not?" I asked.

"What blackmailer worthy of the name asks someone for two hundred pounds?" She laughed. "That's a joke amount. Two thousand at least, or maybe five. Not so much that you drive the victim to the police but enough to make it worth your while."

"I didn't know you were such an expert on blackmail," I said.

"There's lots of things you don't know about me," she said, cuddling up and putting her hand down between my legs.

"No, hold on," I said, pushing her hand away and sitting up straight. "How come you know so much about blackmail?"

"Mark," she said, "don't be so serious. I know because I read Agatha Christie books and watch murder mysteries on the television, that's all."

I leaned back next to her.

"Blackmailers in those stories always ask for a lot. But, I suppose, that's why they usually get murdered. If they only asked for a little bit, no one would bother to murder them, they'd just pay."

Exactly as Austin Reynolds had done, I thought. Was that why the amounts had been so small?

"I saw a film once," Emily went on, "about an American high school where one of the students sends blackmail notes to every one of his graduating class demanding a single dollar or he would inform the school principal that he or she had cheated in the exams."

"What happened?" I asked.

"Nearly all of them hadn't cheated and they just threw the notes away, but four members of the class actually had and those four each gave him the dollar."

"So?"

"The blackmailer then knew which of his classmates *had* cheated and he demanded more from them. Pretty clever, eh?"

18

On Sunday, Emily drove me along the A14 from Newmarket to Huntingdon racetrack, where I was due to commentate on the six-race card.

Racing on Sundays in England was first introduced at Doncaster on July 26, 1992, although, at the start, it still was against the law to charge entry for a sporting event on a Sunday. All sorts of tricks were used, like on that first day when people were charged for listening to the Band of the Irish Guards and then given a free afternoon's racing. And the situation was further confused by the fact that cash betting was also illegal on Sundays then, but using a bookmaker's account or even a credit or a debit card was not.

Since those days, the rules have been relaxed somewhat, and Sunday is now just like any other day of the week, with at least two race meetings held on every Sunday of the year. Indeed, there are now only four days in the whole calendar when there is no racing on British racetracks: Good Friday, Christmas Day, and the two days before Christmas.

The public love the Sunday meetings, and Huntingdon racetrack was already filling nicely by the time we arrived at about one o'clock, over an hour before the first race.

Emily pulled her red Mercedes into the racetrack lot and followed the directions of the attendant to the next space at the end of the parked cars. Only when we had stopped did I notice with dismay and alarm that we had drawn up alongside Mitchell Stacey's car and that he was still sitting in it.

Bugger, I thought. And moving was now impossible as we were hemmed in by other cars parked behind us and with a tape in front. Perhaps Mitchell wouldn't notice.

"Stay in the car," I said to Emily.

"Why?"

"I really don't want to have to talk to the man in the car next to us."

Emily looked to her left, past my nose.

"Who is it?" she asked.

"A man called Mitchell Stacey."

"And why don't you want to talk to him?"

"He's a trainer," I said. "He's got runners here today. And he doesn't like me very much."

"Why not?"

I could hardly tell her that he was my ex-girlfriend's husband and I had cuckolded him or that he had threatened to kill me.

"He just doesn't."

"Kiss me, then," she said, "and he'll go away."

I leaned over and kissed her, long and passionately, as Mitchell climbed out of his car, collected his coat from the trunk, and walked away toward the enclosures. I had no idea if he'd even seen us, let alone if he had recognized me.

"He's gone," Emily said.

We watched him go through the entrance and into the track.

"I'd rather not be here when he comes back."

She must have detected something in my voice. "Are you frightened of him?"

"He has a very nasty temper," I said, "and I've been at the wrong end of it."

"What did you do?" she asked, "sleep with his wife?"

I looked at her in astonishment. "Yes, as a matter of fact, I did."

She laughed. "You men. No sense of decorum. Can't you control your little willies?"

"It wasn't all that little last night," I said with a grin.

"Don't flatter yourself," she said, giggling. "I've seen bigger."

I decided not to continue this discussion for fear of being completely humiliated.

"Come on," I said, getting out of the car, "I've got work to do."

EMILY AND I walked arm in arm into the racetrack enclosures and toward the weighing room and came face-to-face with Mitchell Stacey, who was coming out with a saddle over his arm.

We all stopped, and Mitchell stared at me. If looks could kill, I would have expired on the spot. Then he turned his eyes toward Emily.

"Whose wife are you, then?" he asked sharply.

Emily said nothing but simply smiled at him, which seemed to disturb him even more.

I, meanwhile, also said nothing, although I was tempted to ask him where he'd been at eleven o'clock on the previous Friday evening. I could still feel my sore neck.

"I've had the police round because of you." Mitchell sneered in my direction. "Keep me out of your sordid little business. Do you hear?"

I again said nothing, and suddenly he walked on, brushing past me and disappearing in the general direction of the saddling stalls.

"Not a very friendly chap," Emily said as we watched him go. "He doesn't seem to like you very much."

"No," I said. "But I don't like him very much either."

"When did you sleep with his wife?"

I said nothing.

"Recently, then, was it?"

"She's much younger than him," I said stupidly as if it mattered.

"Are you still sleeping with her?" Emily asked in a deadpan voice, but one with multiple undertones.

"No," I said emphatically, "I am not. I've got a new girlfriend now."

"Oh really," she said, laughing. "Who's that, then?"

I squeezed her waist, but she squirmed away from me.

"Don't touch me, you . . . you . . . serial adulterer!" she cried.

"Keep your voice down," I said, looking around to see if anyone had heard. "How can I be an adulterer when I've never been married? And anyway, you told me you were divorced."

"Only decree nisi," she said. "Technically, for another week or two, I'm still a married woman."

"Come on, then, married woman, I've got things to do."

We went into the weighing room at the base of the Cromwell grandstand and then into the broadcast center.

"Hi, Jack," I said. "This is Emily."

Jack Laver wiped both his hands on his tattered green sweater and then offered his right to her.

"Lovely to meet you," Emily said, shaking it.

"Anything I should know about?" I asked Jack, making him tear his eyes away from Emily's gorgeous figure.

"Nope," he said. "Usual controls. I've already checked that your monitor's working. No problems."

"Right. Thanks, Jack. See you later."

Emily and I went out of the broadcast center and climbed the six flights of stairs to the commentary booth, which at Huntingdon was in a shedlike structure attached to the very top of the grandstand roof almost as if it was added as an afterthought.

The shed also contained the judge's booth and the photofinish system as well as a position for a television camera. It afforded a great view of the course but was not ideal for anyone who didn't have a head for heights, especially when the wind blew hard, which tended to make the whole structure sway slightly.

"Wow," said Emily, moving to the open side, "it's quite high."

Not as high, I thought, as the fifteenth floor of the Hilton Hotel.

"Don't you like heights?" I asked.

"Not much," she said, hanging on tight to the rail as she looked over. "I prefer my feet firmly planted on the ground."

"You get used to it," I said. "And this is much lower than some."

I removed my binoculars from my bag and then checked the non-runners, making notes on my copy of the *Racing Post* that we had stopped to buy in Newmarket. Everything seemed in order for another day at the office.

"Fancy some lunch?" I asked.

"Have we got time?"

There was still half an hour until the first race.

"Plenty," I said.

We descended again to ground level, and I bought some smoked-salmon sandwiches, which we ate perched on barstools at a high table near the window of Hurdles Bar.

"I've been thinking about what you said yesterday—you know, about the blackmail notes and that film."

"And?" Emily said between mouthfuls of sandwich.

"You couldn't just send blackmail notes to everyone. It would be ridiculous."

"You don't have to," she said. "Suppose you only have a slight suspicion that someone has been up to no good. If you sent them a blackmail note asking for a couple of hundred quid, it would sure as hell confirm your suspicions if they then paid up."

"I wonder if that was the case with Clare. Perhaps whoever sent it to her was merely fishing and got more than just a bite when Austin paid."

"Hello, Mark," said a voice behind me. "Mind if I join you?"

I stood up and turned around. "Not at all, Harry. Pull up a stool. Harry, can I introduce Emily Lowther. Emily, this is Harry Jacobs."

Emily held out her hand, but Harry's were both full, a plate of seafood in one and an ice bucket holding a bottle of champagne in the other. He put them down on the table and shook her hand.

"Delighted to meet you, my dear," Harry said. "I'll get glasses."

"No private box today, Harry?" I said.

"No, not here. I'm on my own today anyway. No runners. I only popped along because I was bored at home. Last-minute decision and all that."

He disappeared back toward the bar.

Who is he? Emily mouthed at me.

"Racehorse owner," I said quietly in reply. "I rode a horse for him years and years ago when I was eighteen. We've been friends ever since. Nice enough chap, but a bit eccentric. He's got pots of money, but I don't know where from."

Harry returned with three champagne flutes and proceeded to pour golden bubbles into them.

"Not much for me," said Emily, "I'm driving."

"And not much for me either, thanks," I said, "I'm commentating in ten minutes."

"You're no fun," said Harry with a pained expression. Then he smiled. "But that means there's more for me. Cheers."

We raised our glasses and clinked them together. Emily and I sipped graciously while Harry downed a hefty slug before refilling his glass.

"Now then," he said, "what were you two so intent about? I waved at you, Mark, through the window but you completely ignored me."

"I'm sorry," I said, "I didn't notice you." I laughed. "We were busily talking about sending someone a blackmail note."

The color drained out of Harry's face, and I thought for a moment he was going to drop his glass.

RATHER ANNOYINGLY, at that point I'd had to go to commentate on the first race, so I'd left Emily looking after Harry in the bar, promising to be back straight after I finished.

I later hurried down the stairs to find them sitting on the same barstools as when I'd left. The only thing that seemed to have changed was that the champagne bottle was now empty, being turned upside down in the ice bucket, and the plate of seafood had been half consumed.

Harry was intently studying the floor at his feet.

"Did you see the race?" I asked.

"On the television," said Emily, pointing to one on the wall. She smiled. "And I could hear your voice over the speakers."

"So, Harry," I said, sitting down on the third stool, "tell me."

He looked up slowly. "Tell you what?" His voice was ever so slightly slurred. I wasn't surprised after the quick consumption of nearly a whole bottle of fizz. He again looked down at the floor.

"Tell me who is blackmailing you," I said quietly but distinctly, leaning forward to speak directly into his left ear.

"No one," he said. He suddenly sat up straight and almost toppled backward off the stool.

"I tried to get him to eat something to soak up the booze," Emily said, "but he seems intent on drinking himself into oblivion. I had to restrain him from getting another bottle."

"I'm fine," he said. "I'm not drunk. I'm just a little tipsy, that's all."

"Yes, Harry," I said, "of course you are. Now, where can we take him?" I asked Emily. "Even if we could get him to tell us who's blackmailing him, he's not going to do it here, not with all these people round. How about the commentary booth?"

"Will he get up the stairs?" Emily asked.

"I should think so. I'm quite surprised a single bottle has had such a large effect on him. He's drunk me under the table before now. I'd always assumed he had hollow legs and could drink for England."

"Perhaps he started before he arrived at the races."

I stood up and put my hand under his right elbow. "Come on, Harry, let's go."

"OK," he said, standing up. "Fine by me."

He walked quite steadily out of the bar, Emily and I guiding him around to the stairs that led up to the rooftop shed. Without any hesitation, he followed Emily up quite happily, with me climbing behind him so he couldn't suddenly change his mind and retreat.

There was one chair at the back of the commentary booth, and Harry sat down on it.

"I'm fine," he said again. "Perfectly fine."

"I know you are, Harry," I said. "But just sit there for a bit while I commentate on the next race."

Hell, I thought, I hadn't been to see the horses in the parade ring or check on the colors. But the second race was a moderate two-and-a-half-mile handicap steeplechase with eight runners and all of them had been regulars on racetracks for years. It was like seeing old friends again, and I reckoned I knew the colors already.

Handicaps are the staple of British racing, accounting for more than half of all races. They give the best chance for most owners to have a winner.

All horses in training are given an official rating in a list that is published each week by the British Horseracing Authority. With handicaps, the horses carry different weights according to their official rating: the higher the rating, the greater the weight. In this way, based on previous performance, all horses should have an equal chance of winning.

Without handicaps, the best horses would always win and there would be no real point in owning a moderate horse. And just as soccer teams are also grouped by their performances into "divisions" where they are all roughly the same standard, so horses run in races where they all have approximately the same rating.

Not only does this give every horse in the race a chance of winning, it leads to exciting close finishes because the handicapper is attempting to create a multiple dead heat with all the horses arriving at the winning post at exactly the same moment. Hence they are also great races for the betting public, who always believe they know better than the officials.

The runners for this particular handicap came out onto the track and I described them to the crowd as they made their way around to the two-and-a-half-mile start in the middle of the back stretch.

I'd seen all of these horses racing before, some of them as many as fifteen or twenty times, and I recognized them as much from the shape of their bodies and the shade of their coats as from the colors of the jockeys' silks. Nevertheless, I took a few minutes to make sure. I didn't want to be complacent and end up confusing one horse with another.

"They're off," I said into the microphone as the race began.

The handicapper should have been proud of his work. All

eight horses were still in contention as they turned into the finishing stretch for the second and last time, with just two plain fences left to jump.

Then two of them fell at the second-to-last fence, bringing down a third.

"Now, with just one to jump, it's Twickman taking up the running from Delmar Boy and Coralstone, with Vintest and Felto both making their challenge down the outside."

I smiled at Emily, who was standing next to me totally engrossed in the race.

"And, as they come to the last, it's Twickman by a length from Vintest, with Coralstone third between horses in the green."

Emily started to jump up and down with excitement.

"A great leap at the last from Vintest, who lands alongside Twickman and is quickly into his stride. Just two hundred yards to go now."

It was a long run in at Huntingdon, and plenty could change between the last fence and the winning post. And today was no exception.

"Twickman and Vintest together, but here comes the fast-finishing Felto under Paddy Dean on the outside." My voice rose in pitch with the ever-rising cheering of the crowd. "Into the last fifty yards, and it's still Twickman just from Vintest, but Felto is catching them with every stride."

I clicked off my microphone as the three horses flashed past the finish line stride for stride.

"Photograph, photograph," announced the judge.

"On the nod," I said to Emily.

"What?" she said breathlessly.

"Horses' heads nod back and forth as they run. Those three

were so close that the winner will be the one whose head happened to be nodding forward just as they crossed the line. Half a stride later, one of the others would be in front. When it's that close, it's down to luck as to who wins."

"But it was so exciting," she said. "I've never really watched a race like that before—you know, concentrating on the horses. I've mostly only been to the races for the food and drink and the hospitality."

"Here is the result of the photograph," said the judge over the public address. "First, number four, Felto. Second, number seven. Third, number two. The distances were a nose and a short head."

A great cheer had gone up from the crowd as soon as the number four had been announced. Felto had started the race as favorite and lots of bets had been riding on his particular nose.

"What's the difference between a nose and a short head?" Emily asked.

"Not much," I said. "A nose is anything less than four and a half inches and a short head is between that and nine inches."

Emily made a face. "It hardly seems fair to lose by a few inches after running so far."

"A win is a win," I said. "And as the technology improves and the photographs get better, the margins get smaller and smaller. Dead heats are getting rarer."

Harry Jacobs had sat on the chair at the back of the booth throughout the race, looking more miserable than drunk.

"So, Harry," I said, "tell us who's been blackmailing you."

He looked up at us with clear eyes. "How on earth did you know?"

"We didn't," Emily said. "We were discussing somebody else."

"Oh?" he said. "Who?"

"Two others, actually," I said. "And one of them was my sister, Clare." I felt I had to give him some information in order to establish some trust. "Someone sent her a blackmail note demanding two hundred pounds or they would tell the racing authorities she had failed on purpose to win a race."

"And did she pay?" he asked.

"Sort of," I said. "Someone else paid for her."

"And did the blackmailer then ask for more?"

"Yes," I said.

Harry nodded. "Thought so."

"Is that what happened to you?"

He pursed his lips and went on nodding. "The first demand was so small, I just paid it."

"Why?" I asked. "What had you done?"

"But that's what's so bloody stupid," he said. "I haven't really done anything."

"So what were they using to blackmail you?" I asked.

"It was an offshore bank account I had on the Isle of Man."

"What about it?"

"I opened it in a different name because I thought at one stage I might move all my assets there."

"For tax purposes?"

"Exactly," he said. "Capital gains tax, to be precise. In the end, I didn't go through with it, but I never closed the account. I'd put some money in it, and I suppose I should have paid tax on the interest it earned, but it was so small I didn't think it mattered. Also, I didn't tell my accountant or put any offshore account details on my tax return as I didn't want the tax people to think I was trying to fiddle with my taxes."

"Which you were," Emily said.

"Yeah, well . . . but not using that account."

"But you were fiddling with your taxes somewhere else?" I asked.

"Not actual fiddling," he said, slightly affronted. "I *avoid* tax, not *evade* it. There's an important difference. Avoidance is legal, evasion isn't." He smiled unconvincingly. "But I could really do without being audited by the Revenue. Let's just say it might be awkward, you know, over certain of my interpretations of the tax laws."

"Sailing close to the wind," said Emily.

"Exactly," Harry agreed. "Very close."

"So what did the blackmail note say?"

He knew it by heart. "'I know you are using an offshore bank account to evade paying tax. Just two hundred pounds will make the story go away. Get the cash together. Payment details will follow.'"

"Same blackmailer," I said. "When did you get the note?"

"Nearly two years ago. At a time when it might have been very embarrassing to have had a Revenue investigation. So I paid."

"Were you told to leave the money under your car in a race-track parking lot?"

He nodded. "But he demanded more. About six months later I had to pay a thousand, next it was two thousand, then I got another note yesterday demanding a further twenty thousand. Now, I think that's rather too much." He sounded like someone who had just been overcharged for a meal or a hotel room.

"Have you by any chance got the note with you?" I asked.

He pulled a crumpled piece of paper out of his coat pocket. "I didn't want to leave it at home in case my wife found it."

He handed it to me and I spread it out. It was a computer

printout just like the others, but as on the latest one sent to Austin Reynolds the last zero of the twenty thousand had been added by hand.

I glanced at my watch. The next race was due to be off in fifteen minutes.

"I've got to go down and see the horses in the parade ring," I said. "They're juvenile three-year-old hurdlers and some of them I haven't seen run before. I want to see them in the paddock to help me learn the colors. You two stay right here. I'll be back before you know it."

I skipped down the stairs and out toward the parade ring. Dodging through the crowd, I ran straight into Mitchell Stacey, almost knocking him over.

"Sorry," I said automatically before I even realized who he was.

He stared at me with contempt. "Watch where you're bloody going, can't you?"

We stood facing each other for a moment.

Why, I thought, had Mitchell set up a spy camera in his bedroom to film Sarah and me? How had he known to do so?

What was it that Sarah had said to me in that last call? *I should have paid the little shit.* Paid who? Had Sarah also been a victim of blackmail?

Mitchell turned away toward the weighing room, and I went on to the parade ring to see the horses, but my brain was elsewhere. Instead of learning the colors of the jockeys' silks, I called the Stacey home on my cell phone.

"Hello," said Sarah's familiar voice after two rings.

"Sarah, it's me," I said.

"I told you that it was much better for both of us if we didn't talk again. And we had the police round here this morning asking questions about you." She sounded angry. "I'm sorry, I must go."

"No, please. Don't hang up!" I shouted quickly. "Listen. Were you being blackmailed?"

There was a long pause on the other end, and at one point I wondered if she had indeed hung up but she hadn't, I could hear her breathing.

"Did someone ask you for two hundred pounds to make the story of you and me go away?"

"Yes," she said, "but I didn't pay him. Maybe it would've been better if I had."

I should have paid the little shit.

"But you do know who it was, don't you?"

"Yes," she said. "It was that little shit of a journalist, Toby Woodley."

19

I was not at all sure how I managed to commentate on the juvenile hurdlers.

My eyes had watched the horses being mounted in the parade ring, but none of the data received had reached my conscious brain. My mind had been racing with too much other information and too many unanswered questions.

Had Toby Woodley been murdered at Kempton Park races because of the blackmail?

I didn't even properly learn the jockeys' colors as the horses circled at the start, and, suddenly, the race was under way. I had to keep glancing down to my race program to see which horse was which as they jumped the two hurdles in the stretch for the first time.

Had it been one of Toby Woodley's blackmail victims that had done us all a favor?

It was not proving to be my greatest-ever commentary.

Concentrate, I told myself as the horses swept right-handedly away from the grandstands to start their second circuit. For God's sake, concentrate!

But how could Toby Woodley have sent a blackmail note to Austin Reynolds on Thursday when he'd been murdered on Wednesday night?

The horses galloped down the back of the course, and on two occasions I called one of them by the wrong name, "Woodley," when the horse was properly called "Woodmill."

Could Toby Woodley have mailed the note on Wednesday evening after the last collection so that it hadn't been date-stamped until Thursday?

The horses turned in to the finishing stretch for the second and final time, and by now even the crowd knew the colors better than I did. But thankfully I called the correct names of the leading pair as they jumped the last hurdle together side by side.

But Harry Jacobs had said that he'd received his latest note only yesterday. Could it really have taken three days to arrive?

The two horses fought out another close finish, flashing past the winning post with hardly a cigarette paper between them.

"Photograph, photograph," called the judge once more.

Or had Toby Woodley had an accomplice who was now acting on his own?

HARRY JACOBS insisted on going back to the bar after the third race.

"I need another drink," he said.

"Don't you think you've had enough, Harry?" I said. "Especially if you're driving later."

"I have a driver. I haven't got a license."

Probably lost it, I thought, from having too many boozy days at the races.

"OK," I said. "But a couple of things first. Are you sure that note arrived at your home yesterday?"

"Absolutely certain," Harry said. "It's the sort of thing you remember."

"Do you still have the envelope it came in?"

"No," he said, "I threw it away. Why?"

"I wanted to see when it was mailed and whether it was sent first or second class."

"First class, I think," he said. "But I couldn't be certain. Sorry." He stood up. "Now, where's that drink?"

All three of us went down the stairs from the grandstand shed, but while Harry peeled off toward the bar to order more champagne, Emily and I went through the betting hall to the parade ring to see the horses for the next race, a tricky handicap hurdle with eighteen runners.

"Are all your days as thrilling as this?" Emily asked as I stood silently by the paddock rail making notes on my race program.

I looked sideways at her. "Do I detect a touch of sarcasm?"

"Me?" she said, smiling broadly.

"It's not every day you come across blackmail," I said.

"No," she said, laughing, "only every other day."

"Real blackmail, I mean, not that stuff you watch on the television."

"At least that's exciting."

"How about if I told you that I knew who'd been sending the notes."

"Who?" she said, her eyes opening wider in anticipation.

"I'll tell you over dinner."

"No," she said, "tell me now."

"Over dinner," I said firmly. "I need to concentrate on the horses."

"Well, in that case I'll go and join Harry in the bar."

"I thought you said you were driving," I said.

"So?" She turned and walked away, looking back just once and waving before she disappeared into the bar.

I turned my attention back to the eighteen different silks in front of me and started to sort out which belonged to which horse.

WE STOPPED at six-thirty for an early dinner at the Three Horseshoes, a charming thatched pub in Madingley, near Cambridge.

"How lovely," Emily said as we walked in, "a romantic dinner for two. I can't remember when I last did this."

"What about last night?" I said.

"I'd hardly call takeout from the local Chinese restaurant a romantic dinner."

I smiled at her. "But if I remember correctly, it became quite romantic afterward."

She laughed. "You just got lucky."

We were shown to a quiet table by the window, overlooking the garden and the parking lot beyond it amongst the trees.

After the unwanted attentions of Harry Jacobs all afternoon, I was really looking forward to a couple of hours of uninterrupted time for just the two of us. I'd even left my phone in the car.

"Well?" said Emily eagerly after we'd ordered, "who's the blackmailer?"

"A journalist called Toby Woodley."

She seemed disappointed. "And who is he?"

"Who *was* he, you mean. He was murdered in the parking lot at Kempton Park racetrack last Wednesday evening. And I was there when he died."

Emily's interest was suddenly reawakened. "Did you kill him?"

"No, of course not," I said. "But whoever did may have been a victim of his blackmail."

"See," she said. "I told you it was just like those mysteries on the television."

"There's a problem, though," I said. "Toby Woodley was killed on Wednesday evening and Harry's blackmail note didn't arrive until Saturday. Harry thought it was sent first class, which means that in all likelihood it was mailed on Friday, or on Thursday at the earliest."

"So," said Emily, leaning forward, "who mailed it if this Woodley fellow was already dead?"

"Exactly," I said. "And I think the same person may have inserted the extra zero at the end of the amount. It seems to me that the notes had already been printed and an extra zero was added as an afterthought. It was the same with the note shown me by Austin Reynolds."

"But how do you know it was Toby Woodley who sent the first ones?"

This might be awkward, I thought.

"Well," I said, "you know the man we parked next to?"

"The one whose wife you've been sleeping with?"

"Yes, that one." It was definitely awkward. "She told me."

"When?" she squealed.

"This afternoon. I called her when you were up in the booth with Harry."

"My God! You are a sneaky bastard," Emily said with a laugh. She leaned back in her chair. "I should drive home right now and leave you here."

"I told you it was over between us." I was trying to sound honorable and trustworthy. Even though I'd met Emily only forty-eight hours ago, I suddenly realized that I absolutely didn't want to lose her.

"Anyway, what did she say?"

"She told me that she'd received a blackmail note demanding two hundred pounds to keep quiet about the affair. A note just like the others."

"But how did she know who it was from?"

I thought back to my conversation with Sarah. "She was told to leave used twenty-pound notes in a brown envelope under her car in the parking lot at Newbury races, as the others had. But instead of money, she put strips of newspaper in the envelope, and then she hid and watched to see who collected it. It was this man Toby Woodley."

"What did he do when she didn't pay?" Emily asked.

"I think he was going to write about us in his newspaper. He said something last week about being good to me. It seems his editor wouldn't let a story run because of Clare having just died. I now think the story must have been about me and Sarah Stacey. I think he then told her husband about us to get back at her for not paying."

"Nice chap," Emily said. "No wonder someone murdered him."

A waitress arrived with our starters.

"Do you fancy some wine?" I asked.

"Of course I do," Emily said, "but as you so prudently pointed out, I'm driving."

"We could always leave the car and get a taxi."

"And then how would I get to work in the morning?"

"Where is work?" I asked.

"Cambridge. I work in the university engineering department as a research assistant."

It was now my turn to say "Wow!"

"I'm currently helping with a project to develop needleless injections. It's really interesting."

"So are you an engineer?" I asked.

"No," she said, "I'm more of a medic. But I'm not a doctor. I only did a biomedical degree."

It sounded pretty good to me.

"So I need my car in the morning to get to work."

I suppose I would need a car too. I would have to sort that out, along with lots of other things. Thankfully, I had the day off.

"And I need to go home tonight," Emily said. "I haven't got my things for the morning."

"Do you need to collect your white coat?" I asked flippantly.

She smiled and shook her head. "No. But I do need my university pass, and I can hardly go into the lab dressed like this, so I'm going home tonight to Royston."

I wondered if I was being given the brush-off. I rather hoped not.

"You can come with me, if you like," she said, "but I'm definitely sleeping in my own bed, with or without you."

"With," I said. "But I have to go back to Clare's cottage first to collect my stuff."

Emily smiled broadly. "That's fine, then. We'll make a detour."

We ate our starters with just fizzy water as the accompaniment.

"So tell me," Emily said, "who's the second blackmailer, the one who mailed the note to Harry after this Woodley fellow was killed?"

"I wish I knew. But whoever it is, he's rather more greedy. Toby Woodley never asked anyone for very much, that's why most of them paid him."

"And do you think he asked all sorts of people for two hundred pounds?"

"Yes, I do," I said. "I reckon that's how he got some of his stories for the paper. If he had even the slightest suspicion about someone, he'd send them a blackmail demand for just two hundred pounds to make the story go away. If they paid, then he had the confirmation he needed that he was right and he would ask for more, if necessary backing up the demand with an article in the paper that proved he knew what had been going on, but of course without mentioning anyone by name."

"But enough to frighten his victims into paying up."

"Precisely," I said.

"What's it got to do with the death of your sister?"

"I don't know," I said, "maybe nothing. But she definitely was being blackmailed and that may have had something to do with it."

In truth, I felt nowhere nearer to finding out why Clare died.

"How was the journalist murdered?" Emily asked.

"He was stabbed in the back."

"And you were there?"

"Yes, I was there immediately afterward. I didn't actually see him being stabbed, but I was there when he died a few minutes later. The police thought I might have killed him because he'd written an article about Clare in that morning's paper. But they couldn't find any knife, so they let me go."

And, I thought, they also couldn't find his briefcase.

Had the notes for Austin Reynolds and Harry Jacobs been printed and ready to go in that stolen briefcase? Was the person who had mailed them not an accomplice of Toby Woodley but his killer?

EMILY AND I enjoyed the rest of our dinner free of further blackmail discussion, concentrating instead on learning more about each other.

"So where exactly do you live?" she asked me.

"I rent an apartment in Edenbridge, in Kent. But I'm intending to buy a house. I've even got the details on one in Oxfordshire I like the look of."

That was something else I had to deal with tomorrow, I thought, along with renting a car. I also had to contact Detective Sergeant Sharp about the Hilton Hotel CCTV footage and follow up on the guest list for the Injured Jockeys Fund dinner. Between them, I hoped they might give me some clue to the identity of the mystery visitors to Clare's room the night she died.

So much for my day off.

Both Emily and I decided against dessert and coffee, opting to go.

"We can open a bottle of wine when we get to my place," Emily said, "and have coffee there."

I looked at my watch. It was still only twenty to nine.

"Sounds good to me."

I paid the bill, and we walked out together toward Emily's car.

I was careless. Very careless.

Since the events of Friday night, I had been checking the inside of cars and avoiding all dark places, but, here and now, I had relaxed my guard.

Thinking back, I believe the fateful moment was when Emily took my hand in hers. Perhaps I was preoccupied by the thoughts of what was to come, reliving the excitement of our first lovemaking the previous afternoon. Or maybe it was just due to an overwhelming feeling of contentment that was flooding through me.

Either way, I was careless.

I didn't even notice the darkened car until it was almost upon us.

We were halfway across the gravel parking lot, and just a few yards from Emily's red Mercedes, when the roaring engine to my left finally cut through into my consciousness.

I half turned and screamed at Emily, but it was too late, much too late.

The car hit both of us, spiraling me over the hood while Emily went down under the wheels.

I remembered hitting the roof of the car and, the next thing I knew, I was lying on the gravel, panting madly, wanting to run but unable to get up.

I rolled over, trying to ignore the searing pain in my side.

The car was already out of the parking lot and on the road, traveling fast, and still it had no lights on.

Emily, I thought with panic. Where is Emily?

I gritted my teeth and rolled over again. I searched for her with my eyes, but she was nowhere to be seen.

"Emily." I tried to shout, but the sound came out as more of a croak. "Emily. Where are you? Are you all right?"

There was no reply, and I began to panic further.

I drew myself up onto my knees, and coughed.

Blood, I thought. I can taste blood in my mouth. I coughed again. This time, I knew I was coughing up blood.

Each breath was painful and difficult, and I felt sick.

"Emily," I tried to shout again.

Still nothing.

I forced myself to stand up—if doubled over and clutching my side could be considered standing up. But at least I was on my feet.

I took three small steps over and leaned on a car.

Where was she?

I staggered from car to car, wildly searching in the darkness between them.

I found her lying facedown near the exit of the parking lot. She must have been dragged there under the wheels.

I sank to my knees beside her.

"Emily," I called, touching her shoulder, but there was no reply.

Breathing was becoming very difficult, but I mustered the strength to roll her over on her back. Her face was just a mass of blood, and I couldn't even tell if she was alive or dead.

"Oh my God!" I cried. "I'm so sorry."

Another couple came out of the pub and started to walk toward us.

"Help!" I croaked at them. "Please help me."

They stopped.

"Call an ambulance," I said, tears streaming down my face.

———

I **AGAIN ENDED UP** in Addenbrooke's emergency room, just as I had the previous Friday. But this time I wasn't left alone in a cubicle to recover. I was rushed into a treatment room, where I was worked on by a whole team of medics, and they seemed to be getting more concerned as time went on.

I was placed on my left side, with my head and shoulders slightly raised, and I was wearing what the doctors had referred to as a positive flow oxygen mask strapped over my face.

But the mask didn't seem to be doing much good. My breathing was now so labored and shallow that I was hardly taking in any air at all, and I felt light-headed and close to un-consciousness.

Was this how I would die?

One of the medical staff came up toward my head and into view.

"Can you hear me?" he asked.

I nodded.

"You've broken a couple of ribs," he said. "One of them has punctured your left lung and it has collapsed. We're trying to remove the air from inside your chest cavity so that your lung can reinflate on its own."

I tried to speak, but I didn't seem to have enough breath.

"Don't talk," he said. "Concentrate on your breathing. I don't particularly want to have to put a tube down your throat as it may cause more problems. Our main concern is a rapid buildup of fluid in and round your right lung as well, but we are doing our best to remove it." He smiled a wry smile. I wasn't sure if that was encouraging or not.

One lung collapsed and a buildup of fluid in the other. No wonder it felt like I was drowning.

I desperately wanted to ask him about Emily. When I'd been carried into the ambulance, she had still been on the ground being attended to by paramedics, and I was dreadfully worried because I hadn't seen her move since I'd first found her.

The doctor resumed his attempts to remove the fluid from my lungs, and I went on breathing, albeit with increasingly rapid and shallow breaths.

I tried to take my mind off my immediate medical troubles by thinking back to what had happened in the pub parking lot.

There was no doubt in my mind that it had been a deliberate attempt to run us down. The driver of the car had made no effort to stop. In fact, quite the reverse. He had accelerated across the lot with his engine roaring and had driven off at speed.

He must have been waiting for Emily and me to come out from dinner. He hadn't put on his headlights, but there would have been enough ambient light for him to see us walking through the garden and across the parking lot.

How had he known we were there?

All I could think was that he must have followed us from the races.

But who knew I was at Huntingdon racetrack?

Anyone, I suppose, who'd listened to me either at the track or at home on the RacingTV channel, which had covered the meeting using my commentaries.

And Mitchell Stacey had definitely known.

His car had already gone from the lot when Emily and I came out to her Mercedes, but that didn't mean he hadn't been waiting somewhere near the exit in order to follow us.

The doctor reappeared in my field of vision.

"Right. Now we need you to sit up," he said. "To help the fluid drain."

I hardly had the breath to move a single muscle and I needed the help of two burly male nurses just to swing my legs off the examination table.

I was leaned forward on a high table while the doctor inserted a tube into my back.

"There," he said. "The fluid is now draining out of your chest, and you'll soon be feeling a lot better."

As if by magic, my breathing improved dramatically over the next couple of minutes as three large bottlefuls of pinkish fluid were drained from my body.

Suddenly I began to believe that I might actually survive.

"Is that better?" asked the doctor from behind me.

I nodded. "Much," I gasped through the oxygen mask.

"Good. You were breathing for a time there with only about a tenth of one lung operational. If you'd arrived here just a couple of minutes later, you'd have been a goner."

"What about Emily?" I asked quietly, almost as if I didn't want to know.

"Eh?"

"What about Emily?" I asked him again, this time louder. "The lady I was with."

There was no answer.

"Tell me," I said.

The doctor came around to face me.

"I'm afraid she didn't make it."

20

I lay in the semidarkness of a hospital room in utter despair.

It was my fault.

I should never have placed Emily in such danger.

It was true that I'd known her for only two days, and maybe there had been something of the rebound about our coming together after my breakup with Sarah, but, even so soon, I truly felt that I'd finally met someone I would have been happy to live with, someone with whom to share the rest of my life.

And now she was gone. Snatched away in an instant.

Why?

It was *me* who should be dead, not her.

But why would anyone want me dead? There was no question that they did. Attempted strangulation on Friday and now a hit-and-run in a darkened pub parking lot on Sunday. But why?

Everything in my head came back to Mitchell Stacey.

Who else was there?

That is what Detective Chief Inspector Perry had asked me just as soon as the doctor decided I was well enough to be interviewed by him and another plainclothes policeman.

"You told me I'd be perfectly safe," I'd said to him in an accusing tone.

"I thought you would be," he had said in reply. "I'm sorry."

"How about Mitchell Stacey?" I'd asked. "What did he have to say?"

"Mr. Stacey was interviewed by officers from the Thames Valley Police early yesterday morning and he provided an alibi for his whereabouts on Friday evening. He could not have been the man who tried to strangle you."

"But he could have arranged it, and it might have been him in the pub parking lot tonight," I'd said.

"That will now be up to the Cambridgeshire force to determine." He indicated the other policeman. "DCI Coaker here is dealing with the inquiry into the murder of Mrs. Lowther. I'm assisting him only because of last Friday's incident."

I had spent the next two hours answering the two policemen's questions in increasing frustration and anger.

"Could you identify the car?"

"No."

"Could you identify the driver?"

"No."

"Do you know why anyone would want you dead?"

"No—other than Mitchell Stacey."

They asked me at least ten times about the sequence of events in the pub parking lot and each time I gave them the same answers.

I continually asked them how Emily had died and in the end they told me that her neck had been broken. She must have been rolled under the car for ten or fifteen yards. It would have been enough to break anything.

Now alone at last, I grieved for her, and also for me, and for what we might have been together.

THE MORNING brought little or no relief from my pain, or my misery, and Detective Chief Inspector Coaker came back soon after eight o'clock with more questions.

"Who knew you would be at the Three Horseshoes pub?"

"No one. Going there was a last-minute decision."

"Were you followed there from Huntingdon?"

"We must have been, but I didn't notice. Emily was driving."

Even I could tell that my answers weren't very helpful. But that didn't stop him from asking the same things over and over and over again.

"How about my phone?" I said during a lull in the questioning.

"What about it?"

"It's in Emily Lowther's car," I said. "Along with a leather bag containing my laptop computer, a pair of binoculars, and a few other things. I need them for my job."

"I'll see what I can do," said the chief inspector.

Eventually he had to leave while a doctor came in the room to examine me, placing his stethoscope all over my chest and back while I breathed in and out.

"How are you feeling?" he asked.

"Medically or emotionally?" I replied.

"Both."

"Considering I was convinced last night that I was dying, I'm feeling pretty well on the medical front. My side is still very sore down here." I placed my hand gingerly on my left lower ribs. "But I can breathe all right."

"How about deep breaths?" he asked.

"Very painful," I said. "As is coughing."

He nodded. "But you must try to use all of your lung capacity if you can. It will help prevent complications."

I didn't like the sound of "complications," so I breathed deeply, trying my best to ignore the stabbing pain in my side.

"How long do I have to stay here?" I asked.

"There's no medical reason why you shouldn't go home. Your left lung reflated of its own accord and the function of both lungs is now good, and there has been no recurrence overnight of fluid buildup anywhere in your chest." He smiled at me. "But you must take things easy. No heavy lifting. It will take six weeks for those ribs to heal properly, and they'll give you some considerable discomfort for most of that time. I'll prescribe you something for the pain."

"Can't you strap them up to stop them hurting?"

"We don't do that anymore. Strapping the chest is no longer advised because it's constrictive and prevents you taking those necessary deep breaths. Let me tell you, a bit of pain is far preferable to pneumonia."

It certainly was, I thought. I took yet another deep breath.

"So I can go now?" I asked.

"Yes," he said. "But seek medical advice immediately if you become even the slightest bit out of breath." He paused. "How are you feeling in here?" He tapped his head.

"Pretty bloody," I said. "But staying in bed won't help that."

"No. I'm sorry."

So was I.

MY SISTER ANGELA came to collect me from the hospital around ten-thirty, and we were both in tears.

I'd called her earlier on a hospital pay phone to tell her about Emily, but she already knew, it had been reported on the radio.

"Where to?" she asked.

"Clare's cottage," I said. "I need to collect my stuff."

She drove in silence, too shocked even to ask me what had happened.

I was glad. I'd done enough answering questions for one morning. But I was sure none of my answers had been of any use to the police—or to me, for that matter. Nothing helped to make sense of Emily's death.

But I hadn't said anything to DCI Coaker about blackmail. I couldn't see how it might have been relevant.

Now I wondered if I should have. But surely that would have opened a whole new can of worms and sent the likes of Austin Reynolds and Harry Jacobs running for the hills. Then they would, of course, deny everything, and I'd be left with egg on my face. And did I really want to expose my sister as a cheat and a race fixer if I didn't absolutely have to?

But why else did someone want me dead?

According to Chief Inspector Perry, Mitchell Stacey had had an alibi for Friday night, but he had also once threatened to have my legs broken and he would have needed some help to do that. Did he have some "heavies" he could call on for a bit of garroting to order or was I just being fanciful and maybe also guilty of confusing television drama with real life?

Oh, Emily!

How I wished this nightmare was nothing more than a fictional story line from some screenwriter's imagination.

"I NEED TO GET the key from the stable office," I said to Angela as she turned into the driveway of Clare's cottage.

But I was wrong.

The front door to the cottage was wide open, and a key hadn't been used to open it. The frame had been splintered all around the lock, and there were six overlapping, two-inch-wide round impressions in the door. Someone clearly had used brute force and a sledgehammer to simply smash their way in.

"Oh shit!" I said with feeling. "It's been burgled."

Angela stayed in the car while I moved forward warily to the door. I thought it unlikely that any burglar would still be in the cottage at eleven o'clock in the morning, but I didn't particularly want to disturb some crazy, knife-wielding drug addict who was searching for the wherewithal for his next fix.

"Hello," I called. "Anyone there?"

I stood in the doorway listening for the sound of any movement inside or someone escaping out the back. There was nothing.

"We should call the police," Angela shouted at me through the open car window.

I'd had enough of the police for one morning.

"I'll take a look first," I shouted back.

I stepped inside, expecting to discover that the place had

been completely ransacked, but I was pleasantly surprised to find that nothing much looked out of place. The bags of Clare's clothes were still stacked under the stairs, and the cardboard boxes I'd filled with the contents of her desk remained where I'd left them on the floor of the sitting room.

Indeed, the only things I could see that had been shifted were some of the papers that had been in the boxes, which were now strewn across the carpet.

However, there was something missing.

Not the fancy television set. Not even Clare's collection of silver racing trophies that were still lined up on the mantelpiece.

It was the white envelope containing the two thousand pounds in cash that was missing—gone from the cardboard box where I'd placed it, along with the blackmail note that I had carelessly left in full view on the desk.

Austin Reynolds, I thought.

Who else would only take those items and leave the silver?

Austin Reynolds removing any evidence that could incriminate him. And this time he would have worn gloves.

I went upstairs to have a quick check around and then went back out to Angela.

"It's fine," I said. "There's no one here and nothing seems to be missing, not even Clare's trophies. Perhaps the burglar was disturbed as soon as he broke down the door."

"Maybe someone heard the noise," Angela said, "and investigated."

Possibly, I thought, but the bangs made by a sledgehammer on Clare's front door could have easily been mistaken for a horse kicking the wooden wall of his stall not ten yards away. Race-horse stables were never silent places even in the dead of night.

"Do you think we should still call the police?" Angela said.

"What for?" I asked.

"If only to get an incident number for the insurance."

"But nothing is missing."

"The front door will need replacing and that must cost something," Angela said. "When we got burgled two years ago, we needed a police number before the insurance company would pay for anything."

"Much too complicated," I said. "The insurance will be in Geoff Grubb's name, and there'll probably be an excess on it that'd be more than the cost of the door anyway. Much easier if we just fix it ourselves without involving the police. For a start, we'd be here all day waiting for them to turn up."

Angela shrugged her shoulders. "I suppose you're right."

We went inside.

"It's really strange being here," Angela said, standing in the middle of the sitting room. "You know, without Clare."

I suppose I'd become a little used to it. I went over and gave her a hug while she sobbed gently on my shoulder.

The tears also welled in my eyes. First Clare and now Emily. Was there any limit to grief?

I SAT at Clare's desk, making some phone calls on the landline, while Angela cleared out the kitchen. I tried to tell her that she didn't need to bother, but she'd simply said that being busy would help take her mind off Emily.

I suppose she was right, but a renewed lethargy had come over me. That feeling of *What's the point?* had returned.

After a while, I pulled myself together and rang DCI Coaker.

"Any news about my phone and computer?" I asked him. "I'm desperate for them."

"They're here at police headquarters in Huntingdon."

"Can I come and collect them?" I asked.

"I'm just waiting for clearance from my superintendent," he said. "He may decide that they are evidence."

"How come?"

"Computers are routinely investigated for evidence in all crimes."

"You won't find much on mine," I said. "I only use it to access horseracing data as part of my job. And occasionally for making bets."

"Nevertheless, it will need to be checked."

"How about my phone?" I asked. "I need one of the numbers on it."

"I'll see what I can do. Call me back in twenty minutes."

I spent the time using the Yellow Pages to find a local builder who could send someone around as soon as possible to fix the broken door, and then I called a Newmarket rental company and arranged for them to deliver a car to the cottage.

I didn't know yet how I was going to replace my old Ford, but, in the meantime, I urgently needed some wheels, not least to get to Brighton races the following afternoon and Kempton Park on Wednesday and Thursday evenings, not that I really felt like going back to work.

I was completely wrung out, both physically and mentally.

"What shall I do with all the pots and pans, and the crockery?" Angela asked, putting her head around the door. "Were they Clare's? Or did they come with the cottage?"

"I've no idea." I sighed, dragging myself reluctantly to my feet. "I'll go and ask in Geoff Grubb's office. I need to go in there anyway, and they might know."

Better than that, Geoff's secretary had a full inventory of what was in the cottage when Clare had moved in.

"Don't worry too much if it doesn't match what's in there now," she said, handing me a printed list. "It's been years since Clare moved in."

I gave the list to Angela, who eagerly disappeared with it back into the kitchen.

I checked that twenty minutes had passed and then again called DCI Coaker.

"My super says you can have all your stuff back."

"Great. How do I collect it?"

"The forensic computer guy is just finishing examining your hard drive."

I thought it was a gross invasion of my privacy and I said so.

"Sorry," he said, "but the items were in Mrs. Lowther's possession at the time of her death and therefore they have to be checked."

"So when can I collect it?"

"Where are you now?" he asked.

"Newmarket," I said.

"I'm going to Cambridge shortly. I'll take everything with me. You can collect it anytime after one o'clock from Parkside police station on the eastern ring road."

"Good. Thanks."

"And I've got your phone here for that number you need."

"Oh, thank you," I said. "I need the number for Detective Sergeant Sharp. It should be in my contacts list under S."

I could hear him pushing the buttons of my phone.

"Here you are." He read out the number and I wrote it down. "Can I ask why you want to speak to DS Sharp?"

"He's the Metropolitan Police officer who's investigating my sister's suicide. She fell to her death in London last month."

"Clare Shillingford," he said almost to himself. "Of course, the jockey. Now I recognize the name. I'm sorry."

"Thanks," I said. "It's not been a great couple of weeks."

"No," he agreed.

"What news of your investigation of last night?"

"None that I can give you, I'm afraid. How are you feeling?"

"Rather sore," I said, "but I'll live."

Unlike Emily.

I USED the number DCI Coaker had given me to call Detective Sergeant Sharp, but he was unavailable. I left a message on his voice mail asking him to call me back as soon as possible. "I've got some fresh evidence about my sister's death," I said, "from the hotel."

Angela brought me in a cup of coffee.

"I'm afraid we've only got powdered milk," she said.

I smiled at her. "Fine by me."

Angela sat on the arm of the sofa, the same sofa where Emily and I had snuggled down together on Saturday evening.

"Oh God!" I said, sighing again. "Life is so bloody at times."

"You really liked Emily, didn't you?"

"Yes," I said. "And I feel it was my fault she was killed."

"Why?"

"Because I didn't take enough care. I should have seen the car sooner."

"You can't blame yourself," Angela said, trying to comfort me.

"But I do."

"Have the police any idea who was driving?" Angela asked.

"Not that they'll tell me."

"Maybe it was Emily's ex-husband. From what I hear, he has a fiery temper. Perhaps he didn't like her going out with somebody else."

"She told me at Tatiana's party they were divorced," I said, "but they weren't quite. No decree absolute, apparently. Technically, she was still married to him."

"So he will still inherit her house. Now, there's a motive for murder if ever there was one."

Angela, I thought, was also guilty of watching too much television, but it made about as much sense as anything else.

"I am sure the police will have interviewed him," I said. "Or, at least, they will have inspected his car. There must be some damage to the roof where I hit it." And some blood underneath, I thought, where Emily had gone.

"How are you getting on in the kitchen?" I asked, changing the subject.

"Done," she said, forcing a smile. "I've thrown away the food that was spoiled, and stacked up on the counter everything that wasn't on the inventory. But we need some boxes to pack it in."

"I'll get some," I said, "just as soon as the rental car arrives."

"Do you need me anymore, then?" she asked, getting to her feet.

"Not if you'd rather get off," I said, also standing up. "Thank you so much for coming to get me. It's made a huge difference."

We both hugged each other again, neither of us seemingly wanting to be the first to pull back. I felt closer to my elder sister at that point than I had ever before.

"Is everything all right in your world?" I asked, perhaps sensing something.

"Oh, yes and no," she said with a sigh. "We're just desperately short of money, like everyone else, and that was not helped by that damn party. And then the bank keeps talking about making Nick's job part-time, or even nonexistent altogether, and where would he get another job at his age?"

"But you and he are all right?"

"We seem to argue a lot more these days, mostly about money, but I think we're fine." She didn't sound too convinced. "Though I don't know how we're going to afford Tatiana's university fees next year."

It was she who was now close to tears.

"How about a student loan?" I said. "Get her to apply now."

"But it would saddle her with so much debt for the future."

"Better for her to have a debt in the future," I said, "than to have her parents split up in the present due to worries over money."

"You make everything sound so simple."

"I'd happily talk to Nick if you would like me to."

She laughed. "We always said that you couldn't arrange the proverbial piss-up in a brewery, but now you're more organized than the rest of us."

Was I? I didn't feel like it at the moment.

The telephone rang and I picked it up.

"Hello," I said.

"Mr. Shillingford?"

"Yes."

"This is Detective Sergeant Sharp."

"Oh, right. Thank you for calling back. Can you hold a second?" I put my hand over the mouthpiece. "It's the policeman dealing with Clare's death," I said to Angela.

"I'll go," she mouthed at me. "Call me later."

She gave me a peck on the cheek and left.

"Sorry about that," I said to the detective sergeant. "Someone was just leaving."

"You said in your message that you have some new evidence?"

"Yes," I said. "It would seem that one of the Hilton Hotel staff believes that there may have been a man in my sister's room when she fell from the balcony."

There was a pause on the other end of the line.

"Did you actually interview any of the hotel staff?" I asked. "It seems that my sister's arrival at the hotel caused quite a stir because she had no luggage."

I could tell from his continued silence that the answer to my question was no, he hadn't interviewed anyone at the hotel.

"But the suicide note," he said.

"I don't care about the note," I said angrily. "I want to know why my sister died."

"The inquest will establish that in due course," he said formally.

"But not if no one investigates anything first."

"It's the coroner's staff who are responsible for investigating the death," he said. "The police would be involved only if a crime had occurred."

"But I think a crime might have occurred," I said. "And anyway, the coroner's office hasn't been in touch with me. I haven't even had a copy of the report of her autopsy."

"I did discuss the cause of death with your father, as next of kin," he said somewhat defensively. "And it would not be usual for copies of an autopsy report to be issued to the family prior to the inquest. That's when the coroner will deal with any matters that might have arisen during the examination of the body."

"What sort of matters?" I asked.

"Any medical conditions that might have been present."

"And were there any medical conditions present?" I asked.

"Nothing pertinent to her death."

"Hold on a minute." I took in what he'd just said. "So there *was* something, then, but it didn't have anything to do with her death."

"There was nothing," he said, "other than her being pregnant."

21

What did you say?" I asked him in astonishment.

"I said there was nothing else, other than her being pregnant."

"Pregnant?" I almost shouted it into the phone.

"I assumed you knew," DS Sharp said. "Miss Shillingford was six or seven weeks pregnant when she died."

I was flabbergasted. I sat there staring at the wall above the desk not really knowing what to think.

"But surely you might have thought that being pregnant could have been pertinent to her death," I said.

"In what way?" he asked.

"Well, for a start it might have affected her state of mind, to say nothing of the hormone changes that must accompany pregnancy."

He said nothing.

"And," I went on, "it would have been nice to have known

at her funeral. Prayers could have been said for the unborn child."

"As I said, I assumed you knew. Your father had been informed."

Bloody hell, I thought.

Why hadn't the stupid old bastard said something? Probably because he was embarrassed by the fact that his unmarried daughter was pregnant.

God save me from my parents and their old-fashioned opinions.

"I'm sorry," DS Sharp said finally, "I should have told you."

"Yes, you should have," I said, "but at least you're telling me now. And there is something else I'd like to know."

"Fire away," he said, clearly relieved that I hadn't shouted at him more.

"Is there any CCTV footage from the hotel? Maybe for when Clare arrived and checked in? I've been to the hotel lobby, and there are cameras all over the place, and also some on the elevators. She must have been filmed by lots of them."

"Yes," he said, "I have copies of all the hotel's CCTV recordings for that evening. I suppose you want to see them?"

"You suppose correctly," I said. "Where are they?"

"At Charing Cross police station."

"Can I come and have a look?" I asked.

"I can't think that it will do any good," he said, "but I suppose so."

"Later this afternoon?"

"I'll be here until about six," he said. "Come to the main entrance on Agar Street and ask for me."

I looked at my watch. It was a quarter to one, and it would

take me a good two hours to get there, especially as I had to go
via Cambridge to collect my bag.

And there were a couple of other things I had to do first.

"I'll try and be there by five."

THE MAN FROM the builder's arrived soon after one o'clock,
followed closely by a woman from the car rental company with
a shiny new navy blue Honda Civic.

Suddenly I felt I was back in business. I could now leave the
cottage secure and also get around.

I left the builder's man tut-tutting about the state of the door
and how he would need to replace some of the framing, as well
as the lock, which was bent beyond repair, and drove the Honda
out of Newmarket along the Bury Road and into Austin Reynolds's driveway.

I didn't bother with his front door, which I assumed would
be locked. Instead, I drove down the side of the house to his
office, and then I simply walked in.

There was racing that Monday at Pontefract in the north and
Windsor in the south, and Austin Reynolds didn't have any
runners at either meeting. I'd checked in the *Racing Post* when
I'd been in Geoff Grubb's stable office collecting the inventory
for the cottage.

And just to make sure he was home, I'd called his house
earlier and he'd answered, although I'd hung up without
speaking.

I hoped he might be in his office and I was right. He was
sitting in a leather armchair, watching RacingTV's coverage
from Windsor.

"What the bloody hell do you think you're doing?" he blustered, standing up. "Walking in like this without so much as a by-your-leave?"

"At least your door was unlocked," I said, "so I didn't need to use a sledgehammer."

That shut him up and he sat down again.

Austin Reynolds would have made the world's worst poker player. Every thought and emotion was readable in his face. And he was suddenly scared, shrinking back into the armchair like a small child caught with his hand in the cookie jar.

I shouted at him. "Do you think I'm an idiot or something?"

He shook his head slightly, although I did think that it had been pretty stupid of me to leave the money and the blackmail note in the cottage.

"Where is it?" I asked, drawing myself up to my full six feet two inches and purposefully standing over him in a menacing manner.

"Where is what?" he asked back.

"The blackmail note you took from Clare's cottage."

"I burned it," he said with an air of triumph in his voice. "In the fireplace in the drawing room, along with the other one."

I bet he hadn't burned the money, but I did expect that the envelope had gone the same way. Without the envelope, and the words written on it, the money was meaningless.

"So what are you going to do now?" I asked him, reducing my apparent threat by moving away to his right and perching on the corner of his desk.

"What do you mean?"

"Are you going to pay?" I asked.

"Er . . . I haven't decided yet."

"Ten thousand is a lot of money," I said.

"Yes," he agreed.

"And you've just burned the things I'd hoped to use to catch the bastard."

"I have to protect myself first." He said it in a way that made me think he had rehearsed that line many times before in his head.

"By breaking in to other people's houses?"

"If necessary, yes."

"Have you received the payment instructions?"

"Not yet."

"Let me know when you do."

"Why should I?" he asked.

"Because if you don't, we won't be able to catch him, and he'll simply ask for more next time."

Austin shivered.

"And my advice would be," I said, "don't pay him this time either."

"But he could tell the authorities about me laying the horse."

"Indeed, he could," I said, "but I don't believe he has any evidence to back up his claims." I thought about Toby Woodley's stolen briefcase. "In fact, I don't really believe that the person who sent you the note last week has the faintest idea what he's blackmailing you for. I think he's just an opportunist who's taking advantage of something he found."

And, I thought, he's being far too greedy. If he'd asked Austin Reynolds and Harry Jacobs for a thousand or two, they probably would have just paid and never said anything about it to me, or to anyone else. It had been the size of the most recent demand that had been the all-consuming factor in their behavior.

"Are you certain about that?" Austin asked.

"No," I replied, "I'm not. But I am certain about something else. If you pay the ten thousand, the next demand will be for even more."

He looked absolutely miserable.

"What do you want me to do?" he asked pitifully.

"I want you to pass the payment instructions to me as soon as you get them and then do nothing."

"Nothing?" he said. "How about the money?"

"There will be no money," I said. "You're not paying."

"But . . . what if you're wrong? What if he has got the evidence?"

"What evidence could he have anyway?" I asked. "How did you lay the horse in the first place?"

"I used my wife's credit card account. It's still in her maiden name."

"But isn't her billing address the same as yours?"

He said nothing and just looked down at his feet.

How stupid could you get? I thought.

The bloody man deserved to be blackmailed.

NEXT I WENT into Newmarket, to the offices of the Injured Jockeys Fund in Victoria Way. I'd already called and spoken to Mrs. Green, the lady who had organized the dinner at the Hilton Hotel on the night that Clare had died.

"Did you have a nice holiday?" I'd asked her.

"Oh yes, wonderful, thank you," Mrs. Green replied. "The weather in Portugal was fantastic, just like high summer here."

"Good," I said, laying on the charm.

"But I was so sorry to hear about your dear sister. It was a real shock, especially as I was quite used to seeing her round the town. I live down near Mr. Grubb's stables. She was always so lovely."

"Thank you," I said to her, meaning it. "But the reason I called was that I was hoping you might be able to help me."

"Of course."

"I'm trying to obtain the guest list for your charity night at the Hilton."

"Oh." There had been a slight pause. "I suppose it would be all right to give it to you. The seating plan was on display on the night, so it can hardly be confidential, can it? One has to be so careful these days with that damn Data Protection Act. I wouldn't be able to give you their addresses."

"Just the names will be great."

"I'd rather not e-mail it to you, if you don't mind." Mrs. Green clearly had not been completely convinced that she wasn't breaking some rule or other. "But I could print out another copy of the seating plan, if you'd like. After all, we never had them back at the end of the evening, and you could've just taken it off one of the boards in the hotel."

"Indeed, I could have," I said, playing along with her game.

I had arranged to collect it from the charity's offices and it was waiting for me at the reception desk, sealed in one of those ubiquitous white envelopes.

I sat outside in the car and opened it.

I didn't really know what I was looking for, so I wasn't too disappointed that nothing leapt out at me from the sheet of paper.

Not that I didn't recognize most of the names. I did.

They included many of the great and the good of British racing, coming together to support one of the sport's major charities.

Mr. and Mrs. Mitchell Stacey were listed, as expected, but the other guests at their table were not, at least not by name, simply denoted as "(+10)" after their hosts.

And that was true for lots of the tables, many of which had been taken by the evening's sponsors or by other companies, with only the sponsor or company name shown.

I went back inside the offices to ask Mrs. Green if she had a complete list of everyone who had attended the event.

"Sorry," she said, "the seating plan is all I have. The table hosts put their own place cards out."

I thanked her anyway and drove the Honda back to Clare's cottage to find that the man from the builder's was just finishing the repair to the front door.

"It looks great," I said, inspecting his handiwork. "Thank you."

"Where shall I send the bill?"

"Send it to Austin Reynolds." I started to give him the address, but he already knew it.

"Yeah, we do lots of work for Mr. Reynolds," he said, packing up his tools. "The firm is currently building some new stables at his yard."

I wondered whether Austin would keep his trainer's license long enough to use them.

"**WELL?**" said DS Sharp. "Do you recognize anyone?"

"Quite a few," I said.

We were in a darkened video studio at Charing Cross police station and had spent over an hour looking through the CCTV footage from the hotel lobby the night Clare had died.

"While I was driving down here," I said, "I wondered if

someone had been trying to kill me in order to stop me seeing these films."

"Kill you?" he said, surprised.

"Yes. There have been two attempts on my life this last week and I've been trying to work out why."

I described the two incidents to him, including the murder of Emily, and he suddenly became more interested.

"Have you spoken to the Cambridgeshire Police about the CCTV?"

"No," I said, "nor to the Surrey lot. I only thought that it might be the reason on the way here from Newmarket this afternoon."

"So?" he said eagerly. "Is there anything on the films that was worth killing to prevent you seeing?"

"Nothing that's very obvious," I said.

It had been very strange, and somewhat emotional, to see the silent images of Clare walking into the hotel lobby and up to the reception desk. I'd seen it from about four different angles, but none of them had shown a closeup of her face or given any indication of her state of mind.

The hotel lobby had been relatively empty as she checked in, but later, as the Injured Jockeys dinner had evidently finished in the ballroom upstairs, large groups of dinner-jacketed guests could be seen making their way through to the hotel exit, and it was many of these that I recognized.

Mitchell and Sarah Stacey had been in one of the groups, obviously saying their good-byes to the owners as they all collected coats from the cloakroom.

One of the cameras even covered the area outside the hotel's front door and it had clearly shown people queuing for taxis in a rather strange, silent green-tinged world.

"That camera works on infrared after dark," DS Sharp had said, "hence the greeny pictures and the rather zombie-like eyes."

I sat, looking once more at the moving images, and thought about what had been going on exactly fifteen floors above.

"Did it capture Clare?" I asked.

We both knew what I meant. Did it capture the impact of Clare's body on the sidewalk?

"Yes, it did," he said. "But that has been cropped from this copy."

I was relieved. I didn't have to make the decision to stop watching or not.

I looked up at the clock on the wall. "I thought you were leaving at six."

"I was," he said. "But I've nothing to go home to except an empty, cold apartment, so I'm quite happy to stay here as long as you want."

I, too, had nothing to go home to but an empty, cold apartment.

An empty, cold life.

A wave of pain and grief washed over me. Hold on, I told myself sharply, this was not the time or the place. I needed to make the most of this opportunity.

"How about the cameras in the elevators?" I asked.

"They're not very good," he said.

"In what way?"

"They don't really show people's faces. It's all rather top-down."

He pushed some buttons on the machines, and, in turn, we watched the recordings from each of the four cameras.

As he'd said, the results weren't great. The images were a bit like those filmed for a "Spot the Mystery Guest" slot on television quiz shows, giving only tantalizingly brief glimpses of people's faces, and from unusual angles.

At least we could tell which way the elevator was going as the cameras just captured the lit-up down arrows in the top corner of the images whenever the elevators were going down.

"I think this one is your sister," said DS Sharp. "The timing is right."

I watched as a young woman in jeans, pink shirt, and blue baseball cap entered the elevator and turned around, leaning up against the back wall. After a while she left the elevator. She was alone throughout.

"I timed the elevators," DS Sharp said. "It takes precisely that long to get from the lobby to the fifteenth floor."

"It certainly looked like Clare," I said, "but it's not easy to be absolutely sure with that cap."

"It's also not helped by the poor resolution of the cameras," he said. "They have such small lenses, and that tends to distort the images."

So assuming it had been Clare in the film, she had gone up to the room on her own.

"According to Carlos Luis Sanchez, one of the hotel porters, she was followed up to her room by two men, one after the other, and the first one was wearing a bow tie."

DS Sharp raised his eyebrows in my direction.

"Been busy, have we?" he said.

"I went there primarily to see where Clare died," I said. "But while I was there, I asked some questions."

"Is this Carlos Sanchez the one who says there was someone in your sister's room when she fell?"

"No," I said. "That was his friend Mario."

"Mario?" I could tell from his tone that he was somewhat skeptical.

"Yes, Mario," I said, ignoring him. "Apparently Mario is one of the night porters. According to Carlos, Mario saw the man leave the hotel after Clare had died."

While we had been talking, the CCTV footage from the elevators had continued to play on the screens, and I suddenly saw a face that I recognized.

"Stop!" I said loudly. "Can you play that again?"

He pushed some buttons on the desk in front of him, and the images went slowly backward.

"There," I said. "Stop."

There were three people in the elevator. A young man and a woman, who were too intent on fondling each other to notice anything going on around them, and a second, older man, wearing a dinner jacket and a black bow tie. This second man glanced ever so briefly up at the camera fixed above the kissing heads, allowing it to catch an image of him full face.

"Do you know that man?" DS Sharp asked.

"Yes, I do," I said, continuing to stare straight into the eyes on the screen. "It's a racehorse trainer called Austin Reynolds."

"CAN YOU TELL which floor he got out on?" I asked.

There was a time code superimposed across the top of all the video footage, and DS Sharp inched the images forward frame by frame, measuring the time between Austin entering the elevator and him leaving it.

"Assuming the elevator is going up, it is about right for the fifteenth floor, but it's impossible to say exactly. The camera position doesn't allow us to see the doors, so we can't be sure how long the elevator was actually moving."

"What time did he get in?"

He wound the video back to the exact moment.

"Twenty-two thirty-one and seventeen seconds."

Just after half past ten. Ten minutes after Clare had checked in.

Was that a coincidence? As Lisa, *The Morning Line*'s producer, had said, coincidences did happen. But was this really one of them?

"Do you have a list of those staying at the hotel that night?" I asked.

"No," he said, "I'm afraid not. But we could find out from the hotel."

"Let's check first to see if he leaves."

We went on watching the video recordings.

"Is that him?" I suddenly asked, seeing someone that resembled Austin enter the elevator. I shouted at the image, "Dammit, man, look up at the camera!"

He didn't, of course, and I wasn't very certain it had been him.

"Can you check the lobby films for that precise time?"

DS Sharp again pressed his buttons, and the wide view of the lobby reappeared on one of the screens. He wound the recording on until the time code was the same as for the shot in the elevator. He then let it run.

Austin Reynolds was clearly visible walking from the direction of the elevators to the main exit.

Without being asked, DS Sharp pulled up the shot from outside with its zombie-like eyes. Austin Reynolds had to wait about four minutes in a queue before he climbed into a taxi and was driven away.

"Twenty-two fifty-eight," DS Sharp said, reading the time on the screen. "Mr. Reynolds left the hotel more than half an hour before your sister died."

Surely no one would kill to prevent me seeing that.

"Unless he came back," I said. But even I knew that was unlikely. "Carlos said there was a second man, so let's keep looking."

We spent another twenty minutes looking at the videos from the elevators, but there was no one who I even remotely recognized getting into any of them.

"According to Mario, the second man left the hotel during the commotion that followed Clare's fall."

DS Sharp moved the recordings forward to twenty-three thirty.

I never realized how busy hotel elevators could be. Hardly a second went past without each of the four having people in it, moving in one direction or the other, as the hotel guests came back from the theater, or diners from the high-floor restaurant and bar descended to their rooms or to the street-level exits.

But still there was no one I recognized.

At precisely twenty-three thirty-two and fifteen seconds, a man wearing a dark overcoat and a blue baseball cap entered an elevator already half full with people going down. He didn't look up at the camera—in fact, he seemed to be purposefully looking away from it, and also away from the other people.

"Is that the same baseball cap that Clare had on when she checked in?" I asked.

DS Sharp stopped and reran the film.

"It might be."

"Did you find the cap in Clare's room?" I asked. "Or was she wearing it when she fell?"

The detective sergeant didn't answer.

"Where are her things?" I asked him. "Even if she didn't have a handbag, she must have had her car keys."

"There was nothing left in the room except the note."

"How about her car? Where's that?"

No answer.

"And her phone?" I asked. "Where did that go? And did she call anyone before she died?"

Anyone other than me.

"I'll have to investigate," DS Sharp said, clearly uncomfortable.

Past time for that, I thought. Well past. He had obviously been so convinced by the note that it was straightforward suicide that he really hadn't bothered looking for anything else.

I watched on the screen as the elevator emptied, presumably at ground level.

"OK," I said, "can you find that man in the lobby?"

He fiddled with the equipment, and a wide shot of the lobby appeared on a screen.

"There," I said, pointing.

We watched as the man walked briskly across the lobby.

Lots of other people were running toward the main doors, and some were staggering back inside with wide eyes, holding their heads or hugging one another. I didn't want to think about what they had just witnessed on the sidewalk outside.

The man appeared to be ignoring the disturbance just to his right, marching straight on toward the left-hand side of the main exit.

"Can't you zoom in?" I asked.

DS Sharp tried, but the image became very fuzzy and indistinct.

"I think he's got his collar turned up," the sergeant said. "And maybe a scarf round his face as well."

Why would anyone wear a coat with the collar turned up and a scarf when that particular September evening had been so warm? Was he trying to hide his face from the CCTV cameras?

"Try another angle," I said.

He brought up the image from the camera near the elevators. It showed the man clearly from behind as he walked away. There was no chance of seeing his face from that direction.

DS Sharp went through every camera position in turn, but there was no clear image of the man's features.

"How about the one outside?" I asked, realizing as I said it that any images from out there would also show Clare's body on the ground.

"Are you sure?" the sergeant asked. "I'll have to get the original recording rather than the copy."

"No," I said, "don't. If the man took such efforts inside the hotel not to be seen, he'd hardly let it happen once he was outside. He'd have just gone on walking with his head down."

"I can get it if you want," he said. "We only made the copy without the last bit because we didn't want some unscrupulous idiot uploading it on YouTube. The original is securely locked in my office safe."

I could feel my heart beating.

"No," I said, "I'm sure it wouldn't show anything we can't already see."

"Maybe I'll look at it later," he said, "just to be sure."

"Right." I breathed deeply and was reminded of my broken ribs by a sharp stabbing pain in my left side. But it was in my head that a bell was ringing.

"Could you please show me that shot again of the man walking away from the camera?"

DS Sharp pulled up the images onto the screen.

There was something about the way the man moved—an easy, lolloping long stride, with his head bobbing up and down slightly with each step.

Maybe I didn't need to see the man's face in order to recognize him.

22

I arrived back home at five past ten, and it was as lonely and cold as I had feared. And it was starting to rain.

Ever since leaving Newmarket I'd kept a keen eye on the Honda's rearview mirror to ensure I wasn't being followed, but nevertheless I was very wary when I parked the car on the street outside my apartment and walked quickly to the front door.

I let myself in and put my Chinese takeout in the oven to keep warm while I collected the rest of the things from the car.

Street lighting in my part of Edenbridge could hardly be described as comprehensive. There was a lamppost about twenty yards away in each direction up and down the road, but their meager glow hardly made it to my door. Consequently I was spooked by every shadow, seeing in my mind a potential murderer behind every bush.

My ribs were too painful to carry much at once, so it took

me six separate damp trips to bring in the boxes of Clare's paperwork, plus other things like the racing trophies and some of the stuff that Angela had sorted in the kitchen.

With the help of one of Geoff Grubb's stable staff, Clare's clothes and shoes had been packed into my rented Honda, and I'd driven them to a charity shop in Newmarket High Street. There had been great excitement and giggling amongst the three middle-aged women who ran it when they unpacked the bag overflowing with the black lace undies.

"We normally don't resell people's underwear," one of them said, chuckling and holding up a pair, "but these are beautiful, and I think we'll make an exception. Once they've been washed, of course." She had giggled again, and I rather wished I'd just thrown them all away.

I was very glad when everything from the car was finally in the apartment and I was able to lock my front door with me safely inside. Not that I considered this particular home to be much of a castle. It had taken Austin Reynolds six mighty blows with a sledgehammer to break into Clare's cottage. Looking at the simple latch on my own front door, I thought a well-placed kick might be enough to gain entry. I'd never considered it much of an issue as I had precious little that anyone would want to steal. But was it enough to keep out a murderer while I was sleeping?

I propped one of my two kitchen chairs against the door, tucking its back under the doorknob. It probably wouldn't be enough to keep out an averagely determined child but at least it might give me a few moments' warning.

I then sat on my other kitchen chair at the table to eat chicken chop suey and egg fried rice that I'd picked up at a local Chinese restaurant in Edenbridge. It was not especially tasty, but I was hungry, as I hadn't eaten anything since my bland hospital breakfast at seven o'clock that morning.

Had that really been only this morning? So much had happened since then.

I pushed the empty plate away and leaned back in the chair.

Where did I go from here? I wondered. And I didn't mean only physically.

I cracked open the fortune cookie that Mr. Woo at the Forbidden City restaurant had kindly put in the brown bag with the fried rice and chop suey.

Use your talents wisely. That's why you have them.

I read and reread the Chinese proverb on the little strip of paper.

What particular talents did I have that I should use wisely?

I DIDN'T SLEEP very well. Partly due to the pain in my side, but mostly because of overlapping and disturbing dreams involving both Clare and Emily.

I lay awake in the darkness, trying to think what I should do.

"Can you positively identify that man?" Detective Sergeant Sharp had asked me in the Charing Cross Police's video room.

"What do you mean by positively identify?" I asked him back.

"Could you stand up in a court of law and swear to his identity?"

"No," I said. "Of course I couldn't. I just think he walks a bit like someone I know."

The policeman shook his head. "I'd need much more than

that to interview anyone. Lots of people walk like that. And anyway, there's no law against walking out of a hotel with your collar up and your head down even if there is someone dead on the sidewalk outside."

"But he might have been in the room when Clare fell."

"That doesn't mean there was a crime," he said. "I'll grant you, if there was someone in the room when she fell it would almost certainly be relevant to the coroner and the inquest. The man would be able to testify as to what exactly had happened, but there is no evidence that he was involved in any criminal activity, so I can hardly arrest him. And then there's the suicide note."

"I'm not so sure it's a suicide note," I said, "it's not very specific."

"It's a good deal more specific than some others I've seen." I waited while he'd fetched a photocopy of the note from his office. He then read the last two sentences to me out loud. *"Please don't think badly of me. I am so sorry."* He put the note down on the desk in front of me. "I'm afraid, Mr. Shillingford, that it looks very much like a suicide note to me."

Oh, Clare, how could you?

I TOSSED AND TURNED some more, albeit gingerly, and got up to go to the bathroom just before seven with the coming of the morning light.

I felt dreadful, and my reflection in the mirror showed me as gray-skinned with dark circles under my eyes. I'd probably overdone the amount of weight that I should have attempted carrying with broken ribs.

My side was very sore, but my breathing seemed fine, so I swallowed a couple of heavy-duty painkillers and went back to lie on my bed until they worked.

The phone vibrated on my bedside table.

"Hello," I said, noting the Newmarket number on the caller ID.

"This is Austin Reynolds. I've received the payment instructions in this morning's mail."

"Yes?" I said, encouraging him to continue.

"Just as before," he said, "I have to leave the money in a brown envelope under my car in a racetrack parking lot."

"Where?" I asked. "And when?"

"Kempton. Tomorrow night."

"What does it say exactly?" I asked.

I could hear him nervously rustling the paper. *"Put the cash in used fifties in a brown padded envelope and leave it up against the inside of the offside rear wheel of your car when you arrive at Kempton races tomorrow night. Park in the parking lot, then walk away into the racetrack. Don't look back."*

"Good," I said. "Do you have anything declared for tomorrow night?"

"One," he said. "I've got a new London owner who wants his horse to run. It's in the fourth. What should I do?"

"Nothing," I said. "Just go to the races and walk away from your car. And don't leave the ten thousand."

"I haven't got that sort of cash anyway."

"What car will you be driving?"

"My dark blue BMW." He gave me the registration.

"Will it start?" I asked, remembering the previous Saturday morning.

"Yes," he said, "I've had a new battery fitted."

"Remember," I said, "just park it and then walk away."

"Shouldn't I bend down as if I were putting something by the back wheel?"

"If you like," I said. "Yes, perhaps that will be good just in case our man is watching you arrive. In fact, place a padded envelope there. It doesn't matter if it's empty."

"I'll put a few stones from my driveway in it to prevent it blowing away."

I hadn't quite worked out yet how I would keep an eye on Austin's car at Kempton the following evening, especially as I was due to be commentating there.

"I don't like it," Austin said. "I don't like it one bit. What if he goes to the racing authorities?"

"So would you rather pay him the ten thousand?" I asked.

"No," he said miserably. "I can't."

It wasn't the only thing he was going to be miserable about.

I changed the subject. "Did you enjoy the Injured Jockeys Fund event at the London Hilton?"

"What?" he asked. "But that was weeks ago."

"Less than three weeks," I said. Although it certainly felt like longer. "Why didn't you tell me you'd been up to see Clare after the dinner?"

There was silence on the other end of the line.

"Well?" I said. "Why didn't you tell me, or at least tell the police?"

"I was frightened," Austin said. "People might have thought I had something to do with her death."

"And did you?" I asked.

"No," he answered quickly. "She was alive when I left her."

"I know."

"How could you know?" he asked.

"The hotel CCTV cameras picked you up leaving half an hour before she fell."

"Oh," he said. "Good."

Even across the telephone line, I could hear the relief in his voice.

"So why did you go up to her room?" I asked, not wanting his relief to be too long-lasting. "And how did you know she was even there?"

"She texted me," he said. "It was rather embarrassing, actually. It was during the speeches. I'd forgotten to turn my phone off."

"What exactly did she text?"

"She said she had to talk to me about Bangkok Flyer's race that afternoon and that it might be a problem."

"What time was this?"

"Hold on, I'll get my phone."

I could hear him moving in the background.

"Half past nine," he said. "Nine twenty-seven, to be precise."

About ten to fifteen minutes after she'd left me at Haxted Mill.

"She said she was coming straight to see me in Newmarket, but I texted back to say I wasn't at home, I was at that dinner at the Hilton. She then said she'd come to the hotel."

She must have been really worried.

But she wouldn't have checked into a room just to see Austin. She could have spoken to him in the lobby or in the bar. She must have checked in to stay the night with the other man, her mystery lover.

"How did you know which room she was in?"

"She texted me again later, saying she was there, giving me the room number."

"So you went up to see her?"

"Yes," he said, "as soon as the dinner was over. But I stayed in her room only about ten or so minutes, then I left and went home. I caught the eleven-thirty train from King's Cross. My wife picked me up from Cambridge station. She doesn't really like going to those big events in London."

"What did you and Clare talk about?" I asked.

"Not much, really," he said. "I remember that most of the time I was there she was arguing with one of the hotel security men about unlocking the balcony door. What's the point, she was saying, of having a balcony room if the balcony is locked? Anyway, the man unlocked it when I was there. I'm not really sure what it was about, but Clare kept calling me 'darling' and pretending to the man that she and I were going to spend the night together and therefore the door could be opened."

The "two in a room" rule, I thought.

"So what did Clare say after the man had gone?"

"She said that someone knew about her riding Bangkok Flyer to lose. She seemed quite worried about it. I asked her who it was, but she wouldn't tell me."

"It was me," I said.

"I know that now," Austin replied curtly.

"So what was so urgent that she had needed to see you that night?" I asked. "Why couldn't it wait until morning?"

He didn't reply.

"Come on," I said, "why was it so urgent?"

"Because we had planned to do it again the next day, in the last race at Newmarket, and she knew that I would lay the horse on the Internet early on Saturday morning. But she didn't want to go through with it. In fact, she said she'd never ever do it again. From now on, she was always going to ride to win."

I sat there, holding the phone, with tears streaming down my cheeks.

"Did she say anything about killing herself?" I asked, trying to keep emotion out of my voice.

"Not at all," he said. "She seemed happy, almost as if a weight had been lifted from her shoulders. That's why I couldn't believe it when I heard on *The Morning Line* the next day that she was dead."

"Did she say anything to you about writing a suicide note?"

"No, of course not," Austin said. "I told you, I don't think she was planning to kill herself when I left her."

What on earth had happened in the subsequent half hour?

ALMOST AS SOON as I had put my phone down it rang again, and this time it was my father. What the hell did he want at this time of the morning?

"Hello, Dad," I said as enthusiastically as I could manage. "How are you?"

"What's all this bloody nonsense in the newspaper?" he replied, as always ignoring the normal niceties of polite conversation.

"Which newspaper?" I asked.

"*UK Today.*"

Jim Metcalf, I thought. "What does it say?"

"Something about you being strangled last week." I could tell from his tone that he didn't believe it.

"That's right," I said. "That was why I crashed my car into Angela and Nicholas's gatepost on Friday night."

"What nonsense," he said. "You were drunk. I heard one of those policeman say so. He said you must have been blind drunk to hit that post so hard."

"Dad, I was not drunk. Someone was trying to kill me."

"Hmph." He clearly still didn't believe me.

"And whoever it was tried to murder me again on Sunday night."

"But why would anyone want to murder you?" He said it in a manner that I felt was rather belittling, as if I wasn't worthy of being murdered.

But it was still a good question.

I'd been asking myself the same thing for almost thirty-six hours, since the disaster in the Three Horseshoes parking lot.

And I hadn't yet come up with a credible answer.

"I don't know, Dad," I said. "But I intend to find out."

"And how are *you* going to do that?" he asked, his voice again full of doubt that I could do anything. Our little moment of mutual understanding that had existed at Clare's funeral had clearly evaporated.

I decided to ignore him. He had considered my whole life a disaster from the moment I'd told him, aged seventeen, that I wasn't going to university. In his narrow opinion not getting a degree was tantamount to failure, and the fact that I now earned at least twice what he ever had was completely immaterial.

Use your talents wisely. That's why you have them.

I did have talents and I suddenly realized how I could use them to unravel this mystery. I just hoped it was wise to do so.

I **DROVE** my rented Honda to Brighton races, checking frequently that I was not being followed.

I arrived early, well before the racing was due to start, as there were people I needed to see.

"No problem," said Derek, the RacingTV producer, when I asked him about my plans for the following evening at Kempton. "Night racing is always less frenetic than the afternoons because there's only a single meeting, so we'll have a full half an hour between races. Masses of time."

"Dead easy," said Jack Laver, the technician who ran the racetrack broadcast center.

More of the *easy*, I thought, and less of the *dead*.

I always liked racing at Brighton. It is one of the more unusual of the British racetracks in that, like Epsom and Newmarket, it is not a complete loop but a long, curving mile-and-a-half horseshoe-shaped track that runs along the undulating ridge of Race Hill, part of the South Downs range of chalk hills, two miles to the east of the city center.

The view from the top of the grandstand on that particular October Tuesday was magnificent. The Indian summer of the past weeks had been swept away by a series of Atlantic weather fronts that had finally cleared through overnight, leaving cool, crisp conditions with spectacular visibility.

Away to my right, the bright sunlight reflected with a million flashes off the surface of the sea, and in the far distance I could see a line of freighters making their way eastward toward the Straits of Dover.

To my left, I looked out across the roofs of houses in the valley below toward where the gate was being towed into position at the one-mile start, ready for the first race.

It was a truly beautiful day, the light azure sky contrasting with the lush dark green of the turf and the deep blues of the English Channel.

I sat on the chair in the commentary booth and badly missed Clare. She used to ride frequently at Brighton, often staying the night before or after with our parents at Oxted. She had last been here for the festival in August, and I could still remember her delight in riding three winners on opening day while I'd been commentating.

I smiled at the memory.

There had been nothing strange or unusual about her riding on that occasion, just magnificent judgment and timing, as she had swept up the hill to win the Brighton Mile Challenge Trophy, the big race of the day, by the shortest of short heads.

Commentators were expected to be unbiased and objective, but there had been nothing impartial and balanced about my words that day as I had cheered with delight as she had pulled off the last-gasp victory.

Now it seemed such a long time ago, and I grieved for the loss of any more such joyous days.

I WENT DOWN to the press room to find myself a bite to eat and a cup of coffee.

Jim Metcalf was there ahead of me, and he'd already eaten all the ham-and-mustard sandwiches from the selection provided.

"Did you see my piece today about you?" he asked.

"No," I replied. "But I've heard about it from my father. He says it's a load of rubbish."

Jim tossed a copy of it to me across the room. "It's only what was in that statement of yours."

"Yeah, but *UK Today* must be desperately short of news to have run that today when it happened last Friday," I said. "And anyway, you've completely missed the real story."

"What real story?" he asked slightly concerned.

"Whoever it was trying to kill me had another go on Sunday night, and they killed a friend of mine instead."

He stared at me. "Are you serious?"

"Absolutely," I said.

"Which friend?"

"Someone called Emily Lowther."

He was already typing her name into his laptop.

"The Three Horseshoes, Madingley," he said, reading from the screen.

"Very impressive," I said. "How do you do that?"

"Coroners' database of reports for the Department of Justice. It records every case referred to a coroner in England and Wales. If this Emily Lowther was killed in Madingley on Sunday night, then the coroner for the area would have been informed of her death, probably yesterday, or this morning at the very latest. Either way, it's now been entered on the database."

"Is it legal for you to have access to it?"

"Probably not," he said, "so I don't ask." He read the details on his screen. "This entry doesn't say anything about you."

"That's probably because I didn't die," I said. "Not quite."

"So who was Emily Lowther?" he asked.

"Just a friend."

"Was she that flash bird I saw you with at Newmarket last Saturday?"

"Do you spy on me all the time?" I asked.

"No, not always, but it was a bit difficult not to notice." He laughed. "Not the way you were pawing each other all afternoon."

"Yeah, well." I sighed deeply, trying hard not to lose my

composure. "It was her who was killed, but I think it was really me who was the target."

"Why do you think that?" he said.

"I just do." Although I remembered what Angela had said about Emily's husband having a motive to kill—to inherit her house.

"How was she killed?" Jim asked.

"Run down by a car with no lights on in the pub parking lot. I went over the top, she went under the wheels. I lived, she died."

"Do you want me to write about this as well?"

"Not really," I said.

"Then why are you telling me?"

"I don't know," I said with another heavy sigh, "I just needed to tell someone. I seem to be living a nightmare at the moment. First Clare and now Emily, and the police don't seem to be getting anywhere. They're even suggesting that it might have been a hit-and-run in the pub lot when I'm quite sure it was premeditated murder. And I've got the broken ribs to prove it."

"I'm sorry," he said. "Let me know if there's anything I can do."

I deduced from Jim's tone of voice that he also must believe that the car hitting us was probably an accident. The alternative just seemed too far-fetched.

"Jim," I said, "can I tell you something off the record?"

"Not if it's a news story," he said.

"It's about Toby Woodley."

"What about him?"

"You know you said he had an uncanny knack of sniffing

out real stories amongst all the gossip. Well, I think I know how he did it."

"Tell all," Jim said, his journalistic antennae starting to quiver madly.

"I'm not certain but I think that if Toby Woodley had even the slightest inkling that someone had been up to no good, he would send them a blackmail note asking for a paltry sum like two hundred pounds or he would go to the authorities."

"So?" said Jim.

"If they paid, then he knew he'd been right."

"Bloody hell!" Jim suddenly shouted. "The bastard did it to me."

"You're kidding?"

"No I'm not," he said. "I got this note last year from someone saying that they knew I'd used phone hacking to get a certain story and that if I didn't pay them two hundred quid they would go to the press-complaints people and report me."

"What did you do?"

"Well, as it happens I hadn't used hacking to get that particular story, so I ignored it. But I remember being really worried. I *had* used some information obtained from hacking to get another story round the same time, so I very nearly paid just to shut him up."

"But you didn't?"

"No," he said. "I was even told where and when to leave the money, but in the end I decided not to pay, and I never heard another thing. I'd all but forgotten about it."

"I think Woodley did it to everyone, and when someone took the bait he then demanded more, writing a story in his paper that was close to the truth but without mentioning anyone by name. I believe the stories were solely designed to give his victims the incentive to pay him the new, larger amounts."

"And do you think that's what got him murdered?"

"Yes," I said, "I do."

"The little creep," Jim said with feeling. "Got what he deserved, if you ask me."

"But there's someone else," I said.

"Someone else what?" he asked.

"Toby Woodley was murdered last Wednesday evening at Kempton, and I know of two people who have received blackmail demands that must have been mailed after he died."

"Who?" he asked eagerly.

"Ah, no," I said, "I'm not telling you that, on the record or off it. Suffice to say, they are both reliable sources."

"So who is this someone else?" Jim asked.

"I don't know, but I think it must be someone who was also being blackmailed because he seems to know Toby Woodley's payment method, and I reckon it must be the same person who killed him."

"Why couldn't it simply be an accomplice who's taken over?"

"Partly because I don't think Toby was the sort of man to have an accomplice, and also because of the missing briefcase."

"The famous Woodley briefcase."

"*Infamous*, more like," I said. "I'll bet that far from containing just his sandwiches, that briefcase held his blackmail notes and the details of all his victims. That's why he was always so protective of it. And now someone else is using what was found to go on with the blackmail."

"So what are you going to do about it?" Jim asked. "Go to the police?"

"Maybe," I said. "But that would almost definitely involve breaking confidences." I laughed. "Perhaps I'll just catch the murdering bastard myself."

"Oh yeah?" said Jim sarcastically. "You and whose army?"

23

I hadn't imagined there would be so many policemen. They stood in groups of two or three inside each of the racetrack entrances, with clipboards, asking everyone who came in if they had been there the previous Wednesday, the day of Toby Woodley's murder.

I had arrived at Kempton really early in order to help set up the equipment, but now I wasn't at all sure if the whole thing hadn't been a waste of time.

With all these coppers around, surely only a fool would attempt to collect blackmail money. But the blackmailer had been the one to specify the time and place, and you couldn't actually see the police from the parking lot.

I'd telephoned Austin Reynolds earlier just to check that he wasn't getting cold feet, and also to finalize when and where he was to park his car. I had to take a chance that the blackmailer wouldn't be made suspicious by Austin's parking close to where the RacingTV scanner would be.

"Park close to the big blue television broadcast vehicles that are at the far side of the parking lot, near the fence behind the saddling stalls."

"How can I do that?" Austin had asked. "Don't I have to go where I'm told by the parking lot attendants?"

"There won't be any attendants," I'd said. "They don't have them for the night meetings because parking is free and the crowds are small. People park where they like, mostly as close as they can to the enclosure entrances. There are always plenty of spaces. Arrive at precisely half past four and enter by the racetrack main gate on Staines Road. Drive round toward the television vehicles and try to choose a space with an unoccupied one alongside its right. I promise you the parking lot will not be busy, especially more than an hour before the first race."

"All right." He hadn't sounded very confident.

"Austin," I'd said. "This is all you have to do, so do it right."

I wasn't at all sure that he would even turn up at Kempton, but he did, and at precisely the right time, turning his large blue BMW through the main gate at exactly four-thirty.

I had been waiting for him out on Staines Road in the rented Honda Civic and I now pulled out into traffic and followed him into the racetrack parking lot and around to the TV trucks.

Austin parked in a free space just three away from the scanner and I pulled the Honda into the immediately alongside him on his right. Perfect, I thought. I couldn't have positioned the two cars better if I'd painted white crosses on the blacktop.

I climbed out of the Honda and walked directly to the scanner without looking once at Austin or his car. One never knew who was watching.

"Ideal," said Gareth, one of the bright young RacingTV technicians who had been as keen as mustard to help out. "Anything for some bleedin' excitement."

Gareth had spent the morning and afternoon setting up all the camera equipment around the racetrack, and he would take it all down again later after the racing had finished. He was only there in between times in case any part of the system broke down, then his job was to fix it. He always joked that he was the only member of the broadcast team who actively wanted something to go wrong in order to alleviate the mind-numbing boredom of the actual program.

Gareth didn't really like racing, but he absolutely loved television cameras.

"Can it be done?" I'd asked him.

"'Course it can, me old sugar," he'd replied in his strong London accent. "I can do bloody anything when it comes to cameras. Mr. Bleedin' Magic, I am."

And he was.

He hadn't even wanted to know why I needed a particular car to be kept under constant observation. To him, it was clearly just a game and the reasons for it didn't matter. "Ask no bleedin' questions," he'd said, "and I'll be told no bleedin' lies."

He'd set up one of the small handheld cameras in the back of the Honda so that it pointed out the side window behind the rear door, and he'd shown me how to park the car for maximum coverage. We now sat together in the scanner looking at a monitor that showed the images received from the camera through a link Gareth had established between the roof of the Honda and the signal-relay vehicle.

"Bleedin' marvelous," Gareth exclaimed, staring closely at the monitor. "Crackin' good picture, too, considerin' it only uses a normal Internet wireless link."

The wide-angle lens on the camera meant we could see all the way down the far side of Austin Reynolds's car right down to the ground, with a particularly good shot of the offside rear wheel, behind which I could already see the corner of a brown envelope sticking out.

"Can you run that back?" I asked Gareth.

"Sure," he said, and the image jerked slightly on the screen as he put the recording into reverse. Even when the tape was played backward, it was clear for us both to see Austin Reynolds as he'd climbed out of his car, opened the back door, removed his coat from the backseat, closed the door, put on the coat, and then leaned down to place a brown padded envelope behind the rear wheel before walking off toward the entrance to the enclosures.

"What's in the envelope?" Gareth asked, his inquisitiveness getting the better of him for a moment.

"Just some stones," I said.

"Diamonds?" Gareth was suddenly quite interested.

"No such luck," I said, laughing. "Just a few pieces of ordinary gravel to stop it from blowing away."

Gareth didn't ask me why Austin was placing a worthless envelope behind his rear offside wheel, which I was then going to such trouble to watch—*Ask no bleedin' questions and I'll be told no bleedin' lies.*

"How about the other camera?" I asked.

"No problem," he said, looking at another image on his monitor. "I'll just go and make a small adjustment."

He disappeared outside, and I watched the monitor as the camera moved slightly to the left and Austin's car came clearly into view, with the racetrack entrance beyond. This second camera was attached to the side of one of the receiving-dome frameworks on the roof of the signal-relay vehicle that was parked alongside the scanner.

Gareth returned and seemed satisfied with his handiwork.

"Right," he said. "That should do it. Good thing we've got no girls tonight or we'd be needin' that camera."

"Girls," in this instance, did not refer necessarily to woman-kind. It was the nickname for any presenters, male or female, who sat in the glass-fronted booth overlooking the parade ring and described the horses before a race. Someone once stated that the presenters had chatted away with each other like a pair of schoolgirls, and the nickname had stuck.

The use of such paddock booths was once routine, but now they are seen mostly at the big meetings only, where one of the small cameras is employed to briefly show the girls, mostly men, usually sitting side by side and wearing headphones.

No girls tonight.

Oh God! Don't remind me.

THE BLACKMAILER took the envelope at seven thirty-five just as the seven runners for the fourth race were being mounted in the parade ring and at the precise moment when Austin Reynolds was giving his jockey a leg up into the saddle.

By that time it was dark, and just like the CCTV camera

at the Hilton Hotel Gareth's two small ones had automatically switched to infrared, both assisted by an infrared lamp positioned on the signal-relay vehicle that bathed the area in radiation that was invisible to humans but clear as daylight to the cameras.

I nearly fell off my stool in the commentary booth, from which I hadn't moved since well before the first race. It was good that it didn't happen during a race commentary, I thought, or I would have completely lost the plot.

Jack Laver had worked his magic and installed not one but three monitors in the commentary booth, the extra two showing images from Gareth's hidden cameras.

And there was the blackmailer, bold as brass, walking over to Austin's car, bending down, removing the envelope, and stuffing it in his coat without stopping to open it and count his money—not that he'd find any.

And just for good measure, as he bent down he looked straight into the camera hidden in the Honda from a distance of just a couple of feet. His image may have been monochrome green and he may have had zombie-like eyes, but his features were clear and distinct.

Almost before anyone would have had a chance to react, our man was up and gone, visible now only via the second camera, walking briskly back toward the racetrack entrance, once more to mingle with, and become anonymous amongst, the other racegoers and the attendant policemen.

The man's head bobbed up and down slightly with each step, and I had seen that easy, lolloping long stride before in the video room at Charing Cross police station.

The man who picked up Austin Reynolds's envelope, with

its filling of gravel, was the same man who had exited the Hilton Hotel just minutes after Clare had fallen to her death.

But this time I'd seen his face. And in spite of the greenness and the zombie eyes, I was certain I knew him.

I knew him very well indeed.

"GOT 'IM," Gareth said excitedly, bursting into the commentary booth. "Did you see? Bleedin' marvelous."

To him it was still only a game, but, to be fair, that's all that I'd implied it was.

"Yes," I said almost equally excited, "I did see."

I was thinking fast.

"Take this." I dug into my leather bag and gave him an unmarked DVD. "I need you to do a bit of editing," I said, and I explained what I wanted him to do.

"No prob," he said, taking the DVD. "Give me about ten to fifteen mins." He left as quickly as he'd arrived.

The horses were coming out onto the course for the fourth race, a three-quarter-mile maiden stakes for two-year-olds with seven runners, one of whom, Spitfire Boy, had run at Lingfield in the race when Clare had stopped Bangkok Flyer. That race had been over a mile, and Spitfire Boy had faded badly in the last two hundred yards. Perhaps this shorter trip would suit him better.

I described the colors of the jockeys' silks as the horses made their way to the start on the back stretch, taking particular note of Ground Pepper, the young colt trained by Austin Reynolds.

I tried to concentrate on the horses but my heart was pounding.

If I was right, the man who had collected the envelope had murdered Toby Woodley. I should tell the police straightaway.

Concentrate, I told myself. For God's sake, concentrate on the racing!

Try as I might to learn the colors, visions of the man's face with his zombie eyes kept crowding my consciousness.

"They're loading," I said into my microphone as the horses began to be inserted into the starting gate by the team of handlers.

I flicked my main monitor over to the current betting odds and gave the meager crowd an update.

"Spitfire Boy is the favorite at three-to-one, Ground Pepper at fours, eleven-to-two bar those."

I switched the monitor back to show the horses at the start.

"Mark, coming to you in ten seconds," said Derek into my headphones, *"nine, eight, seven . . ."*

"Just three to go in now," I said over the public address.

". . . six, five, four . . ."

"Ground Pepper will be the last to load."

". . . three, two, one . . ."

As always, I paused fractionally as the satellite viewers came online.

"That's it," I said, "they're all in. Ready." The gate swung open. "They're off, and racing."

I thought I did pretty well, considering the minimal amount of time I had devoted to learning the colors.

I was helped by Spitfire Boy, who was a determined front-runner, taking the lead in the first few strides and setting a strong pace that spread the field around the far end of the course, making their identification easier.

As always, the horses bunched together more as they turned

into the stretch, and, on this occasion, their jockeys' faces didn't remind me of Clare. This time they all appeared to have green faces and zombie eyes full of murderous intent.

Spitfire Boy held on to win by a neck, with Ground Pepper fading to finish fourth of the seven.

As soon as the last horse crossed the line I grabbed my cell phone and called the number of Superintendent Cullen's sergeant. There was no answer. I tried it again. Still no answer, so I left a message asking him or his boss to call me back urgently.

What should I do now?

There were police downstairs by the entrances. Should I go down to one of them or should I call 999?

Gareth's voice came over my headphones. *"Mark, I've done the edit. It runs for just thirty-eight seconds. I'll send it through to your monitor."*

"What the hell are you doing on the talk-back?" I said. "Where's Derek?"

"They've all gone on a bathroom break. We've got commercials for the next . . ."—he paused while he checked—*". . . three mins and twenty. Do you want to see this or not?"*

"Yes, of course," I said. "Put it on."

I watched as his handiwork came up on my main monitor.

The unmarked DVD that I had given to Gareth was a copy that Detective Sergeant Sharp had given to me of the Hilton Hotel CCTV footage of the man with the baseball cap and turned-up collar coming down in the elevator and then walking across the hotel lobby, including the view from behind.

Just as I had asked, Gareth had edited the CCTV footage together with that from the cameras tonight so that the images appeared side by side on a split screen, first with the close-up of the man's face alongside the shot of him in the elevator, then the two views of him walking away from the camera, one in the hotel, the other in the Kempton parking lot.

And it was those final fifteen or twenty seconds of walking that left no doubt whatsoever that the two men in the films were one and the same person.

I glanced out of the commentary booth toward brightly lit bookmakers' boards and the dark racetrack beyond and was horrified by what I saw.

Gareth may have been Mr. Bleedin' Magic when it came to cameras, but he was Mr. Blitherin' Idiot when it came to acting as a producer.

The edited films were not just playing on my monitor but on the huge television screen set up in front of the grandstands.

"For God's sake, Gareth," I shouted through the talk-back, "it's on the big screen."

"Bugger me. So it is. It's bleedin' everywhere."

He thought it was funny.

Derek didn't. In fact, he was furious.

"Was this your doing?" he demanded loudly. *"I go to the bloody toilet and the next thing I know we're broadcasting God knows what to all the television sets right round the racetrack."*

"I'm sorry," I said. "It was only meant to come to mine."

"Bloody amateurs."

I heard him click off his microphone. No doubt young Gareth was getting his earful directly without the aid of technology. I hope it didn't result in either of us losing our jobs.

But Derek's reprimand was not my main worry.

Had the blackmailer seen the film? And did he know it was me that had initiated it?

I'd find out soon enough.

I STAYED in the commentary booth for the rest of the evening, hiding myself away.

Twice more I tried to call Superintendent Cullen or his sergeant, but to no avail. I even tried DS Sharp at Charing Cross, but his phone, too, went to voice mail. Policing was obviously mostly a nine-to-five occupation.

The last two races seemed to go by in a blur, but I must have been all right as Derek, at least, didn't complain about my commentary. He did complain about almost everything else, though, and was even talking about having a bucket installed under the desk in the scanner so that he'd never have to go out to the bathroom again.

"You seem to have caused a bit of a stir!" he shouted into my ears. *"The racetrack chairman has been only one of those we've had down here demanding to know what the bloody hell is going on."*

"What did you tell them?" I asked.

"I told them they'd better speak to you."

Oh thanks, I thought.

I hoped that one of his visitors hadn't been the man with the zombie eyes.

I hung around in the commentary booth for quite a while after the last race, hoping that everyone would go before I made my way down. For one thing, I didn't want to have to explain myself to the racetrack chairman.

The door of the booth opened and I jumped.

"Bye, Mark," said Terence Feynman, the judge, putting his head through the gap. "Will I see you here tomorrow night?"

"Yes, Terence," I said, "that's the plan. Bye, now."

Terence withdrew his head from the gap and closed the door.

Damn, I thought a few moments later. I should have gone down to my car with him. Safety in numbers and all that.

I quickly packed my computer, my binoculars, and my colored pens into my black leather bag and went out into the long corridor after him, turning right toward the exit.

Terence had already disappeared, but another man came around the corner into view, walking briskly toward me, his head bobbing up and down slightly due to his easy lolloping stride.

I stopped.

"Hello, Mark," the man called down the corridor.

That heart of mine was thumping once more in my chest.

He was just fifteen or so yards away and closing in rapidly.

"Hello, Brendan," I said.

My cousin, Brendan Shillingford, smiled at me, but the smile didn't reach his eyes—his zombie eyes.

24

un, my body told me, flooding adrenaline into my bloodstream, ready for flight. But where to? The only way out was past Brendan.

Or was it? I dragged some fragment of memory back into my mind.

Fire escape.

Hadn't I once been told that there was a way out over the roof in case of a fire?

I turned and ran the other way, away from him, sprinting down to the far end of the corridor and up the metal staircase toward the photo-finish booth and the door to the roof, rummaging madly to get my cell phone out of my pocket.

I could hear Brendan coming after me.

I wondered if he'd have a knife. I didn't want to look.

I fumbled with the door and finally turned the lock, tripped over the step, and fell out onto the grandstand roof, dropping my phone in the process. I searched madly for it with my hands, but it had fallen through the metal grille floor of the walkway and my fingers couldn't reach it.

I now could hear Brendan on the stairs, so I moved quickly away from the door, down the walkway and toward the back of the roof, from where I had watched the horses the previous week. I looked down at the now deserted parade ring. Where was a policeman when you needed him most?

The sky above was pitch-black, but there was enough spillage from the racetrack floodlights for me to see across the roof quite well.

There was a junction in the walkway, and I had to make a decision. Which way was the fire escape?

Surely, I thought, there should have been a sign.

I went right but quickly learned that was wrong. The walkway came to an abrupt end after about fifteen yards, next to an electrical junction box.

I turned around and came face-to-face with Brendan.

He was standing about ten or so paces away and looking pretty pleased with himself. Something flashed in his right hand.

"Is that the same knife you used to kill Toby Woodley?" I had to shout over the continuous whirr of the air conditioners.

If he was surprised by the question, he didn't show it.

He took a step toward me.

"And did you murder Clare too?" I shouted.

He took another step forward.

I threw my black leather bag at him, then ducked under the walkway's railing and ran over the corrugated-steel roof.

Brendan followed.

The grandstand roof wasn't flat, and I don't mean just the corrugations.

It sloped up at the front like a giant ramp. And there was a gantry, an enormous structure extending some twenty feet out and up from the front of the roof, that held several banks of floodlights.

I clambered through the main supporting spar that ran right across the middle of the roof. I was trying to double back to the fire escape or return to the door, but Brendan cut me off and drove me on toward the front of the grandstand, toward the sloping part of the roof.

Twice he got so close that I could feel him grabbing for the collar of my coat, but each time I managed to pull myself away.

I was thirty-one and Brendan was nearly ten years older, but I was hampered by my broken ribs that made scrambling over the large steel pipes of the support spars exceedingly painful. He, meanwhile, seemed to skip over them with ease.

I reached one of the walkways, rolled myself through the railing, stood up, and ran.

But still it wasn't the right way for the fire escape.

The walkway ended next to another junction box.

Dammit.

I turned around, kicking something loose on the floor. I looked down. There were several poles, like ones used for scaffolding but smaller in diameter. They appeared to be the same as that used to make the railings of the walkways, probably left behind after construction.

I quickly bent down and picked up one that was about six feet in length.

Brendan was facing me on the walkway.

I jabbed the end of the pole toward him and he stepped back a stride, so I did it again.

We stood like that for what seemed an age, but it was probably only a few seconds.

It was a standoff—me with the pole and him with the knife.

I advanced a stride, jabbing the pole forward. He retreated slightly.

"What are you doing?" I shouted at him. "I'm your cousin."

He didn't reply. He just stared at me with no emotion visible on his face.

"Did you kill Toby Woodley?"

No reply.

"How about Clare?" I shouted. "Did you kill her too?"

"I loved Clare," Brendan said. "And she loved me."

The mystery boyfriend, I thought. The wonderful lover who had made her happy.

Her own cousin.

My cousin.

My married cousin with two teenage children.

"What happened in that hotel room?" I shouted at him.

He said nothing.

"Did you push her off the balcony?"

He continued to stare at me, but in spite of the dim light I thought I could read some pain in his eyes.

"Did you know she was pregnant?" I shouted.

He went on staring at me.

"She was six or seven weeks pregnant."

Still nothing. He had known.

"Was it yours?"

It had to be, but he went on saying nothing.

"Was that why you killed her? Did she want an abortion?"

His head came up a bit. "Shut up."

"So was that it?" I said. "You wanted the child and she didn't?"

He slowly shook his head. "It was the other way round." He spoke quietly, and I had to strain to hear him. "She did it on purpose, to trap me."

It was not an excuse. There can be no excuse for murder.

I thought I could see tears on his face. Crocodile tears.

"It's no good crying now," I shouted at him. "You shouldn't have killed her."

"It was an accident," he shouted back.

"Oh yeah?" I said, mocking him. "Just like it was an accident in the pub parking lot on Sunday? You killed Clare, just like you killed Emily. And you nearly killed me, twice. Why don't you admit it, you bastard?"

"I told you," he screamed at me, "it was an accident! I just pushed her away, and she . . ." He tailed off. "She tripped. I didn't mean for her to fall."

He was mad with anger, and with grief.

That made two of us.

"Did you make her write the note?" I shouted.

"What note?"

"The suicide note."

"There was no note. I told you, it was a bloody accident."

"And was sticking a knife into Toby Woodley's back also a bloody accident?"

"He deserved it," Brendan said with real menace in his voice. "The bastard was blackmailing me."

"He was blackmailing everyone," I said, "but no one else killed him."

"He knew about Clare and me. He said he'd put it in the paper."

I wondered whether Toby had really known or had just been guessing. Perhaps a blackmail note had given him the true answer. It had certainly condemned him to death.

"But you blackmailed people too," I said. I thought back to the handwritten zeros added to the amounts. "And you were much greedier than Toby."

"It seemed like an opportunity not to be missed." He was suddenly smiling as if pleased with himself. I couldn't think why. To continue the blackmail had been stupid and far too risky, and it had finally given him away.

"And what about me?" I said. "Why did you try to kill me?"

"You said at the funeral that you were going to see the video from the hotel."

"And you thought I'd recognize you?"

He nodded.

He'd almost been right.

He suddenly lunged forward and grabbed the end of the pole with his left hand, pulling it sharply toward him, and me along with it.

He slashed at my hands with the knife, and I had to let go or else I'd have lost my fingers.

Now the tables were turned, and he jabbed the end of the pole toward my face, forcing me to duck wildly sideways.

This really isn't funny, I thought, and maybe for the first time I was scared, very scared.

I tried to reach down to pick up another of the poles, but Brendan swung the one he had in a great arc, bringing it down heavily on my back between the shoulder blades. It would have landed on my head and killed me if I hadn't seen it at the last second and ducked.

Even so, the blow was bad enough, driving the air out of my

lungs and causing me to drop to my knees. My broken ribs didn't like it much either.

I sensed, rather than saw, the pole being lifted again for another blow. This time, I thought, it will be fatal.

I rolled to my left, out through the railings of the walkway and onto the roof proper, as the pole smacked down where I had just been.

I was not going to bloody die, I told myself. Not here. Not now.

I stood up, dragged some air into my aching and injured lungs, and ran.

I ran on the corrugated steel toward the front of the grandstand and I could hear Brendan running behind me. I didn't have time to look back, but I was sure he'd have the pole in his hands, ready to strike me down as soon as he got within range.

I ran up the slope of the roof and didn't stop when I got to the brink. I didn't even pause, running like a tightrope walker, straight out from the roof on one of the cylindrical spars of the lighting gantry.

Desperate situations necessitate desperate measures, and running as fast as I could along a metal spar eight inches in diameter with nothing but air beneath for more than a hundred feet was desperate indeed.

And the spar wasn't horizontal. It sloped up at an ever-increasing angle as I moved away from the edge of the roof toward the floodlights. I was tightrope-walking uphill, and my only stability came from movement.

As the slope caused me to slow, I began to wobble.

I went down on my hands and knees, clutching with my fingers at the metal, trying to dig my nails into the smooth, hard paint.

Nevertheless, I began to slide backward, down the spar, back toward the edge of the grandstand roof, and back toward Brendan and his pole.

It wouldn't take much for him to push me off with it.

All there was below me was hard, unforgiving, deserted concrete, a hundred and twenty feet straight down. The fifteenth floor of the Hilton Hotel or the roof of the Kempton Park grandstands—different distances, maybe, but the outcome would be much the same.

I could imagine what would be said: *It's such a shame—Mark never came to terms with his twin sister's suicide, nor the loss of another close friend and the breakup of a long-term relationship. But he found a way out of his pain.*

I managed to turn myself over so that I was now sitting on the spar, with my ankles locked together beneath it and my hands down in front of me on its cold metal.

But still I slid down, inch by inch.

Brendan was standing just short of the edge of the grandstand roof proper, holding the pole in both hands and watching me intently as I moved ever so slowly but inexorably toward him.

He stepped forward and swung the pole at me.

I had time to see it coming, and, keeping my legs tight around the spar, I leaned back flat against it as the pole whizzed past harmlessly just inches from my eyes.

But the sudden movement meant that I slid still farther down.

Next time I'd easily be in range. I knew it and so did Brendan.

I tried my best to climb away from him, but for all my efforts I only managed to slide even closer.

Brendan was smiling again. He was sure he had me now.

Not if I could help it.

As he swung the metal pole at me I purposely leaned forward into it, taking a heavy blow on my left wrist, which made my whole left arm go numb.

However, at the same time, I grabbed the pole firmly with my right hand and pulled hard.

Just as it had done with me earlier, it caught Brendan unawares.

He should have let go.

Even so, he would probably have been all right if the grandstand roof had been flat at the front, allowing him to have a steady stance. But it wasn't. The slope meant that he was leaning forward slightly, and now my sharp tug on the pole had him reeling over the abyss.

I could see the horror on his face as he pitched forward, grasping desperately for the wire stays that crisscrossed the framework to give it added rigidity.

But he didn't fall.

The bulk of his body had gone over the edge of the roof, but he was still supported by the pole that was underneath him, held up at one end by a wire stay.

The other end of the pole was still in my right hand, and Brendan's weight was beginning to rotate me alarmingly around the spar.

I looked across at him and he stared back at me, terror deeply etched in his features, a dreadful realization apparent in his eyes—his zombie eyes.

I thought of my darling sister Clare, and also of the lovely Emily, and what might have been.

Maybe I could have saved him if I'd wanted to or maybe I couldn't.

I'd never know.

I let the pole slip through my fingers and decided to look upward at the black sky rather than downward at the concrete.

I had no wish to witness another of Brendan's "accidents."

EPILOGUE

Two months later, on a bright cold morning just two days before Christmas, a thanksgiving service was held for Clare in Ely Cathedral, and this time I organized everything myself.

The original plan had been to hold it at St. Mary's parish church in Newmarket, but such had been the demand for tickets that somewhere larger had to be found, and the cathedral, just half an hour up the road, was perfect.

There is something very grand about our great churches, and Ely Cathedral is certainly no exception, sitting as it does on a small mound surrounded by the flatlands of the Fens.

The service matched the surroundings, and, unlike at her funeral, there was lots of live music, with the cathedral choir adding to the splendor.

Geoff Grubb read a lesson, as did James and Stephen, while Angela and I both gave eulogies.

Indeed, the Shillingford family had turned out in force.

Even Joshua, Brendan's younger brother, was present, although Gillian, Brendan's widow, and their boys were not.

Life for them had been far from easy.

Not only had their father died that night at Kempton but he had been shown to be a murderer, and the press had not been kind to him.

Toby Woodley may not have been the most popular member of the press but he still was one of their brotherhood and they had devoured his killer like a pack of hungry dogs.

"You can't libel the dead," Toby had said to me at Stratford races.

So right he was.

Jim Metcalf and his fellow journalists had taken full advantage of that fact, dismantling any semblance of good reputation that Brendan had built up over his years as a trainer.

It had even been widely reported by some that Brendan had been the trainer who had layed his horses to lose, the trainer about whom Toby Woodley had written in the *Daily Gazette* the previous May.

That, I was sure, had come as a great relief to Austin Reynolds, although both he and I knew it wasn't true.

The service concluded with a five-minute film tribute to Clare that was shown on big screens set up on either side of the altar and also on a number of screens placed along the nave.

The previous week I had spent a whole day in RacingTV's editing suite in Oxford putting the film together. It started with a montage of photographs of Clare from throughout her life together with some home movies of her riding her pony as a child. Then there was footage of her career, including big-race victories intercut with snippets of interviews and celebrations.

And for the soundtrack I had chosen, appropriately, the song "The Winner Takes It All" by ABBA.

When I had first played the finished film through for myself, it had made me cry, and now as the music echoed around the arches and vaulted ceiling of the Norman cathedral there were many more tears all around me.

But the film wasn't all doom and gloom. Quite the contrary.

There was laughter, too, and spontaneous applause when it finished with a still image of Clare, standing high in her stirrups, all smiles and happiness, punching the air, having just won a race at Royal Ascot.

I STOOD under the West Tower, shaking hands, as the huge congregation spilled out past me through the West Door onto Palace Green.

I suppose I initially had chosen a day when there was no racing in the hope that enough people would come to fill St. Mary's Church in Newmarket. Now it seemed that absolutely everyone I knew in racing, and many more that I didn't, had turned up at Ely Cathedral, and soon my right hand was aching from so much shaking.

It was a good thing that it wasn't my left hand.

That was only just out of a cast after eight weeks.

Brendan had fractured my wrist in six places when he'd hit me with the pole, and it had been almost more than I could manage to get myself off the floodlight gantry and back onto the grandstand roof without going the same way he had.

Detective Sergeant Sharp and Detective Chief Inspector Coaker came out of the cathedral together.

"Lovely service," they both said in unison. "Very moving."

"Thank you," I replied. "Any news?"

"Mr. Brendan Shillingford's car has now been confirmed as the one that hit you and Mrs. Lowther at the pub in Madingley," DCI Coaker said. "It had been repaired by a garage in Bury St. Edmunds. Mr. Shillingford apparently told them that he'd hit a deer in Thetford Forest. But we've been able to extract a sample of Mrs. Lowther's DNA from blood found on the underside of the vehicle."

I suppose I was pleased.

"How about the knife?" I asked.

"According to Superintendent Cullen at Surrey, the knife found on Mr. Shillingford was consistent with that used to kill Mr. Woodley, although they were unable to find any trace of his blood on it."

"Will there be a trial?" I asked.

"Only the remaining inquests," he said, shaking his head. "There'd be no point in a criminal trial."

"Will the inquests name Brendan as the murderer?"

"That doesn't happen anymore. I expect the coroners to record verdicts of unlawful killing in the case of Toby Woodley and Emily Lowther, but there will be little doubt about who was responsible. Mr. Shillingford's verdict will probably be misadventure."

Brendan's misadventure.

The policemen moved away through the door and outside into the pale December sunshine.

I turned to see who was next in the line.

"Hello, Mark," said Sarah Stacey.

I anxiously looked around behind her.

"Mitchell's not here," she said. "I've left him."

I stared at her. "When?"

"About six weeks ago."

"Why didn't you call me?" I asked.

"Because I didn't leave Mitchell for you," she said with determination. "I just left him. Time will tell what happens from now on."

"But where are you living?"

"With my sister," she said.

I hadn't even known she'd had a sister. "What about the prenup?" I asked.

"My lawyer says it's not enforceable. Not after fourteen years of marriage."

"I hope he's right."

"Call me sometime," she said, and then she turned and walked away, out of the cathedral. Was it also out of my life?

I watched her go. Maybe I would call her or maybe I wouldn't. As she had said, time would tell.

Harry Jacobs came bounding up to me.

"A fitting tribute," he said. "Well done. Clare would have been proud of you."

"Thanks, Harry," I said, shaking his hand.

He smiled at me warmly and moved away. Nothing more needed to be said, not today.

In November, I had visited Harry's impressive country mansion near Stratford-upon-Avon to give him the good news that both of his blackmailers were dead and that his guilty secret had died with them.

I certainly wasn't going to say anything to anyone about any blackmail.

We had sat in his conservatory, looking out over the rolling Warwickshire countryside, and his relief had been almost palpable.

"I want to close that offshore bank account," he had said, "but there's more than twenty-five thousand pounds in it, and I can hardly bring that back into my regular accounts without my accountant or tax lawyer asking where it came from."

"Then give it to charity," I told him. "Send it anonymously to the Injured Jockeys Fund."

And that was precisely what he did, right there and then, using his computer and Internet banking.

"Tell me, Harry," I asked him as I was leaving, "where does all your money come from?"

"Don't you know?" he asked, slightly amused. "When I was young and extremely foolish, I managed to borrow an obscene amount of money from a bank to buy fifty acres of industrial wasteland. It was contaminated with all sorts of toxins and heavy metals. Dreadful place. I almost cried when I saw it after I'd bought it."

"Surely you saw it beforehand?"

"I went to the auction to buy something else, but it sold for far too much. The next lot was the fifty acres and the price seemed too good to be true. So I bought it, completely unseen. I'd thought I must be on a winner whatever it was like."

"And were you?"

"I didn't think so just then. I tried to sell it immediately for less than I'd paid for it, but there were no takers."

"So where was the land?" I asked him.

"Somewhere called the West India Docks," he replied, beaming broadly. "East London. It's now part of Canary Wharf, and there's over two million square feet of offices on my land alone." He laughed. "The bank I originally borrowed the money from now pays me a fortune each year in rent for their headquarters building. Money for old rope."

One of the other advantages of having the service on a non–race day was that all my colleagues from RacingTV were able to attend. More than that, Gareth had set up his cameras in the cathedral to record everything for posterity, and I'd even seen Iain Ferguson doing a piece for the camera outside as everyone had arrived.

That should have been my job.

"Hi, Mark," Nicholas said, walking over and shaking me warmly by the hand. "Lovely service."

"Thanks, Nick," I said, meaning it. "And Angela was great too."

"Yes, she was rather good." His tone almost implied surprise.

"How are things?" I asked.

"Pretty good, at the moment," he said. "The bank has realized they can't do without me. Thank God." He smiled broadly. "It seems there was almost a riot amongst the senior management when it was suggested by the chairman that I should be let go. I'd never realized how much I was appreciated. Perhaps I'll ask for a raise next." He laughed. "How about you?"

"I'm finally moving house," I said. "I've bought a place in Oxfordshire, and I move in after the New Year."

"Congratulations," he said. "Although I think it's a bit extreme to go to all that trouble just to get away from your dad."

We both laughed.

"He's not been so bad recently," I said. "Almost human."

I looked across to where my father was standing with my mother on the other side of the West Door, also talking to people as they left the cathedral. As I was watching, he glanced in my direction and smiled at me, a genuine smile that reached all the way to his eyes.

I smiled back. "I think he's been better since the conclusion of Clare's inquest."

Not that the verdict had been quite the one we would have wanted.

The coroner had recorded an open verdict in spite of my assurances that Brendan had as good as admitted to me that he'd been responsible for her death—accident or otherwise. Not that I'd been able to properly get my head around the fact that Brendan and Clare had been lovers and that she had been pregnant with his child.

But at least the verdict wasn't suicide, even though the coroner had still placed great emphasis on the existence of the note addressed to me.

I had tried to explain that I believed it was a letter Clare had been writing to me, after our row at dinner, because she couldn't reach me on the telephone. It was nothing to do with her death, and it had probably been half written, as found, when Brendan had first arrived in her room.

But the coroner had not been convinced and stubbornly maintained that the note, in fact, was strong evidence of her suicide, although, as he'd said, no one could be sure of what had happened in the hotel room that night.

But I knew.

I was certain of it and that was enough.

Whatever anyone else might think was irrelevant.

9/13-16